"I need to apologize for my actions the night that we danced.

"My initial intentions were deplorable, and we both know it. Had my sister been propositioned in such an infantile manner, I would have shot the blackguard."

"I am relieved that my own brother restrained himself from shooting anyone on my behalf that night. If I recall, you looked very dashing that evening, and a bullet hole would have ruined the whole effect. It certainly would have ruined your coat."

"My coat." It was flat, without a hint of humor.

"It was a jest, Your Grace." In truth, he no longer seemed as if he laughed often. He no longer seemed like the impulsive man who had once held her in his arms. This August Faulkner was harder. More intense. A leashed, controlled version of the daring upstart who had made her smile.

Perhaps that was what a duchy did to a man.

ACCLAIM FOR KELLY BOWEN

BETWEEN THE DEVIL AND THE DUKE

"[T]he fun, intrigue, and romance crescendo in a whopping plot twist. Bowen's Regency romances are always delightful, and this is one of her best yet."

—Publishers Weekly (starred review)

"Bowen again delivers the goods with this exquisitely written historical romance, whose richly nuanced characters, unexpected flashes of dry wit, and superbly sensual love story will have readers sighing happily in satisfaction."

—Booklist (starred review)

"Bowen delivers another winner with scandalous heroines and roguish heroes in her A Season for Scandal series. Combining intelligent and somewhat unconventional characters with a clever plot and a bit of suspense, Bowen captures readers' interest from the intriguing beginning to the expected HEA."

—RT Book Reviews

A DUKE TO REMEMBER

"This isn't a Regency comedy of manners. It's way better. This bright, surprising romance sets aside the intricate social rules and focuses on forging trust and love even when it seems like the whole world is against you."

—Best Romance of August selection,
the Amazon Book Review

"Top Pick! 4½ Stars! The powerful emotions, action, adventure and passion are what readers desire, and Bowen delivers, and brings readers her most memorable characters yet. Many will cherish this beautifully rendered tale."

—*RT Book Reviews*

"*A Duke to Remember* has everything you want in a romance...a truly satisfying happily ever after that will leave you misty-eyed." —BookPage.com

DUKE OF MY HEART

"Bowen's irresistible Regency is like the most popular debutante at the ball: pretty, witty, mysterious, and full of coquettish allure. From the first line to the happy dénouement, Bowen builds enough romantic heat to melt midwinter snow."

—A *Publishers Weekly* Best Books of 2016 selection

"In her latest, Kelly Bowen offers up a vibrant, clever heroine in Ivory Moore—think Olivia Pope in a corset. The romance here is deeply satisfying, and Bowen excels in writing secondary characters and scenes. What's more, the nooks and crannies of this book are delightful, much like those in our real world, perfect to be discovered alongside true love."

—*The Washington Post*

"Top Pick! 4½ Stars! Bowen begins her Season for Scandal series with a nonstop murder mystery that sizzles with tension. This suspenseful tale unfolds quickly, and readers will be captivated by the well-drawn characters who move Bowen's inventive plot forward. Readers will savor this unconventional romance."

—*RT Book Reviews*

YOU'RE THE EARL THAT I WANT

A GOOD ROGUE IS HARD TO FIND

"4½ stars! This is a shining example of Bowen's ability to make readers both laugh (at the wry and witty dialogue) and cry (at the poignancy within the romance). With wonderful characters, a quick pace, and heated sensuality, Bowen has a winner."
—*RT Book Reviews*

I'VE GOT MY DUKE TO KEEP ME WARM

"With this unforgettable debut, Bowen proves she is a writer to watch as she spins a multilayered plot skillfully seasoned with danger and deception and involving wonderfully complex protagonists and a memorable cast of supporting characters...a truly remarkable romance well worth savoring."

—*Booklist* (starred review)

"4 stars! In this delightful, poignant debut that sets Bowen on the path to become a beloved author, the innovative plotline and ending are only superseded by the likable, multidimensional characters: a strong-willed heroine and a heart-stealing hero. Get set to relish Bowen's foray into the genre."

—*RT Book Reviews*

"Fans of romance with a touch of suspense will enjoy the work of this new author."

—*Publishers Weekly*

A *Duke* in the *Night*

KELLY BOWEN

FOREVER

New York Boston

Copyright © 2018 by Kelly Bowen
Excerpt from *Last Night with the Earl* copyright © 2018 by Kelly Bowen
Cover design by Elizabeth Stokes
Cover photography by Period Images
Cover copyright © 2018 by Hachette Book Group, Inc.

Forever
Hachette Book Group
1290 Avenue of the Americas, New York, NY 10104
forever-romance.com
twitter.com/foreverromance

First Edition: February 2018

Forever is an imprint of Grand Central Publishing. The Forever name and logo are trademarks of Hachette Book Group, Inc.

The publisher is not responsible for websites (or their content) that are not owned by the publisher.

The Hachette Speakers Bureau provides a wide range of authors for speaking events. To find out more, go to www.hachettespeakersbureau.com or call (866) 376-6591.

ISBN: 978-1-4789-1856-1 (mass market), 978-1-4789-1855-4 (ebook)

Printed in the United States of America

OPM

10 9 8 7 6 5 4 3 2 1

To all the strong women in my life who have gifted me with the courage to believe that I always could.

Acknowledgments

A heartfelt thanks to my editor, Alex Logan, for unerring insight that makes each story better, and to the entire team at Forever, who work so hard on my behalf. Thanks to my agent, Stefanie Lieberman, who has been unfailingly supportive. To my family and friends, who have cheered me on every step of the way. And last but not least, a huge thank-you to the entire romance community—readers and writers. You have made this an unforgettable journey.

Chapter 1

He had danced with her on a dare.

Childish, certainly. Boorish, most definitely. But it was easier to critique such behaviors when one was no longer in the throes of obnoxious youth, surrounded by arrogant acquaintances who snickered and leered and sought entertainment at the expense of others. And to this day, August Faulkner, the twelfth Duke of Holloway, had never forgotten it.

He hadn't been duke of anything then. Though his bravado and self-importance had seemed to make up for that shortcoming. At the time he'd thought Clara Hayward, the eldest daughter of the charismatic and wildly popular Baron Strathmore, would simply be a means to an end.

She had been pretty—flawless fair skin framed by lustrous mahogany tresses shot through with rich ruby highlights. Dark eyes ringed by darker lashes, set into a face that smiled often. An elegant figure displayed by tasteful gowns and a graceful poise that was remarked upon often. All that combined with the staggering wealth of her family meant there should have been earls and dukes and princes falling all over themselves begging for her attention.

Instead her dance card remained empty despite a flurry of proper introductions. And those earls and dukes and princes kept a wary distance—held at bay by the single flaw that illustrious lords could simply not tolerate in a potential wife: an education and an intelligence greater than their own.

August hadn't understood that then. Instead he had foolishly put Clara Hayward in a box labeled *Wallflower*, confident in his superiority. And with the snickers and guffaws of his companions echoing in his ears, he had sauntered up to where she stood at the edge of the dance floor that night and offered her the privilege of his presence.

Miss Hayward had gazed upon him with what looked like bemused tolerance when he had bowed dramatically over her hand. Her dark eyes had flickered over his shoulder to where his cronies watched, waiting for her to stammer or stumble. Instead her full lips had curled only a little further, and her eyes had returned to his, a single brow cocked in clear, knowing amusement, and he knew then that she had heard every crass, careless word. And it had been August who had stammered and stumbled as she took his arm.

He had led her out on the dance floor, appalled at the way his heart was hammering in his chest. She had placed one steady hand in his, another on the sleeve of his coat, and met his eyes directly as the first strains of music floated through the ballroom. August had tried then to recoup the advantage he seemed to have lost and used every ounce of his considerable prowess on the dance floor, leading her in a sweeping, reckless waltz that should have wilted a wallflower into a blushing mess.

But Clara Hayward had only matched him step for step, never once looking away. And by the time the waltz had concluded, the conversation in the room had faltered, every damn guest was staring at them, and August was experiencing a horrifying shortness of breath that had nothing to do with his exertions.

"Good heavens," she had murmured, not sounding nearly as breathless as he. "I was told that you were daring, Mr. Faulkner. And you do not disappoint. You are exactly as advertised."

"And you, Miss Hayward, are not." He'd blurted it before he could stop himself, unsure if her words were a compliment or a criticism. And unsure what to do with either.

She'd grinned then—an honest-to-goodness grin that suggested they were collaborators, complicit in something deliciously wicked. "Good" was all she had said, and his world had tilted. He had found himself grinning foolishly back, disoriented as all hell.

August had left Miss Hayward in the care of her brother after that, and Harland Hayward had gazed upon him with the reproach and pity that August both deserved and hated. He'd not danced with her again, a fact that evoked a peculiar regret if he thought about it for too long. In fact, he had never spoken to Miss Hayward since that night, their paths having seemingly diverged in two completely opposite directions.

He to a duchy he'd never expected to inherit. She to a life of refined academia she'd undoubtedly planned as the headmistress of the most elite finishing school in Britain.

That was, until August had bought that school yesterday.

A property he'd had his solicitors anonymously offer to purchase at least thrice in the past decade.

He glanced down at the papers his solicitors had left on his desk. "Miss Clara Hayward" was written in neat letters on the previous deed of ownership, and the sight of her name still jolted him even now. Which was absurd, because it mattered not which Hayward actually owned the damn school, only that they were finally willing to sell. But seeing her name had triggered a flood of memories and somehow undermined the fierce satisfaction that he should have felt at the prospect of the Haverhall School for Young Ladies becoming part of his vast holdings.

August had made the unforgivable mistake of assuming that the current baron owned Haverhall, along with the shipping empire that had given rise to the Haywards' extensive fortune. But now August was left contemplating why, in a world where women very rarely owned a freehold property that hadn't been conveyed to trustees, Clara Hayward would let it slip away from her.

To anyone else, the *why* probably wouldn't matter. Not when one had gotten what one wanted. There was a whole slew of advice that involved gift horses and mouths that most individuals would heed. But August was not most individuals. He despised questions that did not have answers. He abhorred not knowing what motivated people to act as they did. His sister, Anne, often told him that it was an unhealthy compulsion, his need to pry into the dark corners of other people's lives for profit. But he hadn't become as wealthy as he had by simply accepting what was on the surface. There was something more to this that he wasn't seeing. Information was power, and he could never have enough.

August frowned and reached for his knife, trimming the end of a quill absently. It was ironic, really, that he knew so little about a woman he'd been unable to forget, even after all these years. He knew Miss Clara Hayward had a reputation for graciousness, propriety, and common sense—by all reports she was a damn paragon of politesse. The ton, while unsure what to make of her as a debutante, seemed to have embraced the idea that the woman guiding their young charges was one of their social class—what else could be expected of an otherwise lovely girl with an upbringing and excessive education that had severely limited her prospects?

A headmistress of quality, combined with the limited admission and exorbitant fees of the school itself, had made Haverhall as popular with the most elite of London society as with those young ladies on the fringes of the upper crust who possessed dowries large enough to buy all of Westminster. Even peers with staunch traditionalist views, who closeted their daughters or sisters with governesses, had weakened at the opportunity for their female relations to take painting instruction from Thomas Lawrence or to be coached in the cotillion or quadrille by Thomas Wilson. One did not have to enroll in the entire curriculum to participate in individual classes. An unorthodox system to be sure, but one that had proved shockingly successful. August had to admit he admired Miss Hayward's business model. It was the sort of thing he looked for in the many acquisitions he made.

It was almost unfortunate that none of that would be enough to save the school. Which also evoked a peculiar feeling of regret if he thought about it for too long. And that was utterly unacceptable because inane emotion had no place in lucrative business, no matter how unforgettable Clara Hayward might be.

A hesitant knock on the door of his study interrupted his musings. "Yes?"

The heavy door swung open, and August was not a little startled to see his sister standing in the frame. He could probably count on one hand the number of times she had ever sought him out like this, and her presence sent a rush of pleasure through him. "Anne." He set the quill and knife aside and pushed himself to his feet. "Come in."

She was dressed in a simple, soft blue day dress, which matched her eyes almost perfectly. Her hair, the same shade as his, was pulled back neatly to frame her round face. She advanced into the room, clutching what looked like a small ledger against her chest.

"To what do I owe the good fortune of your company?" August asked with genuine happiness.

"I came to thank you," she said politely.

"Ah, was your new gown delivered?" He had seen the fabric on display in a draper's window on Bond Street, and the brilliant cerulean color had stopped him in his tracks. He had known instantly that Anne would look stunning in the shimmering silk. He'd taken it at once to the modiste who crafted all Anne's clothing, and the woman had turned the silk into an exquisite ball gown worthy of royalty. It was to have been delivered this morning. "Do you like it?"

She hesitated. "Yes, thank you. The gown is lovely." She adjusted her grip on her sketchbook.

"Is something wrong with it?" He frowned at her hesitation.

"It's just…Honestly, it's too much. August, I already have more gowns than I can possibly wear."

"You can never have enough. You deserve it. You saw the necklace that goes with it?" He had found the exotic, smoke-colored pearls the day after he had found the fabric.

"Yes, the pearls were lovely too. I don't think a princess could find fault. Thank you, August."

August smiled. They were indeed fit for a princess. Or his

sister. "Wear them as often as you like. Or put them in your trousseau. Though when you're wed, I'll make sure your husband buys you more."

Anne bit her lip and looked away. August stifled a sigh. He shouldn't have brought that up. The topic of marriage always seemed to be a prickly one with Anne, but it was his duty as her brother and as her guardian to make sure she found a man worthy of her. "You're almost nineteen. You'll be married in a couple of years. I know I've said it before, and you probably don't want to hear it again, but you need to consider your future."

"The future that you're planning." It came out dully.

August shook his head. He had seen firsthand exactly what happened when a good woman married a wastrel. He would not allow his sister to make their mother's mistakes. "The future that I care about," he corrected her. "The gentlemen I suggested to you are good men, Anne. Kind, loyal, wise, and decent men. Any one of them would make an excellent husband."

Anne's lips thinned even more. "They're old."

"Hardly. But they are titled and have the respect of the ton."

"And do I get a say in whom you marry?" Anne snapped.

"I am well aware of my own responsibilities to the duchy, Anne. Responsibilities that I will meet at the appropriate time. You do not need to remind me." He could see the stubborn tilt of her chin and tried to rein in his frustration. "It's my job to take care of you."

His sister looked away, her knuckles going white where they gripped her book. "I am quite capable of taking care of myself. I did it for years, if you recall."

Old guilt needled, and August shoved it aside. He did not have the power to remedy the past, but he certainly had the power to dictate the future. "I know. But you don't have to anymore. I'm here now."

Anne's eyes snapped back to him, sparking with irritation. Her cheeks reddened, and she opened her mouth to say something before seeming to reconsider. "I don't wish to fight with you, August."

"Nor do I wish to fight with you. But you have to trust that I know what's best for you."

"What's best for me?" she repeated softly, shaking her head. "Or best for you?"

"Anne—"

"I came to see you because I had some ideas for the Trenton," she said abruptly, opening the book she carried to where a strip of satin ribbon had been laid to mark the page.

August blinked at the sudden change of topic. "The Trenton?"

"Yes. The hotel you own on Bond Street?"

"I am familiar with it," August replied succinctly, trying to keep from frowning. What did Anne care about the hotel? "What sort of ideas?"

Anne looked down at the pages of her book. "Well, for one, our fresh fish supplier has increased his prices by almost fifty percent over the last ten months. Unless he is gifting us with the golden nets he must be using, I think we should look for a different vendor." She flipped a page. "Also," she continued, "there is a small laundry a street over from the hotel that has come for sale. It's already proven itself extremely profitable. I think we should buy it, not only for its existing business, but we could add complimentary laundry to Trenton's guest services. Most of our hotel's patrons are officers and military sorts, and we are in direct competition with Stephen's Hotel. I think this might give us an edge—"

"Anne," August interrupted her, "where is all this coming from?"

She looked up at him earnestly. "Mr. Down had the books out yesterday, and I just took a small peek. I think that—"

"You don't have to concern yourself with these things, Anne," he said firmly. "I will take care of those sorts of details, or I will instruct my very capable man of business to do so." And he would instruct Duncan Down to keep the books away from Anne in the future. She didn't need to worry about money. She would never, ever need to worry about money again. August had made sure of that.

"But I just—"

"I want you to enjoy whatever it is that you wish to amuse yourself with. Music, reading, riding. Anything you like."

"But—"

"I won't argue about this with you, Anne." His eyes fell on the book she still held and the loose piece of foolscap tucked into it. "Is that a sketch?"

Anne's expression had become tight. "It's nothing."

"May I see it?" August ignored the harshness of her words.

Anne's fingers tightened on the edges of the pages, and her forehead creased before she loosened her grasp and handed him the book. "If you must."

August took the book from her hands and studied the drawing, realizing it wasn't really a drawing at all but a mock-up of a tavern sign. He recognized the name and the graceful swan that dominated the center instantly, because he owned that tavern too. If a sign were to be crafted the way this one was drawn, he had to admit that it would be a vast improvement over the one that currently hung above the tavern's entrance.

It had been a while since he had looked at Anne's work, and the precision and detail of the drawing jumped off the page at him. Each line was deliberate and sure, perfectly executed perspective giving it a three-dimensional appearance that almost made him believe he could touch the object. He frowned slightly.

"You don't like it?" Anne asked in a stilted voice.

August cursed his lack of attention to his expression and schooled his features back into neutrality. "On the contrary. The drawing and design are extraordinarily accomplished. You have a very keen eye."

Anne's lips pulled into a smile, and a faint blush touched her cheeks. "Thank you."

August glanced up at her. That thank-you had been far more heartfelt than the one she had offered him for a silk gown and a string of pearls. He looked down at the pages again. "Yet why are you drawing tavern signs?"

"Because the one that exists right now is appalling. The swan looks like a bat that's had its neck stretched. It gives an otherwise tidy establishment a shabby appearance, and it should be replaced." The smile wavered, and a faintly defiant note had crept into her answer.

August looked down at the book again. On the page that had been hidden by the loose sketch was what resembled a blueprint. A careful schematic drawing of rooms in what looked like the layout of an inn. "What's this?" he asked, tilting the book so she could see.

Her defiant look stayed firmly in place. "A drawing of what the main floor of the Trenton would look like if I had any say."

August stared at her, flummoxed. "What's wrong with it the way it is?"

"What isn't wrong with it? The dining room is completely undersized and stuck at the back of the building like an afterthought. The kitchens might as well be on the other side of the world—your serving staff spend hours in a day walking unnecessary miles back and forth. And the lobby is about as welcoming as the Tower of London. It's cold and stark. A hotel should be warm and welcoming." She paused. "Should I go on?"

"No. And a hotel should be clean and serviceable," August told her. "Unnecessary frills cost money." He stopped and shook his head. This was ridiculous. He wasn't about to debate the merits of running a hotel with his sister. He held up the two drawings. "You're so talented, Anne. Why don't you consider applying your talents to portraits? Landscapes? Anything that you might share with other young ladies of the ton? You might be surprised at the friendships that are realized through a common interest." August knew Anne had had lessons in watercolors and was more than competent, yet these pages were devoid of anything save stark lines of ink and graphite, almost mathematical in their precision.

"I've considered it."

"And?"

"They hold little interest to me." She reached out and snatched her book back. "Landscapes or the young ladies of the ton who go along with them."

August suppressed a groan. "Anne, I—"

"Your Grace?" A brisk knock on his door accompanied the question, and a man with a mop of slightly windblown hair stuck his head into the study. "Oh, my apologies, Your Grace, Lady Anne. I didn't realize you were both in here. I'll come back—"

"No need, Mr. Down," Anne replied. "I was just on my way out." She glanced back at August, folding her precious book under her arm. "Thank you again for...everything."

"You're welcome," August replied, once again at a loss.

He put the drawing of the tavern sign on his desk with a sigh.

"Goodbye, August," she said with finality, hesitating just before the door. "And good day to you, Mr. Down," she murmured, and then she was gone.

Duncan Down eyed her retreating form before turning back to August with a respectful, if sympathetic, look. "Shall I come back at a better time, Your Grace?"

"No," he said tersely as he went to the sideboard to pour himself a very stiff drink. "Brandy, Mr. Down?" He glanced behind him as he poured.

"Appreciate it." His man of business paused at the desk and glanced in dismay at the untidy pile of shavings from the shaft of the newly sharpened quill. "I can purchase you a new set of quills, you know," he remarked. "There is no need to use each until it is a barely recognizable stub. I just finished with your monthly ledgers, and I can assure you that there is more than enough capital to purchase an entire flock of birds, as well as the continent on which they might be found. Just yesterday I saw a lovely set made from swan—"

"Nothing wrong with that quill. Still works just fine. And no point wasting money on swan feathers when ordinary goose writes just as well."

"Yet you buy South Pacific pearls when you could have purchased—"

"Those were a gift for Lady Anne." August cut him off with a black look. "And nothing is too good for my sister."

"Of course, Your Grace."

"Though I will trouble you in the future to keep Lady Anne away from my monthly ledgers."

"Your Grace?"

"She mentioned she took a peek at the books when you had them out yesterday. She was worried about the price of fish being sold to the Trenton, of all things." August scowled. "My sister should not have to worry about the price of anything ever again, Mr. Down. Do you understand?"

Duncan was silent for a second too long before he said, "Of course, Your Grace."

"Is she right?" August asked, almost as an afterthought. "About the increase?"

"She is. I was going to bring it to your attention today."

"Then I trust you will deal with our greedy fishmonger. Get rid of him."

"Would you like me to inquire as to whether he would re-consider his prices? He has, after all, been providing us with a good product for almost three years—"

"Then he's had three years to learn that I do not suffer fools. Find someone else."

Duncan inclined his head. "Consider it done, Your Grace."

"Good." August returned his attention to the glass in front of him before turning and handing it to Duncan.

"The contract to purchase the warehouses on the north side of the London docks will be ready for your signature this afternoon," Duncan said as he took a small sip of his brandy. "The East India Company has already expressed an interest in leasing the warehouse space, as well as their frustration that they were unable to purchase it first. I would reckon the value in those warehouses has just increased ten-fold, should you consider selling in the future. As always, a sound and very profitable investment, Your Grace."

August waved his hand impatiently. "I don't wish to talk about fish vendors or warehouses at the moment, Mr. Down." He stalked over to the door and shoved it closed with his foot before returning to his desk and retrieving the deed to Haverhall. He trusted Duncan with his life but his servants about as far as he could throw them. The ease with which he had obtained information over the years from servants everywhere, either by shrewd conversation or simple coin, had taught him that lesson.

August placed the deed in the center of his desk. He jabbed his finger into the middle of it. "I want you to tell me what you were able to discover about this."

For all of Duncan's talents in law and accounting, his true gift lay in his ability to uncover information from places one did not even know existed. Places a duke could not venture without people taking note. He was a man whose boyish face was rarely noticed and easily forgotten, and it hid a razor-sharp mind. His gentle nature, accompanied by the canny application of charm and coin, made him seem always a friend and never a threat. And no matter what August had asked of him, he had never disappointed.

His man of business took his time settling himself into one of the wide upholstered chairs that sat near the corner of the desk and gave August a long look. "I must ask, Your Grace, was this a test for me?" he asked.

"I beg your pardon?"

"In the course of my inquiries, I was advised that you are already acquainted with Miss Hayward."

August felt a muscle working along the edge of his jaw as he wondered exactly what his man of business had been told. "We crossed paths years and years ago. I haven't seen her since, so I hardly think that qualifies as 'acquainted.'"

"So your previous...encounter was not why you agreed so easily to the absolute secrecy of the sale?"

August set his glass down on the corner of his desk with an irritated thump. "I would have danced an Irish jig naked on the back of an ass if it had been a condition that would see Haverhall finally become mine." He crossed his arms over his chest. "And I would have insisted on confidentiality even if the Haywards hadn't." Almost all of August's holdings were already acquired anonymously through subsidiary companies that he had crafted, not easily traced back to the duchy. That make it easier for the competent individuals he hired to manage his investments on his behalf, and he did not like to advertise the extent of his empire.

August snatched his glass up again. "So no, my previous encounter did not influence my decision to accept her terms. Nor has it provided me the reason why Clara Hayward suddenly and inexplicably decided to sell what seems to amount to her purpose in life. That was your job."

"Ah. Well, I had to ask." Duncan suddenly grinned at him. "You were right, of course."

"About what?"

"When you said that there must be something more to the sale of the school."

August leaned forward impatiently. "Of course I was right."

Duncan took another slow sip of his brandy. "Were you aware that the current Baron Strathmore is a trained physician still practicing?"

"I was, yes." Another eccentricity of the Hayward clan that seemed to have been forgiven thanks to barrels of Strathmore money, though he wasn't sure what this had to do with Haverhall.

"Did you know that he served during the Waterloo campaign?"

"Hmm. That I did not know."

"Departed immediately after he was widowed, though the accepted story seems to be that he spent his period of mourning simply traveling."

"His wife was a shrew. Given what happened at the end

of their marriage, I can understand why he might jump at the chance to shoot things. Therapeutic, I might suggest."

Duncan examined the edge of his glass. "He didn't shoot things. He served as a battlefield surgeon."

August felt another tug of impatience and took a healthy swallow of brandy to hide it. "Very honorable, I'm sure. But get to the point, Mr. Down. What does any of this have to do with Haverhall or the Strathmore shipping empire or—"

"There is no empire."

August's glass froze halfway to his mouth. Carefully he set it aside. "I beg your pardon?"

"There is no empire, though the baron is doing an extraordinarily admirable job of hiding that fact. What remains, as far as I can determine, is the crumbling framework of what used to be a ridiculously profitable import and export company. It could be revived, of course, though I'm not sure the good doctor is the man for the job." Duncan left that last bit dangling.

August tipped his head, an old familiar feeling of heady anticipation starting to tingle through his veins. "Do tell."

"Old Strathmore made the bulk of his fortune on the trade of common goods. He exported furniture, cutlery, glassware, and toys, all purchased directly from the craftsmen. His ships returned with sugar, tobacco, cotton, copper, iron ore, and the occasional shipment of indigo. Nothing glamorous, but all bulk items in high demand. And he increased his profits by distributing and selling them himself."

"What changed?"

"Aside from Lord and Lady Strathmore's indecently extravagant lifestyle?" Duncan drained the last of his brandy. "It would seem extravagance became contagious. The late baron decided there could be more profit in bringing in luxury items from the East Indies. Gold, diamonds, spices, silk."

"He wasn't wrong," August mused, bracing his hands on his desk.

"He wasn't lucky either. Or perhaps he trusted the wrong people. Either way, he leveraged his company to purchase bigger ships to make the journey east instead of west. He committed huge sums of money to secure cargoes, hired more crews with heavier armaments—"

"He overextended himself."

"He borrowed heavily to cover losses. It cost a bit of coin, but I was able to obtain records that document the loss of one of his Indiamen to a storm, three others to pirates. Or maybe mutinies. Hard to say for sure when the crews disappear with the cargo. But all of those ships were laden to the gunwales with a king's ransom in goods already purchased."

"What's left?" This was the important part.

Duncan snorted. "A great deal of debt."

"Ships?"

"Five vessels of varying sorts, including two clippers. The current baron has sold three Indiamen and two large brigs last year. Of his remaining ships, two are active. Two more have been refitted and are now waiting for crews, and the last needs expensive repairs."

"The two ships that are active—where are they?"

"Back to their former routes and former cargoes. Virginia, mostly. It would seem that Strathmore's dependable network of trade partners in the West survived intact."

August straightened with keen interest. Owning a vast fleet himself, he knew just how valuable those trade networks and partners were. "And his distribution arrangements here?"

Duncan made a face and shrugged. "I wasn't able to confirm that. But he's been selling cargo to someone. He, along with his siblings, seems determined to save a sinking company."

"Commendable, I suppose, but with two ships?" August drummed his fingers on his thigh. "He'll be dead of old age before he makes any headway."

"It's a tricky knot, that of requiring money to make more money."

Which was why Clara Hayward had sold Haverhall. The answer was obvious now. Selling any more of their remaining fleet would cripple any chance their family might have at expansion or recovery of the shipping company. "They're trying to get the remaining ships crewed and repaired in a timely manner before they rot at their moorings," August murmured. "I would have done the same."

"The baron does strike me as a resourceful man."

August felt his brows lift. "You spoke to him?"

"Of course I did." Duncan covered his chest dramatically with his fingers. "For the terrible heart palpitations I've been having."

"Palpitations." August shook his head. "The only thing that makes your heart palpitate is money, Mr. Down. And lots of it."

"There is something about a pot, a kettle, and the color black I feel I should mention at this juncture, Your Grace."

"How much trouble are the Haywards still in?" August asked, ignoring the jab. The heady anticipation he had felt before was still buzzing through him.

"There is no agricultural or industrial revenue to subsidize their income—Haverhall is the only land that existed in conjunction with the Strathmore title. But the profits from the school alone weren't enough to cover the loan from

Strathmore's banker that is coming due in six weeks. Capital plus interest."

August didn't even want to know how Duncan had discovered that, but he didn't doubt him for a second. "Strathmore is relying on the ships that are currently in the Americas to return in time with their cargo to counter his debt."

"Yes."

August turned away and paced the room, stopping by one of the towering bookcases. He ran his fingers thoughtfully down the ancient leather spines. From experience August knew that ships were notoriously unreliable when it came to punctuality.

"I want that company," he said to no one in particular. Strathmore's ships would be a welcome addition to his fleet, but it was the baron's trading network that held the real value. A network that could be expanded and exploited to his advantage.

And to have a chance at that, before the baron was forced to put the company up for sale on the open market and ignite a bidding war, August knew that he would need to insert himself into Strathmore's world. Convince him that he was a friend, a confidant, and the answer to all his troubles. Discover exactly what he truly desired and then show him the path to achieving it. Sometimes it took minutes. Other times much longer. But August was a very patient man. And everyone had their price. Everyone had their breaking point.

"Is Lord Strathmore still in London?" August asked.

Duncan smirked, making it obvious to August that he knew exactly what he was thinking. "He is." His man of business made a show of glancing at the mantel clock. "What's more, he can usually be found at the British Museum late on Wednesday afternoons. I am told that he escorts his sisters there regularly." He paused, a sandy brow raised. "Thinking of reacquainting yourself with the baron, Your Grace?"

An unseemly excitement shot through August, different from mere anticipation, though he did a decent job at convincing himself that it was the prospect of adding to his holdings that was responsible for it, not the possibility of seeing Clara Hayward again. "I need to get to Strathmore before he's forced to sell. If he puts that company up for sale on the open market, there will be at least a dozen men clamoring to buy him out. And competition like that will drive the price up well beyond what I'd like."

Duncan sniffed. "I'm surprised there haven't been at least a dozen men clamoring to entice Miss Hayward to the altar before all of this. Surely someone else might have discovered that she owned Haverhall. Surely you're not the only one who's recognized the profit that could be realized by developing that land." He put his empty glass aside and took his spectacles out of his pocket, polishing them on his sleeve. "Men have married for far less, and English law falls squarely in their favor."

August bristled at that and then wondered why he should, especially since Duncan wasn't wrong. "Maybe Miss Hayward has been wise enough to see through those who would court her only for her pecuniary assets. Maybe she has no interest in marriage at all." It came out far more vehemently than he would have liked.

"Then those are things you and Miss Hayward have in common, Your Grace," Duncan suggested with a suspicious amount of nonchalance. "Perhaps it will give you something to discuss if you find yourself reacquainted in your pursuit of the good doctor."

August's heart suddenly tripped erratically, making him

feel as if he were twenty-one again and standing smitten on a ballroom dance floor. He frowned, and the feeling passed.

"Have development plans for Haverhall drawn up, Mr. Down," August said, deliberately changing the subject. "Discreetly, of course. Look outside London for services. Wilds and Busby in Brighton, perhaps—we've used them before and they've proven themselves trustworthy. If and when my ownership of Haverhall is revealed to the Haywards, or anyone else for that matter, it will be on my terms and not through the gossip mill."

"Understood, Your Grace." Duncan looked up at August, sliding his spectacles back over the bridge of his nose and making it difficult to see his eyes behind the reflection of the lenses. "The museum is open for another hour yet. Shall I ask to have your carriage brought round?"

"Yes," August said, reaching for his coat. "Please do."

Chapter 2

Clara Hayward considered the scene before her.

Each line of the sculpture was saturated in unleashed violence. It captured the desperate movement, the raw fury, and the heated anger to exquisite perfection. The centaur's hand was wrapped around the Lapith's throat, intent clear in his carved expression, while the Lapith wrenched a leg up to stave off the assault. Muscles strained as both beings remained locked in an eternal battle, each creature fighting for its life.

Not unlike what Clara was feeling just now.

Well, perhaps that was a little melodramatic. No one was going to die, but life as she knew it was on the brink of changing forever, leaving her feeling empty and a little nauseous at the same time. The papers that she had signed marked the beginning of the end of her tenure at Haverhall, and no matter how hard she tried, Clara was having a difficult time coming to terms with the knowledge that she had sold the legacy that had been left to her.

It had been mercifully quick, the sale, and for that she supposed she should be grateful. It could have dragged on painfully, with her having to endure a host of critical assessments from potential buyers. Quite the opposite, in fact. A faceless company that had previously expressed interest in the property had been contacted—and had immediately and unconditionally agreed to the price and the terms of the sale. Within a day it had been done.

Clara knew that she should be more interested in who had bought it—the faces behind the faceless company—but she couldn't bring herself to pursue it. Because it didn't matter, really, who had bought it. It changed nothing, and dwelling on something that was done and couldn't be undone would bring her only sorrow and despair.

She needed to look forward, not back.

Harland had told her that it would all be temporary. Once they managed to right their finances and the shipping company became profitable again, they could look for a new venue for a school. It was a short-term sacrifice, he had said, and Clara knew that, in theory, he was right. But she also knew that so much could go wrong.

One needed to look no further than the debt her parents had left behind when they had died two years ago. It had come as a shock to Clara and her siblings, catching them all oblivious. There had been a certain amount of humiliation in that, given each one's supposed intelligence. But Clara had been absorbed with her school, Harland with his medical practice, Rose with her art studio, and none of them had been aware of the bleak and disastrous reality that their parents had managed to hide.

And now they were scrambling to recover. Each doing whatever they could, in their own way. She could only hope that it would be enough.

Clara closed her eyes against the heaviness that had settled in her chest and the tightness that had gathered at her throat, grateful that the museum was almost empty at this late hour and no one was witness to her selfish melancholy. She had to believe things would work out. More important, she still had her summer students, those young women who were far more than just—

"Do you suppose it really was the wine, Miss Hayward?" came a low voice behind her. "Or do you think the centaurs and the Lapiths were just looking for an excuse to start a war?"

Clara felt the breath leave her lungs, and her heart seemed to miss a beat before resuming at twice its proper pace. She knew that voice. Even after all this time, she had never forgotten it.

Just as she had never forgotten the way August Faulkner had made her feel the night he had asked her to dance. He might have done so on a dare, and she might have accepted out of sheer spite and an unwillingness to let his arrogance get the better of her. And it might have been more of a contest than a dance, neither one willing to yield an inch, but at the end of it all, she had found a reckless joy in it. And when he had returned her smile, there was a brief moment when she had believed he had actually seen *her* and not the label society had applied. And liked what he saw.

But he'd not seen or spoken to her since, and aside, perhaps, from his sister's recent application to Haverhall, Clara was quite certain he hadn't spared her a thought since that night either.

Clara, of course, hadn't been so lucky. His unexpected title had made sure of that. The moment the Holloway dukedom had come to rest on his shoulders, August Faulkner had been relentlessly pursued across the pages of the gossip rags and newssheets by tales of his wealth, conjecture about his paramours, and speculation about every aspect of his life that the ton decided was relevant. His companionship was sought by popular peers and prospective duchesses alike, all of them hoping for just a taste of the affluence and power he had come to represent.

And now he was here, seeming inexplicably to be seeking her company.

Slowly Clara opened her eyes, the Lapith still struggling desperately in her vision. "I would suggest that excessive drinking tends to bring one's true intentions and feelings to the forefront," she said, relieved that she remembered his question and that her voice was steady. "One might suggest that the fight was inevitable."

"Indeed. I believe I would agree with you." Holloway took a step forward as he came to stand beside her, though Clara kept her eyes firmly on the sculpture. "Who do you think won this particular skirmish?" he asked.

She could feel his presence beside her as acutely as if he had just taken her in his arms again. Her skin prickled with goose bumps, and butterflies assailed her insides. She caught a trace of his scent as he moved, the richness of his shaving soap laced with a hint of leather making her feel as if she were back in that heated ballroom and not in a dusty museum.

Clara cleared her throat, trying to focus on the question at hand and not the man who had asked it. "I don't know. One would assume the centaur has the advantage. Speed, size, strength. But his wits are compromised, and he has given in to base and reckless urges. And history teaches us sheer strength is rarely enough to defeat a cunning, civilized enemy."

"So the Lapith, then. Or at least the superior version of the Lapith that the Athenians believed themselves to be."

For a moment Clara wondered if she might be dreaming all of this. This...surreal conversation with a man she hadn't spoken to in almost a decade, a man she was now, improbably, discussing Greek mythology with. She finally turned to stare at him, half expecting Holloway to shimmer like a mirage and then vanish in a puff of smoke.

He didn't.

But perhaps it would have been better if he had. At twenty-one he'd been handsome. But the man he'd become since then was no less than devastating. His edges had become sharper, his bearing sleeker, his presence exuding a restless, potent energy that seemed to fill whatever spaces in the room his body did not.

He still had thick, dark hair, the color of coffee. It was cut fashionably short, and the slight curl in it reminded her of the styles that seemed so popular for the sculpted Greek art that surrounded them. In fact, there was a lot of him that reminded her of the exquisite marble statue of David she had once viewed outside the Palazzo Vecchio in Florence. Thick, arched brows framed eyes that were set above broad, defined cheekbones and a square jaw. Strong shoulders and a physique that belied power. A height that set him above others.

She forced herself to keep her expression pleasant. The practiced politesse that she relied upon to charm formidable peers was threatening to desert her. Along with most of her wits. Never in her life had she felt so woefully ill prepared.

Though never in her life had she been so thoroughly ambushed.

"You're well versed in mythology, Your Grace," Clara said, averting her eyes and falling back on transparent flattery because she had no idea what else to say.

"I know enough," the duke replied. "Though I suspect that you know more."

Clara snapped her gaze back to Holloway, wondering if he was mocking her, but he was standing square, his eyes focused on the sculpture and his hands clasped behind him.

"I owe you an apology, Miss Hayward. One that comes years too late, but one that I hope you'll accept."

If Holloway had suddenly turned into a unicorn, Clara wouldn't have been more shocked. She managed to close her mouth, realizing belatedly that it had fallen open. "Whatever for?"

"I need to apologize for my actions the night that we danced," he said gravely. "My initial intentions were deplorable, and we both know it. I am no longer that person, trying to prove myself to individuals whose opinions should never have mattered, and it is imperative that you know that. Had my sister been propositioned in such an infantile manner, I would have shot the blackguard."

Clara blinked at him, trying to assimilate his words, cursing her usually capable mind for abandoning her under the force of his brilliant blue gaze. "Are you dying, Your Grace?"

It was his turn to look shocked. "I beg your pardon?"

She cursed herself again. That hadn't been done well. "I've heard of individuals who feel the need to make amends to those they believed that they've wronged before—"

"I'm not dying," Holloway said, looking nonplussed.

"I'm relieved to hear that," Clara replied, trying to salvage this implausible conversation that hovered on the edge of grim and fully in the realm of awkward. "And I am further relieved that my own brother restrained himself from shooting anyone on my behalf that night. If I recall, you looked very dashing that evening, and a bullet hole would have ruined the whole effect. It certainly would have ruined your coat." There, that sounded light. Almost teasing. Something to smooth the conversation.

"My coat." It was flat, without a hint of humor.

"It was a jest, Your Grace." In truth, he no longer seemed as if he laughed often. He no longer seemed like the impulsive man who had once held her in his arms. This August Faulkner was harder. More intense. A leashed, controlled version of the daring upstart who had made her smile.

Perhaps that was what a duchy did to a man.

"Of course." Holloway's face was expressionless now. "Regardless, you have my word that it will not happen again."

"I accept your apology, though it is not required," Clara said into the silence, feeling a sudden sense of loss with the realization that the daredevil who had lingered in her mind and her memories was gone, replaced by a man who would rather blindside her with an austere apology than ask her to waltz again. Although that did make it easier to breathe. And a little easier to think.

"Thank you." He looked away from her, back at the metopes.

"I don't regret it. Dancing with you, that is. You should know that I'm of the mind that regrets are things best reserved for circumstances beyond our control. Otherwise they become mere excuses." She gazed at him and the unyielding lines of his profile. "You should also know that, in the unlikely event that you ever ask me to dance again on a dare, I will take you up on the offer." Those words were out before she could reconsider.

The duke turned to look at her, and she felt the intensity of his piecing gaze crackle all the way through her, making her heart race and her insides twist. The butterflies that she had felt earlier became raptors trying to beat their way out of her chest.

His eyes were narrowed, his lashes shadowing the blue of them. Lashes that were wasted on a man, Clara thought disjointedly. Thick and black and framing eyes the color of twilight. But he was saved from being pretty by the severe, strong lines of his face and the hint of stubble along his jaw. The entire effect was as intoxicating as it was compelling, and it made her want to run her fingers—

Dear God, she needed to pull herself together. Yes, he was a man in possession of sinfully superb looks. And yes, she was a woman in possession of a pulse. But this was ridiculous.

"I'll keep that in mind, Miss Hayward."

Clara forced herself to remain utterly impassive, nodding as if she had just made a blithe comment on the weather and not one that was the height of idiocy.

"Are you here with your brother, Miss Hayward?" Holloway asked, glancing about the room, which was empty save for the sightless figures staring out from their posts and pedestals. "Or are you alone?"

It was as if a bucket of cold water had been dumped over her head, and Clara felt instantly wary. What sort of question was that? Was Holloway actually questioning the respectability of her presence here? Was he really questioning her propriety and decorum?

And suddenly, with an awful bolt of clarity, she understood. The duke's presence here had nothing to do with her and everything to do with his sister. As of tomorrow, Anne Faulkner would be part of what would be Haverhall's last summer term, and Clara was quite sure that this had spurred his sudden visit and apology. His ambush was nothing but a test. One did not, after all, entrust one's sister to the tutelage of a woman who might just be holding a grudge coupled with Boudiccan tendencies.

Her dawning comprehension left her feeling both mortified and deflated. For a moment she had actually deluded herself into believing that the duke had sought her out after all this time for something far different. "My brother is not here, though my sister is just around the corner where I left her, sketching some of the Townley sculptures. We were escorted here by a friend. Even if I were not an ancient spinster, I can assure you that this is all very proper," she felt compelled to add, knowing that it almost sounded resentful.

He frowned. "I wasn't implying otherwise. And you're not ancient."

Clara almost snorted. "That's kind of you to say."

His frown deepened. "If you're ancient, what does that make me?"

"Desirable, if it were a woman asking. Distinguished if it were a man."

"That's not…" The duke trailed off, unclasping his hands.

"That's not your fault." Clara completed his sentence for him, her irritation rising, but giving him a practiced, polite smile to conceal it. "That is just how it is."

He moved then, without warning, coming to stand directly in front of her, close enough that she was now enveloped in his heat and the spicy tang of his shaving soap. In the next breath, he had caught her hand, and Clara knew what he intended long before his lips brushed the backs of her knuckles.

The gesture instantly sent electricity arcing through her veins. It was no wonder women reportedly fought over the privilege of his company, Clara thought. His current gaze and the expression that accompanied it would probably be enough to convince any woman that he had spent eons worshipping her from afar and even more time contemplating how he might worship her up close.

But it wasn't real. It wasn't anything like the look August Faulkner had given her ten years ago. The breathless smile he had bestowed on her then had been genuine, and had dominated her daydreams for a decade. This contrived facsimile, which he no doubt believed partnered well with his apology, was a poor substitute. Gently Clara tried to extract her hand, but he only tightened his fingers.

"May I call on you tomorrow, Miss Hayward?" Holloway asked without warning.

Clara felt her jaw slacken again, and it took every ounce of what was left of her composure not to openly gawk at him. "I beg your pardon?" What was he trying to prove now? Because he would know that she was leaving London the next day, along with his sister and the rest of Haverhall's summer students.

"With Lord Strathmore's permission, of course," he added, her hand still in his.

It was clear he had forgotten. Or perhaps he had confused the dates. Lady Anne had handled the application and arrangements herself, something that Clara never discouraged in any of her students, but perhaps communication between brother and sister had broken down somewhere along the way. He was, after all, a duke with an entire duchy to run, a daunting task at the best of times.

She hesitated, debating the prudence of reminding a man who seemed to revel in control that he had allowed something to slip from that sphere.

"I'm afraid that is not possible," Clara finally said, willing her face to remain serene. It was likely that he would remember soon enough. "I am leaving London tomorrow morning for the duration of the summer," she tried. "My brother has already gone."

"Ah. May I be so bold as to ask where you are spending the summer?"

"Dover?" It came out like a question she was hoping he would recognize the answer to.

"Ah." A crease had appeared in his forehead. "That sounds...lovely."

"Indeed." She kept her smile pasted on her face as she struggled to find words. Any words. Perhaps she should—

"Miss Hayward." A voice behind her ricocheted around the room, bouncing off the marbles with an unpleasant echo.

Clara snatched her hand from Holloway's and spun. "Mr. Stilton." She could feel heat rise in her cheeks as if she were twenty years old again and had just been caught in dishabille with the duke. She smothered that mortifying, juvenile reaction and smoothed her hands over her skirts.

"Your Grace, may I present Mr. Mathias Stilton," she said, her manners thankfully reasserting themselves. "Mr. Stilton, His Grace, the Duke of Holloway." She exhaled, then frowned when neither man made any attempt to continue with the expected pleasantries. In fact, Stilton's expression, usually so genial, was positively frigid. Hostile, almost.

Clara glanced at Holloway. The duke's face gave away none of his thoughts, though he was studying the man intently. Clara frowned, her eyes sliding back to Stilton. She and Rose had, in fact, met Mathias Stilton here in the British Museum on one of their regular excursions not long after their parents' death. They had fallen into easy conversation and had discovered that the wealthy widower shared their interest in history and art.

He was handsome, Clara supposed, with fashionably cut blond hair just starting to silver at his temples, clear gray eyes, a pleasing, broad face, and a slender physique that looked quite elegant in his peacock-blue coat. Clara had once thought that he might have an interest in her sister beyond casual discussions on form and perspective, but both parties had remained romantically indifferent. That hadn't, however, prevented Mr. Stilton from collecting both Clara and Rose to view the exhibits at the museum when their brother was unable to escort them here himself.

Though this particular visit had now become an exhibit itself of antagonistic undercurrents. With no explanations forthcoming.

"Your Grace." Stilton finally uttered something that sounded like a greeting.

"Mr. Stilton," Holloway replied neutrally.

"You are already acquainted?" Clara forced herself to say into the strained silence.

Stilton made a low, derisive noise while Holloway only inclined his head slightly.

"We've met," the duke said.

Clara waited for Stilton to pick up the thread and elaborate, but he remained uncharacteristically mute, and she wondered at his overt discourtesy.

"Well, then," Clara managed with forced cheer, "I think I will collect my sister before the museum closes."

"Excellent," Stilton murmured. "I've already asked for my carriage to be brought around so you don't have to wait."

"How thoughtful." Clara arranged a pleasant smile on her face and turned to Holloway.

The duke's eyes flickered back to her, and Clara was once again pinned under a sea of intense blue. "I didn't realize Mr. Stilton had escorted you here today." He held her gaze for a beat too long before it went back to Stilton as if he were reevaluating the man's motivations.

A strange sort of thrill twisted uninvited through Clara's body. It was almost as if the duke were...not jealous, exactly, because absolutely no logic that existed would support that reaction. *Territorial*, perhaps, was the better word. As if Holloway had some sort of stake in how and with whom she might spend her time.

Not that it was any of his damn business. Not ten years ago and certainly not now.

A faint glimmer of her earlier irritation returned, and Clara grasped it with zeal. Annoyance, when it came to the Duke of Holloway, was much safer than any other feeling the man seemed to elicit from her. "It was a pleasure to see you again, Your Grace," she said with every ounce of distant decorum she could muster. "Please give my regards to Lady Anne." She saw his brows draw together fractionally before they relaxed.

"Of course," he replied. "Enjoy the rest of your day, Miss Hayward." He inclined his head again. "Good afternoon, Mr. Stilton." He said it with no inflection, but out of the corner of her eye, she saw Stilton stiffen all over again.

The duke departed as silently as he had come, and Clara forced herself not to let her eyes linger on his broad back as he exited. She glanced at Stilton, seeing that her escort had no such compunctions. He was watching the duke retreat with an unpleasant curl to his lip.

"Mr. Stilton?" Clara prompted. "Is anything amiss?"

Mathias Stilton's eyes snapped back to hers, and she saw his expression clear. "I beg your pardon, Miss Hayward. I'm sorry if any of that offended you."

She almost rolled her eyes. "I can assure you, I am not offended. Just..." She cast about for a word that might encourage an explanation. "Concerned," she settled on.

Stilton waved his hand. "Business between men," he said

with a beatific smile that didn't quite reach his eyes. "Nothing that you need to worry your pretty little head about. And nothing that will spoil the rest of the afternoon."

Clara gritted her teeth at the banal condescension that had crept into his voice, though she knew very well that most gentlemen would have said the same thing.

The Duke of Holloway wouldn't have.

Clara resolutely ignored that voice, knowing she knew no such thing. A single discussion about centaurs and Lapiths after ten years of silence did not a friendship or a familiarity make.

Stilton held out his arm. "Let's find your sister, shall we?"

"Indeed," Clara murmured, glancing back at the door through which Holloway had vanished.

And reassuring herself that it would probably be another ten years before she'd have to see the Duke of Holloway again.

Chapter 3

Two days later, August sat at the desk in his study, staring into space, still wondering if he had lost his mind. He'd certainly lost his touch.

He'd seen Clara Hayward the instant he'd stepped into that damn museum, and every thought of the baron, expensive ships, invaluable networks, and sound plans had dissolved like mist in the wind. He had kept his distance at first, trying to collect his thoughts and his wits because it was clear that Miss Hayward was no longer the same girl he had danced with.

Then, dressed in a pale, shimmering ball gown and expensive jewels, she had been exceedingly pretty. Now, clad in a simple day dress the color of claret and devoid of accessories, she was stunning. She still possessed the same lustrous hair, though it had been pulled back into a rather pedestrian knot at the back of her head. Her skin was still flawless, free of any cosmetics, and her dark eyes still brimmed with the intelligence he remembered so well. But where she had once displayed tutored poise, she now radiated a rare confidence that was characteristic of those who had truly embraced their individuality and found pleasure and happiness within it. In a man it was admirable. In a woman he found it indecently seductive.

August had followed her discreetly through the museum, not an easy feat considering that the building was almost empty as it approached closing time. She had been accompanied then only by her sister, a petite, fairer version of herself, who showed very little enthusiasm for conversation. Rose Hayward had, however, looked immensely pleased when she was left alone with her sketchbook and a room full of silent sculpture. August knew he should have been disappointed that the baron was nowhere in sight, but instead he had been similarly pleased. Because it had left Clara free to wander into a room stuffed full of Elgin Marbles, gifting him with a sliver of stolen time to spend with her. Precious moments in which he thought he'd charm her.

Instead he'd blundered into a conversation that he'd not adequately prepared himself for. Miss Hayward had been gracious and pleasant and had not given any indication that she found anything odd about his unexpected and unsolicited reappearance. Until, that was, he found himself apologizing to her. Badly. Or badly enough that Miss Hayward had looked at him with concern.

And then asked if he was dying.

His pride had certainly been suffering a slow death, and the fact that his palms had gone damp, his mouth was dry, and his heart pounded did not help. Miss Hayward, in a clear attempt to put him at ease, had accepted his apology with a smooth, lighthearted decorum that was no doubt the cornerstone of the Haverhall School for Young Ladies.

He should have stopped there, retreated even, but instead

he had plowed on and succeeded in making everything worse. The chivalrous kiss and the not-so-chivalrous look he had bestowed upon Miss Hayward were things he had taken great pains to perfect over the years. They were things that promised indecent wickedness without his actually having to do anything more. Once he had mastered the combination, he found he was rewarded with fluttering fans, fluttering lashes, and fluttering giggles. The innocent threatened to swoon. The experienced threatened far more carnal consequences.

Miss Hayward had simply gazed at him, her face set in an expression of mild puzzlement, in a way he might expect her to look while reading a treatise on the Isoptera of England. And then that expression had faded into what looked almost like one of...awkward disappointment, as though she were now faced with a doddering dowager who had fallen asleep in her tea.

August groaned and rested his forehead in his hands. Again he had felt as if he were that youth of his past. Goaded into something he knew wasn't going to end well but unable to resist. What had he thought would happen? The pretty girl who had once matched him step for step, who had stared down his boorish companions and made him grin like a fool, wasn't a girl anymore. That girl was gone, replaced with a beautiful, intelligent woman in possession of a flawless grace and poise. Her sterling reputation had been earned, not fabricated, and he should have known better.

And before August could assure Miss Hayward that he was no longer that gauche youth, seeking to recapture the advantage that he had so spectacularly lost on a dance floor long ago, Mathias Stilton had appeared. August felt his lip curl. The man was a peacock. An egotistical, foolish peacock who had managed to run the profitable lace factory his father had established into the ground within a year and a half of inheriting it.

August had swiftly and unapologetically bought it and the vast tract of land upon which it sat, and it had been one of his first large acquisitions. The purchase price should have been enough to send Stilton away and keep him in moderate comfort, but for almost a year afterward, August had been forced to endure and reject Stilton's constant requests and demands for either a loan or partnership to give back to him what he insisted was his birthright. Another reason August now used benign company names for his investments.

Though what Clara Hayward was doing with a man like that was perplexing. Stilton wasn't intelligent or intrepid. He certainly wasn't the sort of man August had envisioned her with, and a startling animosity had risen fast and fierce. Stilton simply wasn't...good enough for her.

And you are?

The voice in his head came with the reminder that he'd already had his chance and squandered it. Frustration, disappointment, and something far more unsettling rose in his gut. As if he'd once held something valuable in his hand and discarded it, recognizing its worth far too late. Perhaps that was what chafed, because he prided himself on recognizing worth where others did not. It was what he had built his fortune on.

August straightened, pushing himself out of his chair and to his feet. Brooding was pointless. Regret was pointless. He needed to keep his eye on the prize here, and that prize was not Clara Hayward, no matter how beautiful and intelligent and gracious she might be. If he wanted a chance to acquire Strathmore Shipping, he needed a new plan.

Starting, it would seem, in Dover.

"Your Grace?" Duncan stuck his head around the door.

"Perfect timing," August grumbled. "I'd appreciate your assistance."

Duncan sidled in. "Your Grace—"

"We're going to need to make some sort of arrangements to—"

"Your Grace." It was said with greater volume.

"Is there a problem, Mr. Down?" For the first time, August took a good look at his man of business and noted the deep crease in his forehead and the worried expression behind his spectacles. He also realized that Down wasn't alone, and that he was, in fact, accompanied by a young maid. Anne's lady's maid, specifically.

And the woman looked as if she was going to cast up her accounts.

"Mr. Down?" August left that hanging ominously. He didn't have time to deal with domestic problems at the moment.

"It's Lady Anne, Your Grace," the woman wobbled.

Apprehension streaked through him. "What about my sister? Is she ill? Has something happened?" All manner of catastrophes flitted through his mind, each worse than the one before.

The maid now looked as if she was on the verge of tears. "She's not…not…not here, Your Grace."

"I beg your pardon?" It came out far harsher than he'd intended, but he couldn't stand vacillation.

Duncan cleared his throat. "It seems, Your Grace, that Lady Anne has left."

"Left?" August's patience was hanging by a thread. "When did she leave?" he demanded. "Perhaps she's gone visiting or shopping or to—"

"Yesterday, Your Grace."

August blinked in incomprehension. "Yesterday?"

"She told me that she didn't need me yesterday or last night," the maid explained tremulously. "Told me to take the time to visit my ma. So I did." She was wringing her hands. "But then, this morning when I came back and went up to her rooms, I realized that she hadn't slept in her bed."

"Perhaps the chambermaids made it before you got there." It sounded more like an order than a question. As if he could will it so.

She shook her head. "I asked, and they didn't. Tidy the room, that is. And some of her things are missing. Clothes and—"

"Goddammit."

The maid flinched, and Duncan frowned. August forced himself to take a breath. He recalled his last tense encounter with his sister and clenched his hands. Though he was having a very difficult time believing that Anne would run away because she was angry with him. Anne did not run away from conflict. "Did she leave a note? A message? Anything?"

"She did." It was Duncan who spoke. He held out a folded paper.

"What does it say?" August snapped.

"I thought you might wish to read it—"

"What. Does. It. Say?" August growled.

Duncan cleared his throat again. "She has left to attend and take part in the Haverhall School for Young Ladies' summer term. You are not to worry, nor are you to follow her or, ah, interfere in any way. She will return in six weeks."

August stared at Duncan. Duncan stared back. Very slowly, August turned to the maid. "Go. And speak of this to no one, if you value your job."

His man of business frowned again at his rudeness, but August was past the point of caring. The young maid almost fell over herself in her haste to leave, and the door banged shut behind her.

August swung back to the man standing in front of his desk. "Did you know anything about this?"

Duncan bristled. "Of course not."

"Get the carriage," August snarled. "We're going to Haverhall."

Please give my regards to Lady Anne. That was what Clara Hayward had said yesterday, and August had thought her statement just a continuation of her seamless politesse. Instead, it seemed, Clara Hayward and his sister had been in collusion from the very beginning. August wasn't sure whom his anger was best aimed at. Anne, for her duplicity? Miss Hayward, for her silence? Himself, for his utter and complete obliviousness to the entire affair?

"Lady Anne is not at Haverhall, Your Grace."

It took a moment for Duncan's words to sink past the dark cloud that had wrapped itself around him.

May I be so bold as to ask where you are spending the summer?

"She's in Dover."

"Yes." Duncan sounded surprised. "How did you know?"

"Doesn't matter." August became aware that his teeth were grinding, and he tried to relax his jaw before they shattered. "Where in Dover?"

Duncan set the note on the desk. "Avondale. Just north of the town."

"The Earl of Rivers's estate?"

"The very same. It would seem that Haverhall has let it for years. For their summer students. Of which your sister is now one."

August braced his hands on the edge of his desk, the wood biting into his fingers. "Can you explain, Mr. Down, just what the hell my sister needs a finishing school for? A finishing school that extorts a criminal tuition from its students and then drags them seventy miles from London, at that? When I have made sure she has had the best instruction, the best governesses, the best, period? Anne speaks three languages fluently. She can dance, paint, play the pianoforte, make intelligent conversation with impeccable manners. She's smart and capable and accomplished." And August wanted to give her the world, even if she didn't seem to believe it. He pushed himself away from his desk. "What more does she damn well need?"

Duncan merely looked at him. "I can see the appeal."

"I beg your pardon?"

"Miss Hayward's appeal. An individual who seems to have chosen her own path. Defied society to chase her own ambitions." Duncan raised a brow. "Sounds a little like a man I know, now that I think about it."

"I didn't choose a path; I was forced upon it," August growled. "And I didn't defy anything except death to become a duke. Further, I have no intentions of letting my sister defy society. Ever. Society can be horrifically cruel, and I'm sure Miss Hayward will be the first to attest to that."

Duncan sighed. "With all due respect, Your Grace, Lady Anne comes from a very different place than the young ladies of the ton. Her past—her experiences—have shaped her view, and given her an outlook on life that will not be found among her contemporaries. Her ambitions and desires will not be what others may want—"

"Anne is not old enough to know what she wants."

Duncan frowned. "If I may be so bold, I should point out that she is the same age you were when—"

"You may not be so bold, Mr. Down. This discussion is at

an end." Duncan might have good intentions, but the welfare of Anne was not his business. Nor would it ever be.

"Right." Duncan looked as if he wanted to argue.

August glared at him, and he seemed to reconsider. Wise man.

"May we get back to the matter at hand?" August asked testily.

Duncan gave him a long look. "In that case, Your Grace, if you want answers, I expect that your questions are best put to Lady Anne."

Or Clara Hayward.

August's mind was slowly starting to work again. He forced himself to take a deep, steadying breath. Forced himself to think past the betrayal and the fury and the shock because emotion muddled reason and made smart men make stupid choices. His immediate impulse to haul Anne back to London was not in his best interests. She hadn't run away with a band of traveling gypsies. She hadn't run off with a man or, God forbid, eloped to Gretna Green. She had fled London to attend a bloody *finishing school*. Something could be salvaged out of his sister's impetuous, absurd actions.

Because those actions had sent her to Dover. Even if he hadn't been planning on going to Dover before, he certainly was now. He had all the justification he would ever need to go to Avondale.

First and foremost, August had every right to ascertain that his sister was safe—he *needed* to see with his own eyes that she was all right. Second, he had every right to demand that Anne explain herself—though he didn't delude himself into thinking that she would be very forthcoming, given that she had chosen to slink away like a damn thief in the night.

But he recognized that he would need to proceed with caution if he was to stay. Upon his arrival at Avondale, August would need to be firm but not belligerent. Insistent but not boorish. Assertive but not arrogant. Once he'd established his presence, then he'd need to be charming and clever and convincing. No different from many times before.

He just needed a reason to stay.

"Mr. Down, please invite the Earl of Rivers to attend me at his earliest convenience," August instructed in a tone that was downright civilized.

Duncan eyed him circumspectly. "The earl is in reduced health, Your Grace. Has been since the death of his son at Waterloo."

"I thought Eli Dawes was missing."

"And presumed dead, given how much time has passed since Waterloo." Duncan shrugged. "Regardless, the earl rarely attends any—"

"Never mind. I'll go to his Lordship." August was already striding toward the door.

"Now, Your Grace? At this hour?"

"Now," August confirmed. He was of no mind to wait. "And while I am there, please see to the travel arrangements. I'll be departing to Dover first thing on the morrow."

Chapter 4

August had chosen to ride as opposed to taking a carriage.

Not that it got him to Dover much faster, but at the very least, it gave him the illusion of action and control. Riding his own horse had held much more appeal than sitting idle, trapped in a stuffy equipage for hours on end. Though now, as he neared the end of his journey, faint wisps of smoke rising on the horizon to mark the town of Dover, he wondered if perhaps he had been hasty in his decision. He was hungry and weary and dusty and very much looking forward to parting ways with his saddle.

August was quite sure his gelding felt the same.

He reined the animal off the main road, guiding the horse down a worn, rutted cart path that would skirt the town proper. He'd taken this route before, and while it was treacherous for carriage axles, the shortcut would save him almost a mile. He urged his gelding into a reluctant trot. Up ahead, a thick copse of trees rolled down from the crest of a ridge, the leaves fluttering in the early-evening breeze. Once he was on the other side of that ridge, the town would come into view, nestled in its cradle of hills and bordered by the sea. Beyond that, the hulking mass of Dover Castle would be visible on the high cliffs. And somewhere past that, Avondale.

Where August would deal with his wayward, conniving sister and her beautiful, devious headmistress. And then turn his attention to the very real opportunity that dangled, for the moment, just beyond his reach.

The journey here had given August time to think and develop a tentative plan. He had spent more than fifteen years accumulating his fortune through careful and diverse acquisitions. Most everything he bought had been the victim of ineptitude and mismanagement, and occasionally corruption, though Strathmore Shipping seemed more a casualty of bad luck. Change was coming, and those titled, pompous peers who believed themselves insulated from the world would one day find themselves on the wrong end of that change. The late Baron Strathmore seemed to have recognized that. He'd failed in the end, but that failure was not irreversible. Not in the hands of someone with the right experience. Like August.

What if he could make it possible for the current baron to concentrate solely on his medical practice? Even with August's limited knowledge of the baron, he realized doctoring was something Strathmore was committed to and passionate about, given his battlefield experience and the fact that he still practiced. If August could purchase Strathmore Shipping for a fair price, relieving the baron of the grueling responsibility of resurrecting a company with limited means, Strathmore would be free to pursue his first love. And, of course, it would enable the baron to provide handsomely for his sisters at the same time.

It would make everybody happy.

The wide copse of trees and brush in front of August had become a portrait of gilded foliage as the sun began its descent, a low fence running just to the north creating shadows the color of dark amethyst across the tall grasses. The sky was now awash in brilliant, almost blinding color, dotted with crimson- and topaz-lined clouds. August reined his horse to a stop, for a moment simply overwhelmed by the sheer beauty of his surroundings and trying to remember the last time he had actually taken the time to notice a sunset.

He twisted in the saddle, letting his eyes roam over the ocean that he could see stretching out from the far cliffs behind him. So much space, he thought idly. Not at all like London, where roofs and buildings and clouds of coal smoke blocked the sky. Where the noises of the city never stopped, the constant clatter and din and—

His horse shied at the same time August registered the deafening report that shattered the silence. A flock of birds rose from the trees and wheeled away in fright. He managed to keep his seat as his gelding crow-hopped in panic, its ears pinned, its hindquarters bunched beneath him. Bloody hell. Someone was shooting, though August couldn't tell where the shot had come from.

He wrenched the reins, managing to collect the horse, just as something exploded from the trees. No, he realized, not something. Someone. A boy. A mere child, one who couldn't be more than seven or eight years old. Running directly toward him as if the hounds of hell were on his tail, clutching something in a small burlap sack as though his life depended on it.

For a horrible, gut-wrenching moment, August was transported back in time. He had been that boy, maybe a little older, but still running for his life, clutching what he had begged, borrowed, or stolen. Willing to risk everything so that he might keep his family alive for another day.

The gelding snorted. The boy's head snapped up, and he almost stumbled, and August realized that in his flight, against the blinding sunset, the child probably hadn't even seen him. From somewhere on the other side of the trees, a rumble was growing, like the distant sound of thunder. Or the pounding of many, many hooves, punctuated by more gunshots. Without thinking what he was doing, August reached down and grabbed a fistful of the child's ragged coat, hauling him up into the saddle. The boy started to struggle.

"It's me or them," he snapped at the boy, and the child went still.

August jammed his heels into the gelding's side and the horse bolted, only too happy to quit the trees, the gunfire, and the unseen threat on the other side of the copse. The boy, whoever he was, clung to August, one skinny hand poking from a threadbare sleeve clutching August's arm, the other hanging on to his prize.

August aimed the horse in the direction of a long, thick hedgerow, the wind whipping past him and the ground blurring. He chanced a look behind him, but the trees were now hidden by the hills, and the horizon was empty. The gelding started to slow, and August let it, guiding it into the shadows of the hedgerow. The horse suddenly stumbled, and with a frown August pulled it to a stop altogether. The gelding's gait was off.

August swung down, the boy slipping from the saddle almost as quickly. The child tried to dart away, but August caught his arm. He twisted, trying to conceal his front, where something bulky had been stuffed down his shirt. Something soft and yellow, a corner of which was trailing out at the edge of his waistband and looked very much like a length of silk.

August ignored that for the moment. "Who are you?" he asked, staring down into a thin, defiant face. Much, much too thin.

The boy shrugged in a manner August remembered all too well. He had been this child.

In dark, weak moments, he still was this child. And it haunted him.

"Never mind, then," August said. "Tell me who was chasing you."

The boy glanced back in the direction from which they had come, peering through the hedgerow. "Soldiers," he said, as though that should be obvious.

"Why?"

The boy shrugged again and tightened his grip on the bag.

"What did you steal?" August asked.

The defiant look became harder.

"Something worth shooting you for?"

The boy scuffed a toe in the dirt and remained stubbornly silent.

August sighed and snatched the bag from the boy's hands in a lightning-quick move.

"That's mine," the boy cried.

August ignored him and opened the bag. He peered in to find what looked like salted fish mixed with a few loose apples.

"That's mine," the child repeated.

August handed the bag back to him. "You got family?" he asked.

"Maybe." It was sullen and suspicious.

"Here." August reached into the pocket he'd had sewn into the inside of his coat, his fingers finding a handful of coins. He held them out, knowing it wasn't much, but it was better than nothing.

The boy eyed him with incredulity.

"Take them," August urged. "And the next time you need to...borrow something, I want you to come to the Silver Swan in town." August had visions of the boy lying dead in a field, a bullet hole in him for the sake of a half dozen salted herring and a length of yellow silk cloth.

Incredulity turned to bafflement.

"The tavern and inn near the harbor?" August prompted. "There's a sign hanging out front."

The boy's face cleared. "Thought that was a dyin' stork on the sign," he said. "Never knew it was a swan."

August shook his head. "Ask for Charleaux. Tell him Holloway sent you. He'll see to what you need."

"Don't need no charity." The suspicion was back.

"Don't need your family to starve to death either."

Small fingers hesitated and then finally reached for the coins, stuffing them into the bag of food as though the boy was afraid August might change his mind. Slowly he started to back away.

"Remember what I said," August told him.

"Thank you," the boy mumbled, and then he spun and vanished through the thick hedgerow.

August stared at the space he had disappeared through, suddenly feeling a hundred years old. The more things changed, the more things stayed the same, no matter how much time had passed. Only back then, it had not been soldiers chasing him, but other boys just like himself, just as desperate to survive. Then there had been no one to come to his rescue. He'd had to do that all by himself.

August shot another look at the horizon. A half dozen horses and riders had appeared, the red of their coats easily visible in the long rays of the sun even from this distance. They were headed away from where he was concealed in the direction of the cliffs, presumably still hunting a small boy they would no longer find. A small boy with a handful of silk and a bag of dried fish that had been liberated, quite likely, from a larger cache of barrels and crates brought ashore and hidden somewhere.

August was familiar with the soldiers and blockade men who patrolled the chalky coast, hunting for those who slipped through with all manner of contraband. It wasn't something new. But desperate people did desperate things, and while some looked to profit, most looked to merely survive. The war had been hard on these communities, the taxes to pay for it even harder.

August understood survival. He had done and continued to do what he needed to so that he would never have to go back. Back to a time when hunger and cold had been enemies, stalking him with a promise of death just as surely as the wraiths armed with knives and desperation had. Back to a time when he had lacked the power and ability to truly protect and take care of those he loved.

The appearance of that child had reminded him of that. And renewed his resolve to never rest. To never allow the safety net that he had so carefully woven to come apart.

August wearily turned his attention back to his horse. And froze. The gelding had settled and was cropping grass, but one of its rear legs was marred by rivulets of blood that trickled down over its hock. August approached the gelding slowly and bent to examine the wound. There was a furrow the length of his palm across the sleek hide, along the hindquarters, just behind the stifle. Murmuring softly, August traced his fingers along the edge, relieved to discover that the wound was more superficial than serious. It wouldn't require stitches—it had already stopped bleeding for the most part—but there would be bruising, and it would put his horse out of commission while it healed.

August cursed under his breath and ran a hand over his gelding. He would have a word with the garrison captain at his earliest opportunity. The king's men might have their orders, but trigger-happy soldiers running down children and firing wild shots at peers of the realm were not acceptable. That he would make clear. Because there were benefits to being a duke, and having a very loud voice was one of them.

August glanced back at the horizon one last time, but it was deserted. He looped the reins from the gelding's neck and started the odious walk to Avondale.

Chapter 5

The travel was always the most odious part.

The two-day journey had been long but uneventful, which was always a relief. No surprises on the road meant that they had arrived in good time and that the students had finally been able to settle themselves into the warm comfort of Avondale last night. Clara knew very well that some had slept fitfully, anticipating the first full day of summer term. For many of these girls, it was the first time that they had been on their own, unaccompanied by family or hordes of familiar servants. It was their first taste of freedom.

Clara smiled to herself and tugged her shawl tighter about her against the breeze, tipping her face up to the sun and letting the tranquility of Avondale settle into her bones. Almost all the girls had returned, having spent their first day discovering that the Haverhall School for Young Ladies was not all that it might seem. And the excitement and the wonder that was invariably stamped across the students' faces did not disappoint.

A pang of regret and loss came hard on the heels of that thought, and Clara pushed it ruthlessly aside. She might have lost Haverhall, but it did not mean that she needed to lose this as well. Without the school behind her, organizing and managing terms like this would be a little more difficult, but not impossible. But she'd worry about that later. For now she would enjoy every minute.

For now she would enjoy the faint tang of the sea carried on the warm breeze. Enjoy the feel of the sun on her back as it descended in the west, setting each pane of glass on the face of Avondale ablaze. There was a peace and sense of belonging here that she had never found in the malodorous, hectic stew that was London. Perhaps it was the sea that promised adventure and inspired imagination. Perhaps it was the history contained in this place—centuries of lives lived and stories to discover. Perhaps it was the wildness of the cliffs or the grandeur of the sky that opened up around them. Whatever it was, it was one of Clara's favorite places in the world, and it filled her soul as no other place could.

"Good evening, Miss Hayward."

Clara jerked, disbelief making it hard to think. The voice had come from behind her, and if she didn't know better, she might say it sounded suspiciously like the Duke of Holloway's. Which, of course, was impossible. Because she was in Dover set to embark on a wonderful summer term, while August Faulkner was safely in London seeing to whatever needs he or his gleaming duchy might require. He was certainly not standing in the wide, circular walk that led to the rear gardens of Avondale House.

Ambushing her. Again.

"Miss Hayward?" The address came again.

With reluctance, Clara turned to discover that the Duke of Holloway was, regrettably, not a figment of her imagination, and he was, indeed, standing in the walk. The sun hovered low in the west, gilding him in a strange golden light, and Clara took a step sideways so she wasn't squinting against the angled rays.

He was dressed casually in a riding coat and breeches that had seen better days. His boots were dusty, his hair wind-blown, and the lack of polish made him somehow even more attractive than he had been the day he had ambushed her in the museum. Her breath hitched, and butterflies rose again to riot against her ribs, and Clara nearly cringed at the sheer idiocy of her physical reaction to him.

A reaction that was, thankfully, somewhat tempered by the trepidation that was starting to clamor at his sudden appearance.

"Your Grace," she said, aiming for the pleasant, concili-atory tone that she used for handling difficult parents who initially balked at the idea of sending their daughters into the wilds of Kent. "This is a...surprise."

"I can imagine."

Clara felt her smile threaten to falter.

"Did you honestly expect me to stay in London, Miss Hayward?"

Um, yes? Clara tried to make sense of his cryptic com-ment but got nowhere. "Is there something I might assist you with, Your Grace?"

"I had hoped to have a conversation with my sister." The duke's eyes flickered past her as though he expected his sis-ter to pop up from behind Clara's skirts. "I think I'm owed that at the very least, don't you?"

"Lady Anne is not available at the moment," she said smoothly. Lady Anne was, in fact, on her way back from a tavern and inn in Dover. Though her brother didn't need to know that.

"Not available," he repeated in a low voice. "Yes, she certainly seems to be good at that."

Well, then. Clara's mind was racing, and the conclusions that it was reaching were not good, though at least they were smothering the damn butterflies one by one. "Is there something amiss, Your Grace?" she tried.

"Amiss?" Holloway looked at her askance.

"A death in the family? An impending wedding?"

He stared at her. "You lump death and weddings in the same category, Miss Hayward?"

"Depends on the participants in each, I would imagine, Your Grace."

His brow creased, and he continued to stare, unsmiling.

Clara resisted the urge to squirm. She had a sinking feeling that Lady Anne had chosen to ask forgiveness rather than permission when she had committed to this venture. It explained Holloway's presence here, and it explained why he hadn't brought the subject up during their conversation in the museum. Clara had made the monumental mistake of simply assuming that the payments on Anne's behalf had been made at the duke's direction, for very few women had access to the substantial fees that Haverhall demanded.

She would need to speak with Anne later. She didn't blame her, admired her resourcefulness even, but a warning would have been appreciated.

"My sister, Miss Hayward. Please fetch her." Holloway was making a visible effort at patience.

"As I said, Your Grace, she is unavailable. If you wish, you may come back on the morrow, and I will ensure that Lady Anne has time in her schedule to meet with you. It's the best I can do at the moment."

"The best you can do?" He took a step closer, his eyes

not leaving hers. Clara was quite certain many people had quailed under that intense, probing gaze. People who saw only a powerful, ambitious duke and not a boy who had once been dared to dance. "Then perhaps, Miss Hayward, you can give me the answer I came for."

She lifted her chin and met his gaze coolly, without flinching. "And is there a question?"

His lips thinned. "I'd like to know what it is that you think you can give to my sister that an army of expensive governesses and tutors could not. I could not answer that question. My man of business could not answer that question, nor could he explain how my sister had managed to forge my signature on no fewer than two bank drafts directed to you that he failed to notice. So here I find myself forced to ask the very woman with whom my sister hatched her diabolical, secretive plot that brought her to Dover without my knowledge."

Clara felt her brows shoot to her hairline. "You think…" She stopped. "Ah." She supposed it wasn't an unreasonable conclusion to jump to.

"That is not an answer, Miss Hayward."

"No, I suppose it isn't." Clara looked up at the sky, trying to frame in her head the answer he sought before she spoke.

"Is she well?"

That snapped her attention back to the duke, the note of genuine worry in his voice making something inside her melt. For Holloway's all-powerful, devil-may-care reputation, it was obvious that the duke cared very much when it came to his sister. "Lady Anne is very well, Your Grace," she answered. "She is also intelligent and capable and, as it turns out, quite ingenious."

"She is." There was a note of pride now, and Clara felt another part of her melt.

"You should know that I was unaware that you were unaware," Clara said steadily. "Of Lady Anne's intentions, that is. Bank drafts weren't the only documents she signed on your behalf. It would seem that she deceived us both."

Holloway raked a hand through his hair and muttered something under his breath. "Then it appears that I owe you another apology, Miss Hayward."

Clara shook her head, thinking that the duke suddenly sounded weary beyond measure. "Had I known, I would have encouraged her to share her plans with you."

"Encouraged? Not insisted?"

Clara gazed at him, considering. "Tell me, why do *you* think she hatched a diabolical, secretive plot that brought her to Dover without your knowledge?"

She watched with some fascination as a muscle in Holloway's jaw jumped and he looked away. "I couldn't begin to tell you." It came out harshly, but there was a certain unhappy vulnerability in his answer that tugged at her. "I was hoping you knew why she felt she needed a finishing school. And one so far away from London."

Holloway wasn't the first man to question the value of Haverhall. Past experience had taught Clara that there was a fine balance in what peers wanted to hear when it came to their wards. The prevailing attitude that women's natural, and often hysterical, tendencies prevented them from understanding any sort of higher education had to be minded. Even if, after all this time, it made her want to kick something. Or someone.

But Clara had long since learned to use that attitude as a shield, presenting a curriculum that was as familiar as a receipt from a Bond Street modiste. Painting, music, dance, language. A smattering of the geography and history of Kent to justify the travel. Most men nodded and accepted her practiced pitch, either indifferent or more interested in making sure their wards were visibly part of something exclusive and elite than in what those wards might actually accomplish.

The Duke of Holloway, however, was not most men. And he would not be so easily placated.

Clara let a heartbeat pass and picked her words very carefully. "I might suggest, Your Grace, the appeal for Lady Anne lies in the collaborative aspect of many of our classes. Something that a private education with governesses may not be able to provide. I'd like to think that the presence of other like-minded young women offers a unique opportunity."

Holloway was frowning, gazing past her at the facade of Avondale. "Lady Anne is not a dandizette, interested only in whether her latest bonnet should be trimmed in feathers or fruit. She's..." He trailed off, and Clara watched in fascination as he struggled for words.

She didn't dare interrupt.

"I confess I often don't understand her," the duke finally said. "But I do know that she is...exceptional."

Clara already knew this. It had been evident in Lady Anne's interview when she had first applied to Haverhall. It was why she was here at Avondale.

"I'm glad to hear it." Clara focused on keeping her tone light. "Because I believe she will find herself in good company this summer." She paused, wondering just how much he wanted to hear. Wondering just how much she could safely tell him. "I also believe that Lady Anne will find herself adequately challenged. I think she will not only learn a great deal in her tenure here but will be able to contribute significantly as well."

He was silent for several seconds. "Did you know you

are very good at answering a question without providing any real information at all?" he finally asked. His eyes returned from the house to clash with hers. "Perhaps I should get you to teach a class to my stewards on negotiation."

"I didn't realize we were negotiating," she replied warily.

"Everything in life is a negotiation, Miss Hayward."

Clara fell silent for a moment, gathering her thoughts. Perhaps Holloway was right. "This program, this very school, is the legacy that was left to me by my parents," she started. "I have made it my life's work to ensure that each one of my students gets the attention and education that she deserves. Your sister included. And to that end, I hope that you will see the value in Lady Anne's remaining here for the duration of her term."

The duke leveled an appraising look at her. Clara did not look away. Somewhere near the house, a carriage rattled across the drive, and a horse whickered.

"I was told that you were tutored in Latin and Greek by Oxford dons that your parents hired," he said abruptly. "Is that true?"

"Yes." She saw no reason to lie.

"Why?"

Clara hesitated, unsure what he was after. But it seemed as if the Duke of Holloway was doing his best to peer beneath the surface, beyond her explanations and careful delivery, looking for something more. And discovering whatever he found lacking.

"Why were you?" she asked instead of answering.

"I beg your pardon?"

"Why were you tutored in Latin and Greek?"

"Because it is part of the education required for a gentleman."

"But not for a lady."

"I didn't say that." His fingers were tapping slowly against his thigh. "But what good could it possibly do you?"

"I imagine the same good it does you, Your Grace."

He stared at her.

"Do you use it in correspondence? Everyday conversation?" she asked pleasantly.

"Of course not."

"And neither do I. But a mastery of those languages opens up entire troves of philosophy, wisdom, and tales of those who became legends. It would be a shame to miss such learnings from the past when so many of the same lessons can still be applied to the present, don't you agree?"

He was frowning at her again, his eyes narrowed, his dark lashes shadowing the blue of his eyes.

"Are they something that you wish Lady Anne to be introduced to? Latin and Greek?" Clara prompted.

"No. Yes." Holloway's brows were knit, and he looked as unsatisfied with his nonanswer as she was.

Clara remained silent, still unsure what he wanted from her. Unsure what he was looking for in this labyrinth of a conversation where every step Clara took felt like a trapdoor waiting to spring. She needed to redirect this conversation.

"Where are you staying, Your Grace?" Clara asked. "I'll make sure Lady Anne sees you tonight, even if I have to drive her myself. You are right—I think it is the least that she owes you."

"That won't be necessary, Miss Hayward."

"But I thought that—"

"You won't need to drive her. I'm staying here."

Clara felt the bottom of her stomach drop to her toes. He couldn't possibly be serious. "I'm afraid there is a mistake," she said. "Haverhall has let Avondale House from—"

"The Earl of Rivers. Yes, yes, he told me. He also told

me that there are more rooms in this pile than anyone could possibly find use for and a vacant dower house that begs habitation. And he asked me to confirm that things were shipshape for you."

"The condition of this house and its staff is exemplary," Clara said, trying to keep the alarm out of her voice. "As is documented by my brother at the beginning and end of each of our stays. At the earl's request, that documentation is delivered directly to him for review. I suspect his steward does the same thing, though at more regular intervals. I can't imagine why he would require you to be quite so redundant."

Holloway shrugged. "You'll have to ask Rivers the next time you see him."

"I can't allow you to stay in this house, Your Grace." The duke frowned, and so did Clara. "You'll be a distraction," she said, trying to take some of the heat from her voice and regain her composure. She would not be goaded into raising her voice, certainly not to one of her clients. Even if he was a duke acting in the most illogical, insufferable manner. "To the students. To your sister." *To me.*

Holloway made some sort of derisive noise. "I had no intentions of partaking in any of your classes. I will be away most days. You won't even know I'm here." He paused. "Think of me merely as Lady Anne's chaperone."

This could not be happening. Clara could not allow it to happen. She squared her shoulders. "The earl's two widowed sisters live here. If their matronly presence isn't enough, there are nine students, the three lady's maids who traveled with us, the substantial staff who look after this house, and my sister and I. The girls are well chaperoned. They are here to learn, Your Grace, not to entertain themselves frivolously."

"A frivolous entertainment and a distraction. Well, I suppose I've been accused of being worse."

"You mistake me, Your Grace." Clara could feel her fingers curling into her skirts in her effort to remain patient. "That's not what I was implying—"

"It was a jest, Miss Hayward," the duke said with a smile. And it was a smile that reached his eyes. Not the practiced, contrived one she had seen when he had kissed the back of her hand, but the one that had once set her heart pounding. The one that now made her breath catch and wiped her mind clear of every rational thought.

"I already know what it's like to live with one young lady," he told her, his eyes still gleaming. "I have no intention of tossing away what's left of my sanity by moving in with eight more. I'll stay in the dower house."

Clara fought to catch her breath. "You're still a distraction. You are a duke. And you don't need me to tell you that you are handsome, rich, and very, very unmarried. And—"

"An extraordinary dancer."

"And a shameless fisher of compliments." She was aware that a grin was starting to creep across her face.

He held up a hand to stop her. "Your commitment to the reputation and care of your students, including my sister, is admirable."

"You exaggerate."

"I do not. You took a duke to task over an abominably asinine request. It doesn't happen nearly as often as it should."

A decidedly unladylike snort escaped despite her. "You have that many abominably asinine requests?" Clara knew she should simply nod and smile politely, but somehow he was drawing her into this...banter that she had no business participating in. And it was exhilarating.

"You might be surprised." He grinned, and her pulse immediately skipped.

"You know," she said, returning his grin, "I don't think I would."

Something shifted in his eyes. Something hot and possessive. Something that made her knees weaken and an ache settle low in her belly and her breasts.

"There she is," he murmured almost inaudibly.

"Who, Your Grace?" She could feel the blood pounding through her body as he gazed at her. His eyes were searching her face, a strange, yearning expression on his.

He reached out, and for a heart-stopping moment, Clara thought he was going to stroke her cheek. Instead he grasped one of the stubborn, unruly curls that invariably escaped from the knot at the back of her head and tucked it behind her ear. "The girl who once waltzed with me."

She could feel the heat of his fingers as they brushed her skin, and she shivered, every fiber in her body demanding that she step closer to him. Step into his heat and find out what it would feel like if he did truly touch her. Because the way he was looking at her now was infinitely more intoxicating than the way he had gazed at her before.

This time, admiration mingled with desire.

She stepped back slightly. "That girl grew up, Your Grace. I am no longer given to impetuous impulses, just as you are no longer given to imprudent suggestions. Things have changed a great deal, and both of us along with it."

Holloway's hand dropped. "True."

Clara cleared her throat, unwilling to let…whatever this was go any further. Above all, she must remain professional. He was the brother of one of her students, for God's sake. A *client*. If she was going to continue as the headmistress of Haverhall, or if the worst happened and there was ever going to be a hope of resurrecting her school later, she could not...dally with a duke. Her reputation, like it or not, was her currency. No one in their right mind would ever send their gently bred daughters to a school in which the head-mistress was known for her amorous escapades with one of the most visible, sought-after men in England.

"Will your business here take you long, Your Grace?" She steered the conversation back to safer ground.

"Trying to get rid of me so soon?" He wore a smile again, but it was the practiced one she loathed.

Clara kept her expression neutral. "Merely curious, Your Grace." What she needed to know was just exactly how long he might linger and where he might show up, either acciden-tally or purposely. And the faster he could get what he had come to accomplish completed and be away from Dover, the better. For everybody.

She ignored an unacceptable and perilous twinge of disappointment.

"While the Earl of Rivers has insisted that I stay at Avon-dale, he has also asked for my assessment on the current condition of the estate's crops and livestock," Holloway said.

"I see." This was not good. Not good at all. She did not want a duke, specifically this one, on the property, prowling about indefinitely. "You should know that the dower house isn't entirely vacant," she said, aware that she was grasping at straws now. "My brother stays at the dower house when we are here."

Holloway nodded, and instead of inconvenienced, he seemed almost pleased. "Yes, Rivers mentioned as much. But that dower house is as palatial as Avondale itself. I have been told that it has eight bedrooms, two drawing rooms, a music room, and even its own small ballroom. I don't think we'll be tripping over each other, but as I'm sure Lord

Strathmore is also a busy man, I will endeavor to stay out of his way."

Clara grimaced. Clearly there was nothing she could say that was going to deter him. "What do you know of crops and livestock?" A last effort, and one that might be interpreted as rude or insolent, but she no longer cared.

"I've educated myself on the basics," he replied.

"Why?"

"You ask that a lot."

"Yes," she replied unapologetically. "You are, of course, under no obligation to answer."

He considered her for a moment. "Because I own a great deal of land. And crops. And livestock. And I like to understand what I possess." The glibness had gone out of his voice, replaced with a cool bluntness that rang of truth.

Clara felt a shiver race down her spine. The Duke of Holloway was a man who needed to be kept at a safe, proper distance. And the dower house was definitely not far enough.

"Is Lord Strathmore here?" Holloway asked. "I should like to inform him of my presence so he isn't unduly surprised to find himself with a tenant."

"He is here, in Dover, but not at Avondale at the moment." He was, in fact, with three of her students, somewhere in the parish, seeing to the community's medical needs.

"I understand that your brother is an accomplished physician," the duke remarked, as if reading her mind.

"He is." Clara had no idea how much Holloway knew about her brother. Of course he would be aware of Harland's training—that wasn't a secret. Certainly not after Harland's wife had complained loudly about it to anyone who would listen for the duration of their miserable marriage.

"An admirable profession," he offered into the silence.

"Not everyone would agree with you. Most would tell

you gentlemen are not meant for such common...
foolishness." Clara tried to keep the derision out of her
voice, but she wasn't sure she succeeded.

"Only a true fool would believe that a man who has the
knowledge and skills to help a soul cheat death could ever
be considered foolish." August's eyes were shuttered, and in
that moment Clara knew he was thinking about the circumstances that had made him the Duke of Holloway. Spotted
fever, she had heard, which had completely wiped out two
entire generations of Faulkners summering near Bath. August and his sister, who had been in London at the time, had
been the only two survivors.

"I'm sorry. About your family." Her words seemed inadequate.

He started, as if surprised that his comments had been so
transparent. "Thank you." He shifted. "And my condolences
on the loss of your parents."

Clara nodded and looked away. "It was unexpected."
They had been aboard a packet destined for Boston that had
been caught in an Atlantic squall. All crew and passengers
had been lost.

"It always is," the duke mumbled, almost inaudibly.

"Yes," she agreed sadly, wondering how this conversation
had become so melancholy.

"You are fortunate that your brother has so ably taken
the reins of the barony's business. He must be an incredibly
busy man."

"He is busy," she replied, happy to let Holloway direct the
conversation away from death. "But he manages."

"A tough enterprise, shipping," he mused. "One fraught
with risks and unpredictability."

He had no idea. "You own ships as well, Your Grace?"

Holloway shrugged. "I dabble. I have a fondness for

Virginian tobacco. As does half of London. Owning the occasional shipload of it makes me a popular man."

Clara almost rolled her eyes. "Then I must assume you've educated yourself on the basics of that as well?"

He shrugged again. "Of course. As I said, I like to understand what I possess."

"Well, then. You and my brother will have much to discuss."

"I'm counting on it, Miss Hayward. I'm also counting on his ability to play a decent hand of whist or loo if he has the time," he continued. "Dover can be quite dull—"

"August?" The demand came from just behind Clara. She turned to find blue eyes a shade softer than Holloway's flashing with poorly concealed ire and not a little apprehension. "What are you doing here?"

Chapter 6

August felt every muscle in his body stiffen, but he forcibly reminded himself what was really at stake here. He bit back his instant acerbic accusations and fought the urge to stuff his impetuous, wayward sister in a burlap sack, fling her over the back of a horse, and take her back to the safety of their London home. Instead he arranged his features into what he hoped was a mask of cool detachment.

He gazed at Anne, taking in her flushed face and snapping eyes. She hadn't a leg to stand on when it came to righteous indignation, but he had to admire the fact that she had gone on the offensive. Gutsy, that. Instead of looking chastised, she looked as though she wished to run him through.

"You're looking well, Anne. I'm pleased to see you survived the journey from London no worse for wear." He kept his voice pleasant. "Imagine my surprise when I discovered that you were no longer residing in our house."

She had the grace to redden. "I left a note."

"You did."

"With instructions. Instructions that you were not to follow me."

"Indeed. Though had you thought to share your plans with me, I might have given you a ride here. As you may recall, I have interests in Dover that require my attention from time to time. The present being one of those times."

Anne was staring at him as if he had sprouted a second head. "You're not angry with me?"

"Oh, I didn't say that, dear sister." August avoided looking at Miss Hayward. God only knew what she was thinking.

Anne now looked positively mutinous. "Well, I'm not going back to London with you." Her mouth was set in a hard line. "I'm...sorry for whatever inconvenience I might have caused, but I intend to stay. I do not require your supervision. I am perfectly fine on my own without you interfering."

"You'll be relieved to know that Miss Hayward has also conveyed the same," August replied, frustration at her resentment rising despite his best efforts. "It is not my intention to interfere with anything. Though I might suggest that your manners are slipping. I am not the only one I think you owe an apology to."

Anne colored again, and August met Miss Hayward's dark, measuring gaze. He stared stonily back.

"Miss Hayward," Anne said quietly, "I apologize for not being truthful with you. And I apologize for my behavior just now. I was just...surprised to see my brother here."

"That would make two of us," Miss Hayward replied easily, turning to address her student. "Apology accepted. And you should know that I am also well familiar with older brothers who do things that defy reasonable explanation."

A reluctant smile pulled at the corner of Anne's mouth, and August felt the muscles in his jaw tighten.

"I trust that you enjoyed your first day?" Miss Hayward inquired.

"I did. It was…incredible." There was an instant, blinding animation on Anne's face that August hadn't seen in…well, forever. It made her eyes sparkle and her cheeks flush and a dimple appear on the side of her wide smile. He stared at his sister, unable to look away, but she didn't elaborate on what it was that she had found so incredible. Nothing he had ever given her—no gown or slippers or jewels—had ever come close to eliciting such a reaction.

"I'm glad." Miss Hayward inclined her head, a small smile playing around her lips. She didn't offer an explanation either.

"I should go in," Anne said into the silence that had fallen. "I do not want to be late for dinner, and I still have today's reading assignment to complete." She looked at August then, a clear challenge in her soft blue eyes, as if defying him to stop her.

"A good idea," he said.

Anne bit her lip, suspicion shadowing her features, as if his answer had come too easily. And maybe it had, but for now he needed to be at Avondale, and it was better that Anne was here with him than left to her own devices in London, regardless of how that had come about. Here he could keep an eye on her and make sure she was safe while pursuing his own ambitions.

He supposed that he should be grateful that his sister hadn't taken it into her head to see Italy. Or Siberia.

"Thank you, August, for being reasonable." She was still looking at him as if she half expected him to implode.

"When am I not reasonable?" he replied, scowling.

Anne started to speak and then seemingly reconsidered. "Thank you, Miss Hayward," she offered in lieu of whatever she had been going to say. "I'm very much looking forward to tomorrow. And good night, August," she added in a courteous tone. "I hope your business goes well and doesn't take long." She headed toward the house, and August watched her walk away from him, her posture ramrod stiff.

"I apologize on behalf of my sister, Miss Hayward," he said as Anne disappeared into the house without a backward glance.

"Do not make me accuse you of being redundant twice in as many minutes, Your Grace. Lady Anne already apologized." Her words were light and held no judgment.

"Still, she should never have deceived you." *Or me.*

Miss Hayward shrugged. "She's still young. I suspect she acted as she did because she felt you didn't trust her."

"Trust her?"

"To conduct herself in a manner that meets your approval."

August stared at Miss Hayward, aghast. "Is that what you think? Is that what *she* thinks?"

"I can't answer for Lady Anne. But I do think she is fortunate to have a brother who cares as much as you do."

She had done that neatly—softened her refusal to answer his question with a compliment meant to distract and flatter. It was a ploy he used regularly to get what he wanted—usually information—and it was a curious sensation to be on the receiving end.

"That's not it at all." He shook his head. "It's Anne who doesn't trust me."

"Trust you to do what?"

"To take care of her." Why did he need to state the obvious?

"Be more specific."

"What?" The question threw him.

"What, specifically, is it that you believe you can do for your sister that she cannot do for herself?" Again, there was no judgment, only curiosity, and her words held shades of the question he had asked her at the very beginning.

"I can protect her from every manipulative, greedy bastard who will wish to use her for his own gain. To get to me, or maybe just my money. I can make sure that the spiteful gossip that is the currency of the ton never touches her." He stopped abruptly, aware his voice had risen.

"Mmm." Miss Hayward's noncommittal sound was almost as discomfiting as his outburst.

"What's *mmm* supposed to mean?" He had no idea how he'd managed to be drawn into this conversation, but he seemed powerless to retreat from it now.

"Keeping in mind that I too have a brother who cares very much about both my sister and myself—"

"Just say whatever it is that you're going to say." It was rude, but frustration had eroded his patience.

"Very well." She didn't look offended. Or even surprised. "You can't control your sister, even though I understand that your motives are honorable."

"I don't want to control her," he snapped. "I want to make sure she makes the right choices that will ensure her happiness. This role she's found herself in, one of the sister to a duke, does not come naturally to her."

"How so?"

August threw up his hand. This was absolutely none of Miss Hayward's business, but he had been the one to bring it up, and there had been something strangely cathartic about the torrent of words that had escaped. Whether he liked it or not, Clara Hayward was going to be Anne's teacher for the foreseeable future. Perhaps she would be able to talk some sense into Anne.

"She holds herself aloof from the other young ladies of the ton. Makes no effort to blend in socially. Takes no interest in her future." He shook his head. "She refuses to believe that if she doesn't make the right choices, her happiness cannot be guaranteed."

"I see. And what, exactly, are the right choices required for happiness?"

"The same as anyone's. A place in society. A good, sensible marriage—" August stopped suddenly.

Miss Hayward's expression hadn't changed, nor had she uttered a word, but something in her dark eyes had shifted. There was unmistakable disappointment there now. "Ah. You don't want her to end up like me."

"That's not what I meant. That's not at all—"

"I understand, Your Grace. You don't wish your sister to be the oddity at the ball, tolerated because of a title or perhaps because of her wealth, or both. You do not wish Lady Anne to be the girl who gets asked to dance only on a dare." She said it with not a trace of self-pity.

August took another step toward Miss Hayward, needing to say something that would erase the disappointment he'd seen in her eyes. Needing to say something that would ease the regret that had settled heavily in his chest. That feeling that he was losing something—that something was once again slipping through his fingers—returned. God, he was making an epic mess out of this.

"Do not put words in my mouth, Miss Hayward. Because that's not who I see when I look at you." The force of his words made her eyes widen. "I see an intelligent woman, the same one who once put an ignorant buck in his place and taught him that things are rarely as they seem. I wish I had understood that then."

"And what would you have done differently if you had?" she asked quietly.

"I would have asked you to dance again." August reached

for her hand and caught it, bringing it up between them, his thumb sliding over her bare knuckles. "I wish I had asked you to dance again."

She was silent for a long minute, a gut-wrenching, electrifying mix of desire and longing flitting across her usually unreadable features.

Her fingers tightened on his. "I wish you had too," she said, and August felt the breath leave his lungs.

She had told him once that regrets were nothing but excuses, but he was having a hard time recalling what excuse had prevented him from kissing this woman witless. What excuse he might think up to prevent himself from doing it now. All he had to do was catch her face in his hands and dip his head. Capture her lips with his own and be done with wondering what might have been. Be done with regrets and excuses and take control the way he should have a very long time ago.

He gazed at her, the sinking sun kissing her skin a golden color and setting fire to the mass of thick tresses that had surrendered to the breeze and defeated their pins. A curl she had so valiantly tried to stuff behind her ear trailed down the side of her face, the end drifting to touch the skin near the lace-trimmed edge of her bodice. His found his eyes slipping over the gentle swell of her breasts concealed by her modest gown. The deep color of it was the perfect foil for her fair skin, and for a brief second he wondered how she might taste if he pressed his lips to the delicate shadow of her cleavage, her throat, and then her lips. Wondered again what would have happened if he had kissed her that night a decade ago. Wondered what would happen if he did so now. His gaze stalled on her mouth. Her lips were generous, the upper slightly more voluptuous, begging for attention and stirring all sorts of erotic thoughts far south of his brain.

She had never looked more touchable. More perfect.

The air between them had thickened, crackling with tension and anticipation. And then she stepped back, pulling her hand from his, and he almost cursed out loud as a mask of pleasant neutrality dropped over her features. "You speak of marriage being a requirement for happiness, Your Grace, yet you yourself remain unwed. So I might see where Lady Anne remains skeptical of your decrees."

August felt his lip curl in distaste. "I am well aware of my duties to the duchy, Miss Hayward. When I choose a bride, it will be a sound financial and business decision, as all good marriages should be."

"So you're holding out for an heiress." She sounded both cynical and amused.

"If that is what it takes. I've seen what happens when people marry because they believe themselves in love, and it isn't pretty. Contrary to the opinions of poets, love does not conquer all."

"Your sense of romance is overwhelming."

"I do not have the luxury of believing romance and marriage to be the same."

"And what about your sister?"

"Anne will have respect and admiration. Financial security and social standing. Those are the foundations necessary if love within a marriage is to be achieved. And I will make sure she has those things."

And what does she have to say about that?"

"It doesn't matter."

"I might suggest that your sister needs a brother, not a dictator," Miss Hayward said evenly, in that damnably composed way of hers.

He took a deep breath. "I'm not her dictator. I'm her protector."

"I fail to see the difference in this case."

"Anne is not you. You are stronger than she is," he said.

"Then you underestimate your sister, Your Grace."

August looked away. How the hell would she know that? She didn't truly know Anne, not the way he did. This was all so...impossible.

"What is she reading? The assignment she mentioned?" August asked abruptly, knowing that this change of topic was wholly transparent and not caring. He might not be able to control everything—the rise and fall of the tides was a bit beyond him—but there was no excuse for prolonging an ill-advised conversation he never should have started.

"I'm sure it's of little interest to you."

"Then you'd be wrong."

"It's titled *Marriage*," Miss Hayward said with a measure of irony.

"I've not heard of it."

"No, I don't suppose you would have. I received my copies shipped from Edinburgh only last week."

"A Scotsman wrote it?"

A small smile played around Miss Hayward's lips. "No. A Scotsman most assuredly did not write it."

"I don't understand."

"You don't need to, Your Grace. As you pointed out earlier, you are not a student of the Haverhall School for Young Ladies. Unless, of course, you feel the need to determine what Lady Anne is and isn't allowed to read while she is under my tutelage." She said it genially, but August could hear the steely challenge beneath.

Dictator indeed. "Of course not."

"I'm glad to hear it. You are welcome to read it yourself, if you like. I can have a copy sent over to the dower house."

She hesitated. "Perhaps that would give you an alternative topic of conversation in which you may engage your sister."

August frowned. He didn't need any more of Miss Hayward's advice when it came to Anne. He'd already disclosed far more than was wise, and he did not like to give anyone any kind of leverage. "No, thank you. I'm quite sure that I'll have other things that will occupy my time." Like focusing on the real reason he was here.

Because he didn't accept failure. Failure was for weak people like his father.

"Would you join me for dinner?" he asked. He needed to get back on track. Start making some inroads with the Haywards that didn't involve his own family tribulations.

"I beg your pardon?" Miss Hayward stared at him, those liquid brown eyes widening in startled uncertainty and a beautiful flush creeping into her cheeks. August tried not to be too pleased.

"The invitation, of course, extends to your brother. And your sister too, if she's so inclined. I am, after all, trespassing somewhat, and it's the least I can do." And it was something that the Duke of Holloway did when courting an investment. Invite the stakeholder to his club or to his home and lavish him with good food and better liquor. An expensive strategy, but one that invariably paid off in spades. It was easy to disarm his next prospective opportunity when he was drunk on extravagance.

Though he suspected that none of the Haywards would be impressed with such extravagance. Especially since it had been part of the demise of their fortunes, an obsession that had cost their parents almost everything. No, the Haywards would require something a little different, yet no less memorable.

"I'm afraid I'm going to have to decline, Your Grace."

"Wonderf— Wait, what?" He stared at Miss Hayward. Dammit, why was she making this so difficult? A dinner invitation from a duke seemed to be something the rest of society fell all over itself to accept. "Why? Is it a requirement that you eat with your students?"

She frowned. "Not at all. In fact, I try to give them space to socialize amongst themselves. They'll see enough of me in the coming days, but I do make it a point to be available the first evening to ensure they've settled in and address any concerns and questions."

"Tomorrow, then."

"Your Grace—"

"You need to eat. Why not with me?" He was not taking no for an answer.

"Um."

"There is a tavern on the north side of town that serves excellent lamb with mint and an even better selection of wines. The kind of wine that has had the privilege of being crafted in France."

"The Silver Swan."

"You know it?"

"Yes," she said slowly.

"Good. We'll take an equipage from Avondale. How does six o'clock sound?"

"It sounds delightful, but I don't think—"

"I insist. It's the least I can do in return for your gracious hospitality. And, of course, Lord Strathmore's." He smiled in his most disarming manner. "Even if he doesn't know it yet."

Miss Hayward gave him a weak smile, and he could see her teetering on indecision. No doubt weighing the consequences of refusing a duke a request. Though a request that was not asinine, but entirely proper and sincere. At least on the surface.

"I promise not to dare you to dance. Or do anything else that would give your brother leave to put a bullet hole in my coat."

She laughed then, a low, musical sound, and it was as if the sun had broken through a cloud. Her eyes crinkled at the corners, and August thought that time might have stopped for the briefest of moments. He had never, in all his life, wanted to kiss a woman as badly as he did right now. He thought he might ask her to dinner every night just to hear her laugh again like that.

Until he remembered he was not asking her to dinner to woo her. He was asking her to dinner to extract whatever information he could from her and her family to use to his own advantage. Potentially.

He was disturbed at the guilt that instantly stabbed at his conscience. August reminded himself that he wasn't deceiving her—not really. Further to his purchase of the school, he was simply...exploring a mutually beneficial opportunity, even if the Haywards didn't know it yet. And there was no room in good business for guilt.

"In that case, I thank you," she said, though she had moderated her smile, and now it was simply one of polite acceptance. "That would be lovely."

Chapter 7

The library at Avondale House was a thing of beauty.

Someone, or, more accurately, a long line of someones, had taken great pains to select and assemble a stupefying collection. There were manuscripts centuries old, and aside from the glimpse into the past they provided, the hand lettering and illuminations made them works of art in their own right. There were treatises on agriculture and veterinary care. Books about the creatures of the world and the exotic lands in which they were found. Collections of maps and drawings. There were entire shelves of novels, plays, and poetry, and dissertations on history and politics. Clara rather thought she could live out the rest of her life in this room and not be unhappy.

The staff, efficient as always, had pulled the curtains from the tall windows that lined the south side, and the early-morning sunlight flooded in to reveal a cavernous room that was positively gleaming. Three long tables were positioned in the center, each with lanterns and candelabras resting on its polished surface and each with a collection of beautifully matched chairs surrounding it. Larger, upholstered chairs were scattered around the grouping, fairly begging a body to curl up within their comfort with a good book.

It was this room that had been the deciding factor when Clara had gone looking for a house to let for her summer program. Well, that and the fact that the Earl of Rivers had gifted them the use of Avondale. Apparently he was exceedingly grateful to her brother for his attention to and treatment of his many ailments, and he had offered his Dover estate to Haverhall as a favor. Which pleased Clara to no end.

Many other homes had spacious and refined accommodations and efficient and capable staffs, but none had a library like this. Her students spent a great deal of time here, and Clara wondered if the elderly Earl of Rivers truly comprehended what a treasure he possessed in this house. It was one of many that he owned, though it had been years since he'd been well enough to make the trip to the coast.

Clara wandered over to a pretty rosewood writing desk, positioned in a sunbeam, and ran her hand over the smooth surface before picking up a delicate glass ink pot. It, like everything else in the library, was in a state of readiness, sparkling and newly filled with ink. She would have to add a footnote to Harland's report and express her appreciation of the dedication and attention to detail that the staff—

"Was that the Duke of Doxies I saw you speaking to in the driveway last night?"

Clara jerked and nearly dropped the inkpot on the immaculate rug under her feet. With great care she replaced it on the desk and turned.

"Rose. I didn't hear you come in." She eyed her sister, who was leaning just inside the door, her arms folded over her chest, a cynical smirk twisting her delicate features.

"I gathered." Rose stepped farther into the library, and the sunlight coming in through the window set alight the loose strands of strawberry-blond hair that rested along her cheek. "Was I correct?"

Clara frowned. "About what?"

"The Duke of Doxies. Here, down in Dover." Rose paused. "Hmm. I feel like that could be the beginning of a very fine limerick."

Clara frowned at Rose's tone. "The Duke of Holloway is indeed in Dover," she said evenly. "And yes, I was speaking to him."

"Why is he here? Spying on his sister?"

Quite possibly. "Lady Anne, it seems, failed to mention to the duke that she would be spending the summer here with us when she made the required arrangements. He discovered her plans only after she left."

Rose's elegant brows lifted. "Hmm. I'm beginning to like Lady Anne more and more."

Clara sighed.

"Let me guess. His Grace stomped all the way out here to drag her back to London?"

Clara sighed again. "Worse."

"Worse? What could be worse?"

"He's here to stay."

"At Avondale?" Rose's voice was an octave higher than usual.

"At Avondale," Clara confirmed.

"Why? Surely he can spy from a distance?"

"The Earl of Rivers has requested that he evaluate the property. Lands and stock and such."

"Now?" Rose looked horrified. "When is he leaving?"

"I don't know."

"His presence is rather inconvenient, don't you think?"

"We'll work around it." Clara tried to inject some confidence into her words. "He invited us to dinner tonight."

"Dinner?" Rose cocked her head, seemingly unimpressed. "How does that improve anything? And have you forgotten that this man once tried to make a fool out of you? I was there, if you recall."

"Good Lord, Rose, that was ten years ago."

"And I remember very clearly that he behaved like a damn swine."

"A great deal has changed since then." Clara scowled. "And when you're done with my sister, Circe, I'd like her back so that I can have a civilized conversation."

Rose unfolded her arms and sighed. "Fine. I apologize."

"Thank you. So did he, you know." She hadn't told Rose the details of the conversation she'd had with Holloway in the museum, and she didn't care to examine the why of that too closely.

"Who?"

"The duke. Apologized for his actions that night."

Rose leaned on the back of a gold-and-blue brocaded chair. "Was he drunk?" she speculated into the silence. "When he apologized, I mean. That he was drunk back then is rather a given."

"He was not drunk now or then," Clara replied evenly. "I would imagine he apologized because he is no longer a boy. He is a man willing to take responsibility for his actions and make amends for those that may have been unwise. He has been nothing but a perfect gentleman." She winced inwardly, wondering if her defense of the duke sounded too fervent.

"A perfect gentleman?" Rose's smirk returned. "That's not how I've heard him described."

Clara pinned her sister with a quelling look. "By whom?" She regretted that question the second it was out. For their purposes it didn't matter if the Duke of Holloway was the devil himself in disguise or if he danced naked around bonfires fornicating with the queen and her entire court. So long as he stayed out of their way.

Rose raised her hands in mock defense. "The ladies who have graced my old London studio. Not that anyone was complaining," she said. "On the contrary, his rumored lack of... gentlemanly habits between the sheets was being extolled." She let her hands drop and ran her fingers over the stitched braid along the back of the chair. "Discussed at great... length."

"The ladies who frequent your studio should pay heed to the fact that their conversations are probably not as private as they would like to think," Clara admonished, trying to ignore the heat that had suddenly ignited deep in her belly.

Rose sniffed. "I'm just the humble artist. If I repeated everything I heard, I would probably be accused of being a spy and hanged for treason by half the members of Parliament, the House of Lords, the army, and most definitely the navy. Sailors are a sentimental lot when it comes to wives and mistresses and wishing to have a memento in their image. It's intriguing what secrets pass for pillow talk."

"I'll take your word for it." Clara made a face.

"I've never done a portrait, boudoir or otherwise, on behalf of the Duke of Doxies," Rose mused.

"Holloway," Clara corrected sternly.

Rose ignored her. "It can't possibly be from lack of money, even given what I charge. I wonder if it's because he can't decide which mistress is his favorite? Or if by the time I was finished painting one, he'd already have moved on to the next?"

"I find your sudden zeal for spiteful gossip rather unbecoming, Rose." Annoyance was prickling, and Clara decided it was because Rose was being so contrary. It certainly had nothing to do with who August Faulkner chose to keep company with.

Rose looked away, her features drawn. Clara studied her younger sister, seeing the tautness in her petite body and the way her fingers were curled along the back of the chair, and she suddenly understood.

"The Duke of Holloway is not the same as Anthony," Clara said gently. Though the resemblance was there, both in appearance and, it would seem, rumored popularity with women.

"Of course not. The Duke of Doxies does not appear to be dead yet." Rose's lips twisted.

Clara looked down at her hands. Rose's fiancée had broken not only her heart but her trust as well, and had he not been killed at Waterloo, Clara might have done it herself. And while Clara didn't really know Holloway intimately enough to pass judgment on his true character, there was no conceivable way he was as contemptible as the late Anthony Gibson. "Rose—"

"Who doesn't appear to be dead yet?" Harland Hayward asked as he strode into the room, pulling off his coat as he came. "Bloody warm out there already," he grumbled as he dropped the offending garment on the surface of one of the long library tables and looked at his sisters expectantly.

"The Duke of Holloway," Clara said with a sigh.

"The Duke of Holloway was indeed very much alive last time I saw him," Harland said with a slight frown. "In London. Though that was a good while ago."

"So you didn't see him last night?"

Harland stared at her. "Last night?"

"The duke is not in London," Rose offered. "He's here."

Harland blinked in confusion. "The duke's in Dover? And he's dying?"

"Ooh, my limerick keeps getting better and better," Rose murmured.

"He's not dying," Clara told Harland, ignoring her sister. "He's here on business for the Earl of Rivers." That seemed like the simplest explanation at the moment.

Harland flopped into one of the upholstered chairs and ran his hands over his face. "So he doesn't need me to save him. Good. That's one less thing for me to do. I don't need or want to know anything else."

Clara studied her brother. He looked exhausted. His hair, darker than Clara's but still possessing the same red highlights, was disheveled and in need of a scissor. He had pronounced shadows under his eyes, and the angles of his face had become sharper, his long, muscle-roped limbs leaner. "Did you even sleep last night, Harland?" Clara asked.

He made a derisive noise and let his head tip back on the chair, closing his eyes. "I'll sleep when I'm dead. Too much to do right now."

"Harland—"

"The duke has invited all of us to dinner," Rose piped up. "Tonight."

"Tonight?" Harland's eyes popped open. "Why?"

"Because he's here, he asked, and one generally tries not to offend dukes by refusing their invitations. It did not seem advantageous." Clara felt her pulse skip. Which was unacceptable, because that meant that somewhere deep down she believed that he had asked her to dinner for the sake of asking her to dinner. To spend more time with her, or some other foolish nonsense.

"You accepted, then?" It wasn't really a question.

Rose blew out a disgusted breath. "Of course she did. You can share a carriage."

Harland frowned. "Wait, what do you mean when you said that he's *here*? In Dover?"

"Avondale," Rose corrected waspishly. "His Grace is moving in."

"*What?*" She saw her brother's hands curl into fists before they relaxed again almost immediately.

Clara grimaced. "He's staying at the dower house."

"Why? And how long does he intend to stay?" Harland didn't sound happy.

Clara sighed wearily. "I'm not sure. Rivers asked him to take a look at the land and livestock."

"Now? Why?"

Clara threw up a hand helplessly, ignoring the pointed look Rose was giving her. "Both of you can ask Rivers the next time you see him."

Harland seemed to be waging a war within himself to find words. "Damn his titled timing all to hell," was what he finally came up with.

"Language," Clara admonished half-heartedly. "But agreed."

"Did he say anything else?"

"He hoped you would be available for a hand of loo."

"Loo?"

"Or whist."

Harland pinched the bridge of his nose. "Bloody hell, Clara."

Clara didn't bother to hide her own displeasure. "I couldn't very well demand that he leave, now could I?"

"You could have," Rose said, jumping back into the conversation. "You just didn't."

Harland closed his eyes. "Clara is right, Rose. One does not simply order dukes about. But dammit, having August Faulkner here is the last thing we need."

"I didn't realize that you don't have a very high opinion of him," Clara said, and she could hear the edge of accusation in her own words. "You and Rose seem rather united on that front."

Harland opened his eyes and sat up. "On the contrary," he said. "The man's raw ambition has made him quite formidable. You will not meet a more ruthless, cunning adversary than Holloway when he goes after something he wants. He may hold the title of duke, but for all that, he is completely self-made. That is not something that one should ever dismiss lightly." He shifted his attention to Rose. "You disagree?"

"Self-made?" Rose repeated with disbelief. "Come, Harland, dukes are not self-made. They're victors in the game of accidental birth."

"Did you know his father was in debtors' prison?" Harland asked, giving Rose an irritable look. "Ten years before Faulkner became a duke."

Clara stared at her brother. Even Rose looked surprised. Holloway would have been fifteen when his father had been incarcerated.

"I didn't know that," Clara said.

"No, I don't suspect many people do. At the time he was only a distant footnote on the ducal family tree and therefore of little interest."

"But why was his father in prison?"

"I imagine the same reason everyone else winds up in Marshalsea."

"But surely someone in the family would have wanted to assist to keep him out of prison? If only to preserve the family name?"

"For whatever reason, that did not happen. His father was estranged." Harland shook his head. "But that's not the point. My point here is that August Faulkner, in five years, managed to make enough money to pay off his father's debts and buy his release. Two years after that, he had made enough to purchase back the lifestyle that his family had once enjoyed. Not that his father lived long enough to appreciate it much. As I understand it, the man never did recover his health once released."

"How do you know all this?" Clara asked.

"I attended his father as a medical student while he was in prison," Harland said. "He suffered from dropsy."

Rose sniffed. "Was it cards or horses?"

Harland frowned. "What?"

"Did the duke get lucky at a gaming hell or a racetrack? After all, that is how men like him—"

"The duke has made his money on industry. He buys broken things and breaks them apart further before building them back up into profitable ventures." He looked faintly troubled, even though his words held respect. "His empire is bigger than most people realize. Much, much bigger. If we possessed even a fraction of his capital..."

"Still no word from London?" The familiar foreboding settled heavily in Clara's gut.

Harland scrubbed his face with his hands before letting them drop. "Not yet. If I thought it would help, I would stand on the edge of the London Docks and wait for those damn ships. But that's all I would be doing. I can do more to help here than there."

"I have two sittings this week," Rose said. "And two more next week. All have agreed to pay up front. I'm sorry I can't paint faster—"

"Stop it." Harland cut her off. "We've all discussed this a

hundred times. We're all doing everything and anything we can."

"'The end crowneth the work,'" Clara murmured.

Rose shot her a long-suffering glance. "Do we really need another Elizabethan quote?"

"The woman managed to keep her head and her throne while living amidst a pack of jackals."

"I'd settle for my head and the surety that there will be a roof over it in a year's time." Rose sighed.

"Let's change the subject, shall we?" Harland suggested. "Before we all drown in self-pity." He glanced at Clara. "Where, exactly, is our dinner invitation with the illustrious duke?"

"The Silver Swan."

Harland seemed to perk up at this. "Well, then. As much as I rather resent His Grace's presence, at least he has good taste in food."

Clara turned to Rose. "Will you come with us?"

Rose looked down. "I think I'll need the time to finish setting up my studio," she said.

"I can help you. The students have a free morning, and I'm not meeting with them until—"

"No, thank you. I'll take care of it."

Clara recognized the stubborn shade to Rose's tone. She glanced at her brother for help, but Harland was already pulling his coat off the table where he had left it.

"You may wish to change your mind once you remember how good French wine tastes, Rose," Harland said.

"I don't think so."

"Suit yourself. I assume we'll leave from here," Harland tossed over his shoulder, already halfway out the door. "What time?"

"Six," Clara told him. "Where are you going now?"

"An appointment," he replied vaguely, not breaking stride.

"For what?" Clara called after him, but he was already gone. "Why does he keep doing that?" she asked into the silence.

"Disappearing?" Rose moved past her and shrugged. "I don't think I want to know."

Chapter 8

Clara loved this part.

Because, like their very first day here, this would be unlike anything her students had expected. And no matter what happened, even if this was her very last chance to do this—especially if it was her last chance—Clara was determined to enjoy every minute.

She led the nine students from the house through the gardens and out onto the expanse of grassland that topped the cliffs overlooking the sea. In the late-morning sunlight, the ocean was silvered with a sheen that danced and glittered as if a thousand suns had been strewn across its surface. Long wisps of clouds drifted over their heads, almost like elongated angel wings pushed westward by the wind. To the south the distant shape of Dover Castle partially blocked the view of the town that sprawled away in its shadow.

Involuntarily her eyes swept the empty fields around them and back toward Avondale, though the house was no

longer visible beyond the rise. She knew what she was looking for—the tall, dark-haired figure who might be out wan-
dering around the property, examining barley or ewes or
whatever else might catch his fancy. She hated that she felt
she had to search, and she resented the feeling of hope that
she just might see him. She didn't want to see him anywhere.
She forced him out of her mind.

Clara closed her eyes and breathed deeply, letting the
scent of salt and vegetation fill her lungs as the wind
tugged at her hair. She turned back to her charges, who
were standing behind her, looking at her with the expected
expressions of anticipation. They ranged in age from sixteen to eighteen. Half were from rich, titled English families, and four more were from extraordinarily wealthy
families of the landed gentry or the nouveau riche. The
remaining student was an American heiress, despised and
sought after by the ton all at the same time. And all had
been painstakingly selected by Clara from the long list of
girls who had applied.

"Have a seat," she said, gesturing to the wild grasses
swaying in the wind. She picked up her skirts and lowered
herself to the ground, tucking the fabric around her knees.
She hid an inward smile as some of the girls hesitated. There
were no blankets, no servants scurrying forward with chairs,
only a mat of grass and wildflowers.

"On the grass?" It came from a fair-haired student. She
was the youngest daughter of a marquess, and given what
she knew about the family, Clara rather suspected that this
was probably the first time the girl had ever been asked to
put her backside on something that wasn't padded.

"On the grass," Clara confirmed pleasantly.

"But—"

"Don't worry, people have been doing it for thousands

of years. And we'll all have creased skirts and grass stains when we're done and no one to judge us for it."

There were a couple of titters. Patiently she waited as, one by one, they finally sat, some more gingerly than others.

"Welcome to our first class," Clara said. She saw a few exchange uncertain looks and hid another smile. "A rather beautiful classroom, do you not agree?"

There were nods, these less uncertain.

"I trust you all found the excursion that each of you participated in yesterday . . . appealing?"

This was met by shy smiles and outright grins and curious gazes at their fellow students—especially from the three who had been on their own.

"Good. We'll get back to that," Clara said. "In the meantime I'm assuming that some of you may know each other already, either from prior familiarity, from being stuck in a carriage, or from the time you might have spent together yesterday. But I'll ask you to humor me and introduce yourselves again. Tell us your name and something important about you that you'd like us to know."

More curious glances around the group.

"Why don't we start with you?" Clara gestured at the blond girl, who was, even now, trying to smooth out her skirts.

"Oh," she said, blinking at Clara. "Very well. My name is Lady—"

"Just your Christian name will do," Clara interrupted gently.

"I beg your pardon?" The blonde's mouth hung slightly agape.

"Your name. The prefix of *Lady* gives an indication of who your family is. I'm not interested in your family, and I'm not interested if your families are attached to titles. I'm not interested in how much money or how many houses they have or where they have theater boxes. I'm interested in you."

She ignored the new round of wide-eyed, uncertain looks being exchanged. She could well understand why this would be shocking for many.

"But—"

"But nothing." Clara smiled at her. "Tell me your name and something you want me to know about you."

She stared at Clara and then gave a slight shrug. "Very well. My name is Lydia. And I enjoy riding. Fast. Not that I've ever been allowed on one of our racing thoroughbreds."

"Yet," Clara said, and Lydia looked up with interest.

"Yet," she repeated with a slight curl to her lips.

"Thank you." Clara looked at the platinum-haired, green-eyed girl next to her, daughter of a man whose family had made a fortune in prospecting and mining.

"Amelia," the girl blurted and then looked around her almost shyly. "My name is Amelia."

"Good," Clara said and gave her an encouraging smile. "Go on."

Amelia looked around. "My favorite color is red?"

"Is that a question?" Clara asked.

The girl flushed slightly. "No."

"What kind of red?" Clara asked.

"Crimson. Like the crimson China roses that are twined over the trellises near the fountain at the back of Avondale. It's the soil, I think, and the application of—" She suddenly clamped her mouth shut as if she'd said too much. "Never mind. They're just ... pretty."

"I agree," Clara nodded, thinking how very different this conversation would go a week from now. Her eyes slid to the familiar dark-haired girl next to her.

"My name is Anne." Holloway's sister was looking around her with interest. "And I have a brother who drives me crazy."

This was met by giggles, and Clara could feel some of the uncertainty break.

"Your brother is a *duke*," Lydia whispered, looking just a little scandalized.

"And he still puts his trousers on one leg at a time." Anne twirled a piece of grass between her fingers, looking unimpressed.

Clara gestured to the student sitting next to Anne, not wishing to get into a conversation that had her imagining Holloway putting on or taking off any item of clothing. "Go ahead," she encouraged.

"My name is Phoebe," said a pretty girl with hair the color of chestnuts and eyes to match. Her eyes slid to Anne. "I grew up in Boston, and my parents think I should marry one. A duke, that is."

"Excellent," said Anne crisply. "I have one you can have, so long as you promise to take him back to Boston with you."

Phoebe snorted. "I never said *I* wanted one."

"That's too bad. Is there room for negotiation? Everything in life is a negotiation, really. Perhaps I can throw in a good horse or two to sway you?"

"Ladies," Clara warned, though she was smiling. She wondered if Anne had any idea how much she sounded like her brother just then. "Let's continue."

One by one they went around the circle until everyone had introduced herself. By the time the last student had finished, the tension had dissipated. Missing from any of the questions and reactions had been the snobbery that she saw in so many of her students who attended her programs throughout the year. Missing were the class divide, the preconceptions, and the prejudices. This was not a surprise. She had chosen these girls for exactly this reason.

"Thank you, ladies," she said. "Next activity. Lie back in the grass."

Lydia sent her a skeptical look, though the shy Amelia was grinning. With a couple of scattered giggles, the girls reclined so that they were gazing up at the sky.

This part, Clara knew from experience, was easier when each girl did not have the eyes of all the others on her. When each student felt as though she might be alone in the world, alone with her dreams on a cliff high above the sea with only the gulls and the breeze for company.

Clara gazed around her, the girls almost invisible among the waving grass. "Think back to when each of you came to my office and I interviewed you. Now think about the application I gave you to fill out while you were there." She paused. "You all filled out the same application. Do you all remember what the last question was?"

Heads nodded in the grass.

"Good." Clara snapped a pretty horseshoe vetch bloom from beside her and looked out over the ocean. "I want you to tell everyone what your answer was. Whenever you're ready."

There was a long pause. She could almost hear the thoughts swirling around her. Was this a trick? Was this a trap? Was there going to be some sort of consequence for disclosing publicly what had been written in private? No one wished to say what she had probably never shared with anyone out loud before. Clara snapped another bright-yellow flower and added it to the one already in her hand. A third joined her small bouquet.

"Hotelier." It was Anne who finally spoke up, the word clear and steady as she gazed up at the drifting clouds.

"Barrister," Lydia said almost immediately after, and there was a note of wonder in her declaration.

"Physician." Phoebe added her voice.

"Landscape gardener," Amelia whispered.

And so it went. This year she had an ambitious hotelier, two students who were fascinated with the intricacies of law, three aspiring physicians, a landscape gardener, an artist, and an architect. The last student spoke, and Clara let a new silence fall.

"You can sit up now."

The girls pushed themselves upright, each looking around with comprehension dawning in her eyes.

"Thank you for your honesty," Clara said. "For your courage and willingness to share." She added a final flower to her collection. "The places and people you spent yesterday with outside Avondale—you will continue as you did yesterday two or three days of each week. You will be expected to contribute as well as learn, and I suggest you take notes and ask a lot of questions of each of your mentors."

Progressive, generous, and discreet mentors who had been part of her program for years, starting with her brother, who was as good at teaching medicine as he was at administering it. Mentors who valued clever, intelligent minds over everything else.

A buzz of excitement rippled through the group as each realized that her ambitions and desires were suddenly no longer things to be hidden, but things to be embraced. That an opportunity that she might never get again was right in front of her to seize.

"I would think it's only fair that I answer the same question I asked you all." Clara's voice carried over the whispers and murmurs, and she waited for them to fade. She smiled at each of her students. "Professor. Cambridge, or Oxford, though I'm rather partial to the classics, so it might have to be Oxford." She passed her newly assembled bouquet to Anne, who was watching her with wide eyes. "That's what I would be if I were a man."

～

August still hadn't managed to find Harland Hayward.

He'd cleaned his gelding's wound again that morning, pleased with how it looked, and seen the animal turned out comfortably, once again horrifying the stable boys by his refusal to hand the animal over to their care. He didn't bother explaining that his horse was like everything else he owned—his responsibility and therefore deserving of his complete attention when required. August had, however, offered a cursory explanation of how the wound had come about, leaving out the part that involved a small child and letting his displeasure at rash and reckless soldiers be known. There had been a few knowing nods and a few glances exchanged, leaving August with the distinct impression that this sort of behavior was not surprising.

Which firmed his resolve to seek out the officer in charge at his earliest opportunity.

In the meantime, August went looking for Harland Hayward, hoping to have a conversation with the baron before this evening. But Strathmore remained stubbornly elusive, and after a few hours, August gave up and set out in the direction of the calving sheds. He still wasn't entirely sure if Miss Hayward had believed him when he'd trotted out his reason for remaining at Avondale, but he'd been telling the truth.

When August had visited the elderly Rivers, he'd told the earl that he would be in the Dover area evaluating a prospective property, and had offered to look in on Avondale. He'd experienced a brief, Machiavellian satisfaction when Rivers had agreed and then insisted that he simply stay at the estate, giving him a watertight excuse should any of the Haywards actually wish to verify his story.

From what August had seen thus far, the estate was a model of good stewardship and management, but he had no intention of reneging on an agreement, no matter how contrived. He would hold up his end and report back to Rivers as promised. And in the continued absence of one Harland Hayward, August had no good excuse not to get to it.

He was in the calving sheds when he saw Anne and the rest of the students following Miss Hayward out across the windswept fields and toward the sea like the pied piper and his collection of children. They did not have any books; they had no papers or easels; they had nothing to suggest that they were doing anything scholastic. Instead they looked as if they were heading out for a picnic. Less any baskets, food, or blankets.

Without considering what he was doing, he followed at a judicious distance, skirting the edge of the long stone fence that ran parallel to the ridge and the edge of the cliff far ahead. He saw Miss Hayward glance back surreptitiously, which only piqued his curiosity and suspicion further. What was she up to? Where were they going? And what could they possibly be doing?

August hunkered lower behind the ancient wall, the moss soft against his fingertips where it grew on the stone. He felt as if he were ten years old again, spying on one of his father's card games at the public house that had been just down the road from the tumbledown building he'd grown up in.

What the hell kind of ladies' finishing school had its pupils sprawled out in the middle of a field on what was supposed to be the first day of classes? August shuffled forward a little farther on his knees, tying to get a better view.

"Have you lost something, dearie?"

August nearly knocked a loose stone off the top of the fence with his elbow, so fast did he shoot to his feet, biting back a muffled curse as a bolt of pain shot through his arm. He wrenched himself around and was presented with a tall, angular woman flanked by a shorter, rounder version of herself. Both had silver hair pulled back neatly from their lined faces, and both had the same pale-gray eyes set above a healthy flush in their cheeks. The taller of the two was wrapped in a faded rose-colored shawl, while the shorter wore a similar garment in a deep green.

"No." August's heart slowed as he straightened his shoulders, and he leaned back against the stone fence. Bloody hell, he hadn't even heard them, so wrapped up had he been in the scene out on the field. "I haven't lost anything." Except, perhaps, his dignity.

"Have you taken ill?" It was the taller who asked, shifting the basket she held over her arm. "Should we fetch someone for you? Perhaps we should alert Miss Hayward—"

"No." It came out a little louder than he would have liked. "There is no need to fetch anyone. I'm perfectly fine."

"Are you sure? You were crouched on your hands and knees for some time." It was said kindly enough, but the shorter woman's sharp eyes were dancing with poorly concealed humor that let August know she knew exactly what he had been doing.

"I am quite sure. Thank you for your concern," he replied curtly. Not that he needed to explain his actions to anyone. Especially these two. He subtly examined the two women further. Their clothes were plain but of fine quality. Sturdy, somewhat battered leather shoes peeked out from just beneath their hems, but there was nothing battered or plain about the emerald brooch pinned at the shoulder of the deep green shawl or the large sapphire on the finger of the taller woman where it rested on the top of a walking stick. "Lady Tabitha and Lady Theodosia, I presume?" The Earl of Rivers's sisters. The ones who lived out here in Dover.

"A pleasure, Your Grace," the taller replied. "But most just call me Tabby. And you can call her Theo." She gestured at her sister.

August started at the address. "You know who I am." He didn't know if he should be relieved or mortified.

"Of course, Your Grace. Your clothes are far too fine for you to be a tinker," Lady Tabitha quipped, doing an admirable job of suppressing her amusement. Her sister wasn't as successful. "Simple deduction, really."

"Well, it might not have been so simple. He might have been an apothecary," Lady Theo suggested to her sister. "Collecting plants and herbs and whatnot."

"True. Or a biologist," Tabby mused. "Looking for crickets."

"Or fossils."

"Or perhaps examining animal leavings."

Animal leavings? August closed his eyes briefly, wondering if they had forgotten he was still standing there. "I'm very pleased to meet you, Lady Tabitha, Lady Theodosia," he replied deliberately. No matter the saucy cheek of these two old ducks, he would not be reduced to calling a woman old enough to be his grandmother *Tabby*. Or *Theo*. Not even in a middle of a field at the very edge of England.

Lady Tabitha pulled her shawl a little tighter around her shoulders against the breeze. "Welcome, Your Grace. My brother sent word that you would be staying up at the dower house, evaluating the . . . livestock." Her eyes slid past August to the group of students out on the plain, and August had the uncomfortable feeling that she might be laughing at him again.

"The livestock and the land," August repeated firmly. "I had just started out when I came across Miss Hayward and her students. I did not wish to be a distraction." Why was he explaining himself? "I do hope I haven't put you out of your residence," he said, gesturing in the direction of the dower house and deliberately changing the subject. "I didn't think to—"

Lady Theodosia waved a plump hand to cut him off. "Tabby and I haven't put ourselves out to pasture quite yet," she said with a wry chuckle. "My sister and I live in the main house. Where the action is."

"The action?"

"The young ladies of Miss Hayward's school. We're so pleased to have her company, and that of her students, every summer."

"Special woman, Miss Hayward is," Lady Tabitha interjected.

"She is. Makes an old soul feel young again." Theodosia beamed. "And here they come now." She was once again looking over August's shoulder.

August turned to see that Miss Hayward and her students were indeed returning to Avondale. She was talking animatedly to one of the girls, her hands as expressive as her features. Her face was pink from her walk or the breeze or both, and her hair had again lost its battle with its curl and the wind. The urge to yank the last few pins from the back of it and watch it unfurl down her back was almost overwhelming.

August had a sudden vision of her sitting on the edge of those cliffs, only this time it was he who was with her.

This time it was he who lay back in the grass, drawing her down with him. Baring her until she wore nothing but sunlight and that glorious curtain of fire that tumbled over her shoulders—

"Miss Hayward, good afternoon," Lady Tabitha chirped.

August jerked, trying to haul his thoughts out of the dissolute depths where they had slid.

"Good afternoon, Tabby, Theo," Miss Hayward replied, and some of the laughter in her expression disappeared as her gaze settled on him. "Your Grace."

"Good afternoon," he managed.

Miss Hayward turned back to her students. "Head on up to the house, girls," she instructed. "I'll meet you in the library very shortly."

August had already braced himself for the irritation he would no doubt find in his sister's expression. But instead she was deep in conversation with a pretty brunette with an American accent and merely gave him a distracted nod as she passed.

Huh.

"How was your walk, ladies?" Miss Hayward asked.

"Oooh, it was lovely, dearie." Lady Tabitha beamed. "We found three fossilized urchins and a lovely bivalve specimen on the lower beach. Oh, and we found His Grace. Though he was a little higher up." She poked the end of her walking stick in his direction, which made August suspect that he measured up rather poorly to a fine urchin specimen.

Miss Hayward once again turned her attention to August, and he found himself the object of another one of her indecipherable stares. Her eyes skipped down his body, lingering on the bits of grass still stubbornly clinging to the knees of his breeches. He saw her lips thin slightly and a faint crease mar her forehead. But as always, good manners won out, and her expression flattened into one of pleasant neutrality. "You're up and about early, Your Grace."

Early? August scoffed. "It's midafternoon, Miss Hayward. I've never much been one for lying abed when there is work to be done."

He saw her brows rise slightly, and she might have flushed, though it was difficult to tell beneath her wind-reddened cheeks. "How commendable," she said in a way that suggested his particular work this afternoon was anything but.

August was aware of the sisters' gaze upon them. "Can you join us for a cup of tea, Your Grace?" Lady Theo asked. "Miss Hayward will be busy with her students, of course, but we'd love the company."

"Er, thank you, but no. I have a great deal to get done today. Perhaps another time." He'd been the object of their entertainment for too long already, and he had no intention of prolonging it. Though he had no one but himself to blame.

"Of course." Lady Tabitha shrugged slightly and linked her arm through her sister's. "Come along, then, Theo. Let us not stand in the way of . . . important work."

August inwardly grimaced.

"I'll be right in," Miss Hayward said. "I just need a quick word with His Grace."

The sisters nodded and cheerfully headed off in the direction of the house, moving at a surprisingly swift clip.

"They walk the beach every day," Miss Hayward said.

He frowned at her words. The beach? "But that has to be two hundred feet down."

"And two hundred feet back up."

"Why?" August was aghast.

"They like to collect fossils. And they tell me the exercise is good for their constitutions." She stared at him with that unreadable expression he despised. "Is that what you were doing this afternoon, Your Grace? Exercising?"

"I was checking the calving sheds, if you must know."

Miss Hayward made a great show of looking around her. "The calving sheds."

"Yes."

Her eyes dropped to the knees of his breeches. "Must be a time-consuming task if you have to crawl around on your hands and knees to do so," she commented with a calm, infuriating logic.

"I was not crawling around on my hands and knees," he bit out. That was true. He had been walking until he got to the fence. And then he had been more...*crouching*.

She smiled, but it didn't come anywhere close to her eyes. "If you are going to insist on spying on me, your sister, and the rest of my students, I am going to have to insist you leave."

"I was not spying on you." But it was hard to argue with grass stains.

"Of course you weren't." Her lips turned up in the cynical quirk he remembered so well.

He went on the offensive, abhorring the accusation. Probably because it was true. "I was out walking when I stumbled upon...whatever the hell you were doing out there in that field. Having the girls lie on their backs in the grass like a bunch of dairymaids about to be tumbled."

He hated the words the second they were out of his mouth. Because before they'd disappeared in the long grass, they hadn't looked like a bunch of maids about to be tumbled; they had looked like a bunch of beautiful young girls laughing in the sun.

Miss Hayward's immaculate composure slipped, and fury crossed her face, her eyes flashing and her hands fisting at her sides. "Have a care, Your Grace. That is your sister you are speaking of. And eight other women who don't deserve such inconsiderate, ill-mannered remarks. Those sort of comments may find you popularity in the back rooms at Boodle's, but they will not be tolerated here."

August ran a hand over his face. Not eight others. Nine. She hadn't included herself in her defense of her students. What was wrong with him? His job with Miss Hayward was to be charming and personable and get her to open up to him. To get her to trust him. To bloody well like him. And right now he didn't even like himself.

"You're right. That was thoughtless."

She blinked.

"It was just... It wasn't what I was expecting."

"Not what you were expecting?" She still sounded furious, but it looked as if she was fighting for patience. "You may be Lady Anne's brother and guardian, but that does not give you the right to pass judgment on something you don't understand."

"I saw my sister laughing." That was not what he had intended to say. But this woman seemed to provoke him into fits of honesty that were as terrifying as they were liberating. Given his reason for being here in the first place, the irony was not lost on him.

Miss Hayward stilled and then blew out a long breath. She looked away from him and gazed out over the expanse of the sea. "Do you know why I bring them out here?"

August remained silent.

"To take them out of their element and put them in mine." She ran her fingers lightly along the top of the stone fence.

"I'm not sure I understand."

She laughed softly, still looking out over the glittering expanse of water. "You, Your Grace, should understand more than anyone, I should think. Your worth in society is measured by your title. Yet I would argue that your true merit as an individual should come not from where and to whom you were born, but from what you did with the time between then and now."

Miss Hayward fell silent, and August simply watched the play of emotion that creased her forehead and brought a pensive aura to her being. Something strange was pulsing through him, a reckless feeling of acknowledgment that this woman saw him. Saw the very thing that drove him and haunted him at the same time.

She finally looked back at him, her eyes searching his. "In this class I have girls who call dukes and earls family. I have girls who are daughters of bankers and miners and factory owners, one of whom isn't even English." Her beautiful lips twisted. "You tell me how this group of women would be encouraged to interact in a society ballroom."

He knew the answer because he had lived it. He had recovered his father's fortune and then desperately tried to repair his family's good name within the ranks of society. The debacle that had led him to dare Miss Hayward to dance had been part of that desperation. But it had been damn near impossible until the title of Holloway had unexpectedly fallen onto his shoulders.

"They wouldn't." She was right. He did know that better than anyone.

Miss Hayward inclined her head and seemed to be choosing her words carefully. "For the duration of my program, I wish my students to have the chance to be recognized for their own merit. Not an accident of birth or the ledger totals at the bottom of their family's quarterly earnings statement. Not the type of lace used to trim their ball gown or the appearance of their hair. Not the label that society gives them because they come with a preconceived, baseless checklist of traits that has been ruled either acceptable or unacceptable."

August stared at her. It sounded ridiculous. Preposterous, even, because that simply wasn't how the world worked. Yet he had never, in all his years, seen Anne as carefree and as joyous as she had been sitting in a field of wildflowers.

Nor had he ever seen Miss Hayward as unguarded as she had been. As she was now.

And he realized that it was because she had lived it too. She had been allowed to exist along the fringes of society just like him, tolerated but not welcomed. But unlike him, she had not inherited a duchy.

"Is that what you wanted? To be measured by your merit?"

She gave him a long look. "Don't you?"

"I know who I am. And I care very little for the opinions of others."

She made a noise in her throat. "Spoken like a man and a duke."

August scowled. "That's not fair."

Miss Hayward didn't look away from him. "It isn't, is it?" she asked, and now there was an edge to her words.

August tapped his fingers on the top of the stone. "Are you trying to be obtuse on purpose?"

"Not at all. I'm trying to make you consider, just for a moment, what it might be like to not be a duke, or even a man, in a world that gives precedence and value to both of those things over all else. Consider what it's like to navigate—" Miss Hayward stopped suddenly and clamped her lips together.

The reckless passion and heat that had been in her voice were making it impossible for him to look away. This was the Clara Hayward he had never forgotten.

"My apologies, Your Grace," she said, looking down. "This is not at all a suitable conversation for—"

"Stop apologizing." He reached out and tipped her chin up, forcing her eyes back to his. It was hard to read what was in those liquid brown depths, but he wasn't going to let her retreat behind the composure she wore like a cloak.

He felt her breath on his wrist as she exhaled. Very slowly she reached up and drew his hand away from her face, though he didn't let her withdraw her fingers from his. Her hand stayed trapped in his, hidden by her skirts. He had let her go once before, and he wasn't ready to let her go again.

She was shaking her head. "Your Grace—"

"Pretend I am not a duke," he said impulsively. "Pretend, just for a moment, that I am a young idiot again, who needs at least part of the world explained to him."

"You were never an idiot," she said, with a weak smile.

"Debatable." His fingers tightened on hers, and she made no move to withdraw her hand.

"Well, you were the only man who ever asked me to dance who wasn't doing it as a favor to my father." She said it wryly.

"Then I would suggest that proves I'm a bloody genius, and the rest of the lot are all bottleheads." He kept his words light even as an intense, possessive anger rose on her behalf.

She sniffed, though it sounded a little like a chuckle.

"Please finish your thoughts, Miss Hayward."

She drew in another deep breath and let it out slowly. "Very well. I was going to ask you to consider what it's like to navigate your world in my shoes. Or, more importantly, in those of your sister."

August remained silent, waiting for her to continue.

"As the sister to a duke, she must be gracious and beautiful, though not so much that she might inspire envy or jealousy. She should be firm, decisive, and capable, but only in those areas that you or her future husband allow her to be. She should not show an unattractive interest in subjects that have been deemed unladylike or beyond her comprehension. Which isn't to say she shouldn't be intelligent. Just so long as she doesn't accidentally prove her intellect superior to that of the gentleman seated on her right at the dinner table."

August could feel his nostrils flare.

"Ah. You're angry."

"I'm not."

"You're crushing my fingers."

He relaxed his grip. "Sorry."

"None of what I said was meant as a criticism of you, Your Grace."

"It sounded like it."

Miss Hayward sighed, sounding defeated. "That was not my intention." She turned away from him slightly in the direction of the house. "I should get back to my students."

"Not yet." August didn't relinquish his grip on her hand. "What was?"

"I'm sorry?"

"Your intention. What was it, if not to censure?"

"What is your greatest passion, Your Grace?" she asked suddenly.

"I beg your pardon?"

"What is it that gives you the most joy out of life? The thing that gets you out of bed every morning?"

Ownership. Acquisition. Building something from nothing. He knew he should probably say something flippant like cards or whiskey or snuff. "Business," he hedged instead.

She considered him. "Are you good at it?"

The best. "Yes."

"Now just for a moment, pretend Lady Anne didn't approve of what you did." She pulled her fingers from his and stepped away. "And now, just for the moment, pretend she had the control and the power to stop you from doing what you loved."

Chapter 9

Clara paced across Avondale's hall.

The clock near the bottom of the stairs ticked loudly, and Clara wondered why she had never noticed before that this house had so many wretched ticking clocks. Five minutes to six. No sign of her brother. And no sign of the duke.

Which, after the conversation, or rather the lecture, she had given Holloway earlier, was probably understandable, though the duke hadn't sent word canceling his invitation. Clara wasn't sure what it was about the man that provoked her into blurting truths that had no business being aired, especially to the paying clientele of Haverhall. Perhaps because he had trapped her hand in his, his steady warmth giving her courage to be more honest with him than was wise or safe. As though by keeping her with him, her fingers clasped within his, he was promising to at least try to understand her words.

That gesture of possession still sent chills through her, accompanied by a strange feeling of vertigo. Much the same way she felt when standing on the edge of the cliffs, looking down at the crashing sea far below. Not safe or wise at all.

"You're pacing, dearie." The voice came from the stairs.

Clara looked up and saw Lady Tabitha coming down the wide staircase. She was dressed in one of her walking outfits. "On your way out?" Clara asked.

"Yes." She pulled her shawl a little more tightly around her shoulders. "Theo is waiting for me outside. There is a section of the beach where the cliffs have sloughed in the last day that we'd like to take a look at. You never know what you're going to find in unexpected places."

"No, I suppose you don't," Clara muttered.

"A gentleman stopped by earlier asking after you," Tabby said. "While you were with your students."

"A gentleman?"

"A Mr. Stilton? He mentioned that he was in the area visiting friends and that he would return at a later time to call on you."

Clara frowned slightly. Stilton hadn't mentioned anything about traveling to Dover the last time she had seen him.

"Is he someone you would rather avoid?" Tabby asked, her eyes narrowed.

"No, no, of course not. He is a London acquaintance who has graciously lent his company for an occasional outing."

"Mr. Stilton asked after His Grace as well. Are they also acquaintances?"

Clara shook her head. "They are familiar, but from what I could tell, I don't think that there is much love lost between those two."

"Mmm." Tabby gazed at her. "Well, speaking of His Grace, I understand you are dining with the duke this evening," she commented casually. "At a tavern."

"Yes." All thoughts of Stilton's unexpected appearance evaporated at the mention of the impending evening.

"Not that I've had a great deal of experience dining with dukes, but one might have thought he'd insist on a proper dinner in a proper dining room. We have a perfectly opulent one here."

"His Grace does not always conform to the expected." Clara glanced at the clock again.

"Including punctuality?"

Clara squirmed. "I'm not sure he hasn't rescinded his offer of dinner entirely. I might have incensed him beyond repair."

"The duke does not strike me as a man who easily gets his breeches in a twist."

"I don't think that applies when broaching the subject of his sister."

"Protective, is he?"

Clara sighed. "I believe I might have accused him of being a controlling dictator. And suggested that he alter his behavior before he further alienates the very person he wishes to understand."

"Yes, well, Julius Caesar learned that lesson the hard way, didn't he?" Tabby murmured.

"I did not point that out," Clara said, though she felt a smile tug at her lips. "I didn't think it would help the situation."

Tabby shrugged. "I was married for thirty-seven years, dearie. Sometimes men need to figure these things out on their own."

"Figure what out on their own?"

Clara's head whipped around as the Duke of Holloway strode through the door, pulling at his gloves. He was dressed in rough breeches, an unadorned coat, and dusty boots, and save for the unmistakable aura of power that emanated from his person, he might have passed for a simple country gentleman just coming in from a ride.

Except that a simple country gentleman would never steal Clara's voice and scatter her wits the way this man did with a single smile. A simple country gentleman would not turn her insides into molten heat. The room suddenly felt suffocating.

"Figure out that a lady does not like to be kept waiting," Tabby said smoothly into the silence.

"I wouldn't dream of it, Lady Tabitha," Holloway said with a charming smile. "Which is why I am"—he pulled a battered-looking watch from his pocket—"a full three minutes early. Though I confess that our ride is somewhat delayed. I had a hankering to drive, so I asked for the earl's barouche to be prepared, only to discover that one of the horses had thrown a shoe. It is being reshod as we speak, and should be ready shortly. I did not wish you to believe that I had abandoned you." He looked around with interest. "Is Lord Strathmore not here yet?"

As if on cue, a footman rounded the corner, his heels ringing over the polished marble floor of the hall. "Miss Hayward, a message from his Lordship." He held out a gleaming silver tray with a creased, smudged, and hastily folded scrap of paper on it.

Clara plucked it from the tray, and the footman disappeared as quickly as he had arrived. She opened the note, although she already knew what it was going to say.

Late. Meet you at the S. Swan. H.

"It would seem my brother is running a little behind schedule," she said, using the note as an excuse not to have to look at Holloway. She wasn't sure if she was ready yet to weather the full attention of those intense eyes. "He asks if we will meet him at the Silver Swan." She smoothed the paper with her finger, frowning at the rust-colored stains at the edge. Good Lord. Was that blood?

"That works for the best, doesn't it?" Holloway replied amicably, and Clara did look up at him then, wondering at his cheerful, charming demeanor. After leaving him angrily scowling in the middle of a field earlier, she'd rather expected at least an air of reserve. Even Lady Tabitha was eyeing him somewhat suspiciously. "I am honored that his Lordship entrusts me with your safety and well-being."

"I've been ensuring my own safety and well-being for almost thirty years, Your Grace. I'm a capable woman, not a capricious lapdog. I promise not to throw myself out a moving equipage after a squirrel. At least while we're traveling at high speeds."

"I'm glad to hear it, Miss Hayward." His eyes crinkled at the corners as he grinned at her, and Clara felt rivulets of longing run down her spine. No man had the right to look that handsome when he smiled. "Would you care to join us, Lady Tabitha?" Holloway continued. "I should have thought to extend the invitation. My apologies for my oversight."

"No, thank you, Your Grace. My sister and I have an evening of collecting planned." Tabby shifted her basket to her other hand and moved toward the door. "And I've kept her waiting long enough. Perhaps another time. Enjoy your evening, Miss Hayward, Your Grace."

Clara watched the woman depart, excruciatingly aware that she was now alone with the duke. She turned back to face him warily. "Your Grace—"

"I can have the equipage brought around while you wait here, Miss Hayward," Holloway interrupted her before she could say anything further. "But it is a beautiful evening that would be made only more beautiful by your company. Perhaps you would walk with me back to the dower house to collect our transportation?"

Clara blinked. *Yes*, the reckless part of her hissed. *Absolutely not*, the more prudent part of her countered. "Um."

"Don't do that," he said.

"Do what?"

"Look for excuses to hide behind as to why you should not. You didn't do it ten years ago. Don't do it now."

Clara could feel her heart thrumming in her chest. She looked up at him, completely at a loss for words. Simply lost, period.

"I'll ask again, Miss Hayward. Perhaps you would like to walk with me a bit before we depart?"

"Yes," she heard herself reply. "I'd like that."

"Very good, then." He offered her his arm.

Clara stepped forward, her hand sliding around his arm. Instantly his other hand came up to cover hers, and she could feel the heat of his palm bleeding through her thin gloves. She could also feel the steely strength of his arm and the way his body brushed against hers as they moved. She closed her eyes and told herself again that he was not escorting her to a night of wicked revelry but to a casual dinner with her brother. Which meant that if this night was to be bearable, it would be better if she cleared the air with the duke before they ever reached the tavern. She did not want to draw Harland into what had been an ill-advised topic of conversation.

She cleared her throat. "Your Grace, I've been thinking about our last conversation, and I believe I should apol—"

"Yes, I've been thinking a great deal about our last conversation as well," he said, leading her down the steps into the early-evening light.

"It wasn't my place to—"

"Please let me finish," he said, and Clara made a funny noise in her throat. He looked at her quizzically. "What?"

"You will not offer me the same courtesy? You haven't let me finish a sentence yet," she murmured.

"For good reason, Miss Hayward." He led her around the far side of Avondale and toward the path that would take them across the expanse of field and through the small copse of trees separating the dower house from Avondale. "You've been trying to apologize for something that requires no apology. In fact, I rather feel you've apologized to me far too much of late. And that, I can only conclude, is borne of a fear that, when challenged, I'll conduct myself in a manner befitting a temperamental two-year-old, collect my sister, and storm my way back to London in a self-righteous rage."

Clara turned her head to stare at him. "That sounds very...dramatic."

"Doesn't it?" His hand tightened over hers. "And that is not I. And that is not Anne either. She rarely complains of anything. Which is probably why I have done a poor job of considering her point of view of late. And I should be thanking you for drawing that to my attention."

It suddenly became difficult to draw a full breath. They were walking very close together, and she could see the flecks of sapphire scattered in the azure of his irises. His eyes were even more startling given the sun-darkened planes of his face, and they had her firmly in their thrall. Should winged dragons start spewing from Avondale's chimneys at that moment, Clara doubted she'd even notice.

"I see," she managed to utter, because that was the only thing that her addled mind could come up with. Holloway had shaved just recently, and she could smell the sharp, clean scent of the soap he'd used. Near his ear was a slightly reddened mark where the blade had pressed a little too hard, and she suffered a sudden urge to rise on her toes and press her lips to that skin.

"I love my sister very much, Miss Hayward. And I do not want to see her unhappy."

Good Lord, but if she didn't remember how to breathe again soon, she might simply drop like a sack of onions at his feet. "I'm glad I could be of some small help, Your Grace."

"Don't ever stop," he said in a low voice, searching her face.

The aching need to kiss him unfurled into a need for something far more wanton than mere kisses. Her nipples hardened against her bodice, and an unmistakable dampness had gathered between her legs.

"Stop what?" she whispered. When had this gotten away from her? When had this conversation turned into something so dissolute in her head? Because all she could imagine was what it might be like to have him at the mercy of her hands and her lips and hear him say, *Don't ever stop*.

"Don't ever stop asking me difficult questions," Holloway said. "Don't ever stop making me accountable for my actions."

Clara shook her head, not trusting her voice.

"You did it the day I first met you, and you did it again yesterday. And I think I might just be a better man—or at least a better brother—because of it. Because of you."

"I rather think you're doing just fine on your own." It sounded a little uneven. "I very much doubt you need my help." Clara's eyes slid from his, focusing on a small white butterfly that was fluttering near the edge of the grassy path.

Holloway didn't answer. They continued walking, the path now following a low stone fence that ran to the edge of the wind-buffeted trees. Here, away from the house, the sound of the surf was louder, the breeze a little stronger. They were almost to the trees when the duke stopped.

"I should have kissed you," he said suddenly.

"I beg your pardon?" Her eyes flew back to his.

"That night when we waltzed." He held her gaze. "I wanted to kiss you then. I want to kiss you now."

Clara swallowed with difficulty. Not only was she having trouble breathing, but the ground beneath her feet suddenly felt unsteady.

"Why?" It slipped out, and Clara cursed at the awkward inanity of such a question.

Holloway chuckled. "Only you would ask that." The mirth slid from his face, replaced with a smoldering heat. His hand slid slightly, and his fingers gently caressed the exposed skin of her upper arm.

"Why did you really invite me out here?" she asked abruptly.

"Why do you ask?"

She bit her lip. "You're getting better at that, Your Grace. Turning the why back on me."

"Before I met you, I believed myself to be one of the best at it. You, however, have proven me wrong."

"I'm not sure if that is a compliment."

"It is."

"And you have yet to answer my question."

"That's true."

Clara ran the fingers of her free hand over the cool, rough stone. "I'd appreciate the truth."

The duke was silent for a long minute. "Because you fascinate me. You're extraordinary."

Clara felt her cheeks flush. She cast about for a suitable response but could find none.

"I've made you uncomfortable." His voice was low.

"You just surprised me with your flattery."

"Not flattery. The truth."

"Your Grace—"

"August. I want you to call me August."

Clara's mind was racing, but not as fast as her heart was slamming in her chest. "I'm not sure that is appropriate given my position as—"

"As what? A beautiful, brilliant woman? Because right here, right now, that is who you are." He ran a finger down the side of her face before slowly threading his fingers through the hair at the back of her head. She could feel pins tumble to fall soundlessly into the grass. "The woman I once let get away."

His fingers caressed the nape of her neck.

"You were right, you know," he said, stepping closer so that the backs of her legs were pressed against the stone wall and the front of her was a whisper away from the entire length of him.

"About what?" she managed to whisper.

"That regrets are nothing but excuses. And I'm done with both." His other hand came up to catch her face.

Clara closed her eyes, every nerve ending she possessed on fire. Time seemed to have slowed. A strange sense of inevitability enveloped her, as though this moment had been unavoidable since the very second she had said yes to a waltz. His fingers dropped from the side of her face to trail along the side of her neck, along the ridge of her collarbone, and down to the edge of her bodice.

The heat that had been chasing itself across her skin pooled low in her belly and between her legs. Her breasts felt heavy, and her nipples hardened. She kept her eyes closed, focusing solely on the feel of his hands and the warmth from his body as he closed the distance between them and pressed against her.

And then she felt him move again, and his lips brushed hers, softly, deftly. She remained perfectly still, lust screaming through her limbs. His hand that had been resting at the edge of her bodice lowered, stroking the side of her breast and coming to rest at her waist, urging her more firmly against him. She could feel the hard solidity of his body through the light fabric of her skirts, and she sucked in a breath, her arousal sharpening and a pulsing restlessness stealing whatever coherent thought remained.

And then his mouth returned to hers, controlled and soft again as he teased her lips. It was an exquisite, gentle torment, as though he feared she might shatter. Clara brought her own hands up, slipping them inside his coat and sliding them over his waistcoat to his shoulders, feeling his steely strength under the soft linen of his shirt. Her hands roamed farther under his coat and down his back, intoxicated by the way his muscles flexed beneath her touch.

He made an incoherent noise and deepened their kiss, though still with the same careful control. Not enough. She opened her mouth, catching his lower lip and tracing it wickedly with her tongue.

It was as if she had branded him. His head jerked back, and he stared at her, his breath coming quick and shallow, his hands still holding her in place. "Bloody hell," she thought she heard him groan.

Clara wasn't sure if she should embrace her confusion or her mortification first. What was wrong with her? What had she done?

"Was it something I said?" she murmured, willing the ground to open up and swallow her so that she wouldn't need to hear him answer or face him when he did.

"I am not the first man to kiss you," he blurted, sounding just as confused as she felt.

Clara goggled at him. "What?"

"I thought...I mean to say...I wasn't expecting..."

"Bloody hell indeed," she breathed. "You thought I'd never been *kissed*?"

He had the grace to redden. Good Lord, that was exactly what he had thought. Well, that might explain why he had been so very, very careful. She wasn't sure whether to be moved by his gentleness or appalled by his astounding arrogance.

"Why would you have thought that?" she breathed.

August shook his head. "I'm not...I can't..."

A very inelegant snort escaped. "Because I was the wall-flower at the ball? The bluestocking who never married and became a spinster?"

"I despise how you make that sound," he growled. "As if you are...less. You are not."

"While I am touched by your words, let me assure you I have never considered myself less. Different, of course, but not less for it." She paused. "Have you?"

"Have I what?"

"Been kissed. Before tonight, that is."

"That is the most idiotic question I've ever been asked."

"I take that as a yes. But you're not married."

"Of course not." Now he sounded cross.

"Do you see my point here?"

"I'm not a half-wit," he growled. "It just...took me by surprise."

"Would you like to stop?"

His head dropped, and Clara saw his lips twitch. "That's what I was prepared to ask you."

"Ah. Well, I think you had my answer. Before you reacted like a scalded cat."

His hand tightened at her waist. "I resent being compared to a cat."

"And I resent being kissed like a schoolgirl." She wanted those words back the second they were out. Because the humor was wiped clean from his face, to be replaced with something dark.

"I can assure you, Miss Hayward, it won't happen again."

She swallowed. "Perhaps that is for the best." It was true. Her mind seemed to have regained its grasp on sanity, and this kiss, however short and sweet it had been, shouldn't go any further.

"You misunderstand me." The duke shifted, bringing his leg forward so that it was wedged between hers. The hand that still rested at the back of her head lifted and stroked the hair that had tumbled down, coming to rest at the small of her back, his fingers splayed possessively. "When I kiss you again, it will not be like a schoolgirl."

Clara's mouth went dry.

"Who kissed you before me?" he asked in a low voice.

"What?" It was hard to concentrate with so much of him pressed against so much of her.

"The man who kissed you. Were you in love with him?"

Clara shook her head. "The woman you kissed before me. Were you in love with her?"

Holloway laughed, a low rumble she could hear in his chest. "That was well done."

"It was a reasonable question. At the least, as reasonable as the one you asked me."

"Touché." His hand at her back slid back up to the nape

of her neck. "So tell me, Miss Hayward, was kissing part of your impressive education?" he whispered.

"Yes."

He drew back. "What?"

"Yes. It was."

"I was jesting, Miss Hayward."

"And I was not."

"I don't understand."

Clara brought her hands to the front of his coat and ran them down the lapel, picking her words with careful concentration. This was not something that she had ever intended to discuss with this man. But here they were, and she would not retreat. And if he could not accede to what she was about to say, then it was better that everything stop here and now. "The idea that a gentleman should go to his marriage bed well versed in the art of bed sport, while his fine lady should go to that same marriage bed utterly ignorant, is a bit of a conundrum, isn't it?"

She felt him still. "I beg your pardon?"

"Did you know that when my mother, as a very sheltered daughter of a baron, married my father, she didn't know how babies were made? She didn't know what parts were supposed to go where. She was told that marital relations were painful, but her duty, and something to be suffered through." She looked up at Holloway. "I can't imagine that is the speech given to most young lords, is it?"

The duke was staring at her.

"In fact, as I understand it, if a titled man hasn't taken his son to his favored courtesan or mistress by the time the young buck is sixteen, he's failed in one of his principal duties as a father." She tilted her head. "Am I wrong?"

Holloway was frowning fiercely now.

"Luckily, my mother married a very loving, very patient,

very open-minded man. Not every bride is quite so lucky. So when she had daughters of her own, she encouraged us to...educate ourselves. At the very least understand exactly how it is that children are conceived. Empower ourselves with knowledge and understanding. And yes, experience, though that is a personal choice."

Holloway still hadn't spoken.

"You don't approve."

He shook his head. "Don't do that. Put words in my mouth again."

"Your Grace—"

"August." He touched his finger to her lips. "I asked you to call me August." He made a funny sound of amusement. "Given the nature of this...entire conversation, I think we are well beyond proper titles. And I don't think it's my place to approve or disapprove."

Clara traced one of the buttons on the front of his coat with her thumb, something squeezing relentlessly in her chest. "I appreciate that, but I'm not sure that is entirely true."

"What do you mean?"

She kept her eyes firmly on the button beneath her fingers, reluctant to look up. "There is an old midwife who lives just outside Dover," she went on. "During the summer, I hire her to speak with my students. Fill in any gaps in their education when it comes to...amorous congress and childbearing. Answer questions about a woman's health that most of the world they live in deems inappropriate or scandalous to ask. Some of my students are fortunate enough to have women in their lives who have already taught them much, but others are as ignorant as my mother was." Clara paused. "Your sister will be part of that class."

The duke stepped back from her, his hands falling away, taking his heat with him. Part of Clara, the part that had managed to find a little sanity, was relieved. The other part of her wanted to weep with frustration, loss, and regret. She tried to read his expression, but his features gave none of his thoughts away.

"If ever there was a time you'd like to collect your sister and storm back to London in a self-righteous rage, now would be it," she muttered.

"Have you lost your mind?" Holloway demanded.

Clara's chin came up along with her indignation. "I've had young girls confess to me that they thought they were dying the first time they got their monthly courses because no one had taken the time to explain even that. I cannot abide by such—"

"Stop. You misunderstand me again," he said, sounding a bit strangled. "Completely."

"Your Grace—"

"August."

"August." She squared her shoulders.

"Thank you. And I'm not…" He trailed off, as if searching for the right words. "I am not sure that I am the…source of guidance my sister needs when it comes to…feminine matters. The fact that you have taken it upon yourself to provide such guidance is a relief." He exhaled heavily. "So, yes, you've lost your mind if you think *I* think I can do better. If that makes any sense."

"Oh." The strange feeling that had been squeezing her heart returned.

August braced his hands on the stone wall and leaned forward, studying the horizon. "You are full of surprises, Miss Hayward."

"Clara."

He turned his head.

"Given the nature of this entire conversation, I think we are well beyond proper titles." She echoed his words, trying to make it light, but she wasn't sure if she had been able to keep the longing from them.

"Well, then, I'm glad we got that sorted." He straightened and stepped toward her again. "Clara."

The sound of her name on his lips set her pulse pounding. Cocooned as they were by their sun-kissed privacy, it was tempting to forget that reality existed. "I understand if you're scandalized. Horrified. Given what—who—I am supposed to be. Though I'm not prepared to apologize for it."

"Which is what? What are you supposed to be?"

"A woman of modesty and virtue. A woman who is deemed fit to tutor her young charges not because of her experience and knowledge of the world, but because of her lack of it."

"I don't want the woman you're supposed to be," he said, his voice low. "I never have. I want the woman you are, and everything that that encompasses. I wanted her ten years ago, and I want her now." He stepped closer to her, his hand coming up to toy with the ribbon at the front of her bodice. "A woman who knows her own mind. A woman who can make a man lose his. Make him do reckless things."

"August—"

He closed the remaining distance, once again pressing her back against the stone fence. His hands went to her lower back and then suddenly they dropped to her buttocks, and she was being lifted up, coming to sit on the edge of the cool stone. He ran his hands down the backs of her thighs, shoving her skirts up slightly and bringing her legs to rest on either side of his hips.

Desire streaked through Clara. She tightened her legs

around him, her heels pressed firmly against the small of his back. August made a guttural sound of approval and leaned into her, and she could feel his own arousal, pressed firmly against her core.

His breath brushed against the side of her neck, and she shivered. "You should be kissed, and kissed often," he whispered. "Kissed often by a man who knows how. A man who will kiss you until you can't breathe. Can't think. Someone who will set your blood on fire and make you feel like the only woman in the world."

Clara was pretty sure he had accomplished everything on that list before he had even kissed her. His hands roamed over her rear and then up her back, urging her even closer. "But tell me what you want, Clara."

"I'd like to be kissed by a man who knows how," she whispered back. "Until I can't breathe. Can't think." Her fingers found the sides of his face, skimming over his cheeks before she let them delve into his hair the way she had longed to, tangling them in the silky thickness. She brought her mouth to his, starting the way he had. Gentle, soft brushes of her lips over his. Controlled, measured tastes. He let her, for long seconds, and only the increasing pressure of his fingers at her shoulders betrayed the steady fraying of his control.

And then his hands moved, and he caught the base of her head, curling his fingers in her hair and tipping her head back so that his mouth could slant over hers. She gasped, and he angled his head farther, his tongue now stroking deep against hers as he claimed her. This wasn't a gentle kiss. This was hot and hard and demanding and stole every lucid thought other than her need to belong to this man. She kissed him back, all the pent-up emotion and longing she had ever suppressed channeled into a language he seemed to understand perfectly. It could have been seconds or minutes or hours that he kissed her, but it was difficult to tell, because time ceased to have meaning. Sensation coursed through her, making her ache and throb with need. She tightened her legs around his hips, and he made a tortured noise, his hands sliding from the base of her skull to skim her bodice.

He cupped her breasts through the fabric, filling his hands with them, rubbing his thumbs over her aching nipples. It was excruciating to have him touching but not touching. To not have his hands on her skin. His mouth dropped to her neck, his tongue and lips leaving trails of fire everywhere they went. Her head tipped back as she arched against him, her breath coming in shallow gasps.

"Clara," he whispered against her skin.

She could hear her heart thundering in her ears, growing louder with each passing second. It vibrated through her veins, a relentless pounding that couldn't be ignored. Her head fell to the side, her gaze unfocused, spots of color dancing before her vision.

And then she blinked, and with horror she realized that the thunder was not just that of her pulse, but also that of two dozen horses pounding their way across the grassland below them.

August suddenly yanked her hard against him, gathering her tight and dropping to his knees just behind the wall. His hands were wrapped around her back, keeping her steady. She looked up at him in the pale light, and he nodded, releasing his grip slightly so that she was able to relax her legs and slide away from him. She came to rest on her hands and knees and cautiously peered over the top of the wall, praying that they hadn't been spotted.

The soldiers didn't seem to have noticed them at all. Instead they had reined in their horses and had their attention fixed on the glittering sea. Clara could hear faint shouts as orders were issued, though the breeze was not strong enough to carry their words. The horses milled about restlessly for a minute before the riders split into two groups, one heading farther north, and the other angling inland, back in the general direction of the town.

"Do they ever stop?" August whispered roughly beside her. "The damn soldiers?"

She turned to him in surprise. "What do you know of them?"

"Enough."

She frowned slightly at his incomplete answer. "It's going to be a clear night with a full moon. Easy to see anyone out who shouldn't be. Anyone along the beaches. Small craft out on the water. They must have received a tip." Her heart rate was slowly returning to normal. She slid back down the stone fence and turned, leaning her back against it. "The soldiers come to Avondale from time to time. Asking if Tabby and Theo have seen any suspicious activity, given the proximity of the house to the coast. On occasion they interrogate Harland when we're here."

"Why?"

"Because he's a doctor who gets called out at all hours of the day and night. And there is probably little that he hasn't seen in his travels."

"Will the soldiers go there now?" August was frowning. "To Avondale?"

"I don't think so." She pushed herself to her feet. "We should go." The men were distant smudges of color down the coast, while the soldiers who had gone inland had vanished over the rise.

"Yes." August stood beside her but caught her arm before she could turn away. "Are you... Are we good?"

"Good?"

"I don't want what just happened to make things awkward between us."

"You're having regrets already?"

His expression hardened, and he suddenly pulled her to him, kissing her long and hard, ravaging her mouth and promising far more carnal things to come.

She should pull away. She kissed him back instead.

"Does it seem as if I have any regrets?" he growled against her lips.

"No," she replied a little unsteadily.

"Then I'm glad we got that sorted too." He raised his head slightly. "Because I'll kiss you again."

"Is that wise?"

"I don't care if it's wise. It's what I want. And I think what you want."

Yes, she wanted to tell him. *Yes, yes*, and whatever else he thought she wanted when it came to him, *yes* to that too. Because he would be right. And that wasn't wise at all.

"Where is this going?" she asked suddenly.

"This?"

"Us."

He reached up and pushed her hair away from her face. "Wherever you wish it to."

"August, I don't regret what just happened here either. But it can't ever become…anything," Clara said, loss and loneliness stabbing at her as reality took hold. She shoved it back. "I cannot be the mistress of a duke and still have any hope of running Hav—a school for young ladies. If it became known that *we* were an *us*, I would lose my reputation and my livelihood. And I will not sacrifice that for a temporary tryst."

His expression was unreadable, and he remained silent.

She went up on her toes and brushed her mouth against his. "Let's go," she said, and this time he let her pull away.

Chapter 10

The stable boy who came out to take the horses wasn't a boy at all, though it was rarely noticed.

"Good evening, Your Grace," she said as August drew the barouche to a halt in the busy stable yard. If the thirteen-year-old was surprised to see him, she hid it as well as she hid her gender.

"Good evening." He jumped out of the equipage. "I trust your brothers are about?"

"They're about all right," she said, sounding slightly out of breath. "Busy night."

"Good." He took a moment to survey the bustling yard and the tavern that was already alive with light and noise beyond it. Out of proprietary interest, of course, but also to give himself a moment to collect his wits before he faced Clara.

Temporary tryst.

The words continued to flicker through his consciousness like a peat fire that could not be extinguished. It sounded almost...tawdry. As if they were simply a pleasing diversion to each other in which a modicum of pleasure might be found and then discarded once they tired of it. No different, really, from any of his past relationships, if one could even call them that.

He had never really cared to get to know a woman the way he wanted to know Clara. So long as he and his paramour rubbed along well enough in the scant time they spent together and the bed sport was enjoyable, that was enough. Until they inevitably wanted more from him. Broad hints of marriage or a more permanent arrangement as a mistress. More jewels, a fine house, expensive clothes. They all wanted more. Predictable.

Clara Hayward seemed to want less.

And now that he'd kissed her, that was simply unacceptable. She had shaken him to his toes. Just the thought of her mouth on his, the memory of how her thighs had wrapped around his waist, had him hard and restless all over again.

It was a good thing August had insisted he drive. If he'd had to make this journey seated next to or directly across from Clara, he was quite sure he would have done something exceedingly ill advised. Like pull her into his lap and kiss her. And then skip dinner entirely so that he might take her someplace and finish what they had started. Which would have been equally unacceptable.

Because until he had pulled into this damn stable yard, he had forgotten why he was really here. And now that he had been reminded, an unpleasant guilt was starting to brew, seeping into the crevices of his mind and undermining his sense of purpose. He'd never intended to reveal his ownership of the school—certainly not while he was still in pursuit of Strathmore Shipping. But then, he'd never intended to become wholly besotted with the school's headmistress either.

August hardened his conscience. He had never experienced such a feeling before, and he didn't like it. It reeked of weakness. Flawed ambition. And August Faulkner had never been weak. What was done was done. If he hadn't bought Haverhall, someone else would have. Feelings and emotions did not have a place in business, because feelings and emotions made clever men make stupid decisions. One never knew what was around the next corner. What disaster might occur, what emergency might crop up. He needed to ensure his family was looked after forever, even after he was gone. He needed to make sure that what he had survived, and how Anne had been forced to live, would never be repeated. Not while he could control their circumstances.

August squared his shoulders and turned from the yard, making his way to the side of the barouche. "Your servant, Miss Hayward." He gave her a slight bow as he opened the small door.

She'd repaired her hair admirably on the drive, but her cheeks were still flushed the way they had been when he had had his mouth and his hands—

Arousal streaked through him instantly, and he averted his eyes.

"Your Grace—"

"Dukes can still open doors for their ladies, just as easily as they can drive themselves places," he said, pleased with how smoothly that had come out. "I've discovered that becoming a duke hasn't impeded my mobility or my coordination overmuch. Though it often creates an unwelcome distraction wherever I go. I'm generally not recognized in Dover, and I prefer to keep it that way. There's only so much bowing and scraping and clinging a man can take."

"Ah. No fancy clothes, no carriage with a coat of arms." She sounded amused. "No footmen, no drivers—"

"And I left the heralds and the horns and the flower-throwing maidens at home this evening as well." He returned her smile, unable to help himself.

He heard her catch her breath slightly as she took his hand and stepped out of the barouche. "Pity," she said, releasing his fingers once she was firmly on the ground and Miss Baker was smartly leading the team away. "Spectacles are vastly underrated," she continued. "I've always wanted to walk under a shower of rose petals."

"I'll keep that in mind next time I ask you to dinner." Except it wasn't dinner August was imagining but a bed covered in the velvet softness of scarlet petals, their fragrance as intoxicating as the woman who would be lying in their midst. He would start by—

"The girl who took the horses. She knew who you were, even though you're not dressed as a duke and were driving." Clara was watching the retreating horses with suddenly narrowed eyes. "Why?"

"A keen observation," he said, firmly grasping the change in topic that offered a respite from his lewd imagination. He offered her his arm. "Most don't notice Miss Baker is a miss at all."

"And you never answered my question."

August felt her hand come to rest delicately on his arm, as if she were determined to keep a more civilized distance. "Miss Baker and her brothers work for me." He saw no reason to hide the fact from her.

Clara stopped abruptly. "They work for you," she repeated slowly. "You own this tavern."

"I do." He paused. "Ah. I imagine you thought Monsieur Charleaux owned it."

"Yes." Her voice was faint.

"My ownership isn't entirely a secret, but it's something

that I—and Charleaux—certainly don't shout from the rooftops. I can't be in all places at all times, so I hire competent people to manage my assets. Charleaux—and other individuals I've hired in similar positions—are better able to make daily decisions if the vast majority simply believe them to be owners."

"Your sister did not mention that you owned property in town." She had a peculiar expression on her face.

August hid a frown. "She's only been to the Silver Swan once, and that was years ago, just after I purchased it and long before I had it renovated. Is it important?"

Clara muttered something that August didn't catch. "Forget I mentioned it. Please, tell me about Miss Baker."

August started forward again. "In truth, it is her older brother who is the crown jewel in the Baker family, as it were. A bloody wizard when it comes to managing stable yards and everything that goes with it. I poached him from one of the busiest coaching inns in London."

"And he just agreed to leave?"

"Mr. Baker wished to be able to protect and ensure the well-being of his family. Something I could understand. At the time I hired him, his sister was only eight, his brother ten. My willingness to employ both his siblings and leave them under his tutelage has made him a loyal employee." He paused. "And Miss Baker especially has proven herself an unexpected asset. She is a fine hand with horses."

"I see."

"I have developed it substantially. Kept the tavern, improved the dining room, and expanded the inn. It was in rather deplorable condition when I bought it, but the location is second to none. It is one of the first buildings a thirsty sailor happens upon and the first lodgings a weary traveler sees. Now that the wars are over, there has been a greater influx of passengers crossing to France. The shipping trade has similarly increased, and business is brisk."

"I see."

August glanced at her. She was saying that a lot.

"Come, let's see if your brother has arrived. Will he have come by horse?" He glanced back at the yard, but the trio of Bakers was nowhere to be seen. He should have asked Miss Baker when he had the chance.

"I assume so." Clara sounded distracted. "What else do you own?"

August waved his hand dismissively. "A collection of other investments. None of which will interest you, I'm sure." He didn't want to get into a long discussion of his holdings. Quite frankly, it would take all night, and it would detract from his objectives if they were discussing profit margins, taxes, and land titles. No, August needed to get the Haywards talking about the Haywards. And what he could do to make the Haywards happy and solve all their financial woes.

"Did you run out of money?" Clara said as they approached the door.

"I beg your pardon?"

She gestured above their heads to the sign hanging above the door. "The exterior has very clearly been repaired and upgraded, yet your sign looks like a holdover from the Children's Crusade."

August glanced up at the battered wooden sign that had come with the building. "What's wrong with it?" It was still perfectly legible, if perhaps a little faded. Well, perhaps a lot faded and a little cracked at the bottom. And perhaps the bird looked more like a turkey than a swan. But it served its purpose. And it was familiar to the residents of Dover.

Clara shot him a dubious look. "You went to the trouble

of improving this establishment but left it represented by a crooked flamingo?"

"It's a swan, not a flamingo. And you sound like my sister, though she called it a bat," August grumbled.

"You should have listened to her."

August paused, his hand halfway to the door. Perhaps Clara had a point. Perhaps, in an effort to bridge the gap between them and reassure Anne that he had not intended to be dismissive of her talents, he could have a new sign made. One that would be crafted from her sketch. He had no doubt it would please her immeasurably. And it would prove to her that, while he was still her brother and responsible for her future, he was making an effort to listen and not simply trying to control her life. What harm could it do, really?

Anne's drawing would still be on his desk. He would send a note to Duncan to have a new sign made and shipped immediately.

"Come, Miss Hayward," he said, buoyed by his decision. He grasped the heavy iron door handle. "Tell me about your brother. What made him want to pursue medicine?"

Clara stepped past him into the din of the tavern. "Why don't you ask him yourself?"

August followed her gaze and gestured to a man sitting against the far wall, a tankard of ale in his hand, speaking with an individual dressed like a seaman. It had been a long time since August had seen Strathmore. The baron had nearly the same dark mahogany hair as his sister and the same dark eyes. He was dressed neatly, his hair pulled back into a queue, but his tidy appearance couldn't disguise the weary, worried lines of his face. August recognized that look. He had once worn the same haggard look for too many years. Perhaps this would be easier than he expected.

August strode toward the far side of the tavern, weaving

his way through the long tables and benches. The tavern was busy tonight, just as Miss Baker had said, and it pleased August to no end to see trays of ale and bowls of stew being served with a most satisfying swiftness.

Strathmore must have seen them coming, because he broke off his conversation and rose. The man he was speaking to turned, and August noted his battered coat and the old-fashioned tricorne he held in his hand. A sea captain perhaps, though one who looked more like a pirate, given his dark beard and the small braid at his temple.

The baron stepped forward, grasping Clara's hands and kissing her lightly on the cheek before he turned to August. "Your Grace, it is a pleasure," he said. "My apologies for the change in plan. I hope it didn't cause you any inconvenience."

"Not at all," August replied, avoiding looking in Clara's direction. "And the pleasure is all mine. I did not mean to interrupt your conversation." He let his gaze settle on the sea captain.

"Captain Black at your service, Your Grace," the man said, not waiting for introductions and sketching a brief bow. His dark eyes returned to August for a second before they settled on Clara. He swept his tricorne in front of him and his bow became exaggerated. "And you must be Dr. Hayward's beautiful sister, who he speaks of so often."

"One of them," Strathmore said drily. "Clara, may I present Richard Black, captain of the *Azores*. Captain, my sister, Miss Clara Hayward."

"Enchanted," the captain said, smiling widely at Clara.

"A pleasure," Clara replied, looking amused.

"It could be," the captain replied with a wink.

August stiffened, but the baron merely laughed. "You'll excuse us, Captain?" Strathmore said.

"Of course, of course." Black settled his tricorne on his

head. "I must be away as well. People to see, ships to sail. Enjoy your evening." He tipped his hat and melted away into the crowd.

August watched him vanish in the crush. A man to remember, August thought to himself. Not because he particularly wished to make the man's acquaintance, but because any sea captain clearly so familiar with the baron might just be an invaluable source of information when it came to Harland Hayward. Or Strathmore Shipping.

"I'm sorry if we interrupted your conversation before you could finish," August said to the baron. "Would you care to have him fetched back? He would have been welcome to join us—"

"Hemorrhoids," Strathmore said succinctly. "We were speaking of hemorrhoids. More precisely the means by which one may reduce them. Not a suitable conversation for dinner, I can assure you."

"Of course." August eyed the baron. That had been neatly done. A subject meant to stall a conversation before it ever got started. "Shall we make our way into the dining room then?" He gestured toward the wide, arched door that led farther back.

"Yes, please." It was Clara who spoke. "I'm quite famished."

August led them into the room, characterized by ordered tables with proper tablecloths and proper tableware laid out and a noise level that was a third of that in the main tavern. The tables were all occupied save for the largest one on the far wall, set in front of a wide window overlooking the harbor.

"Please." August gestured for his guests to sit. The baron pulled out a chair for Clara, and once she was seated, both men took theirs. He had barely gotten comfortable when a server materialized at the side of their table.

"Good evening," he said, and August was pleased to see that the man's appearance wouldn't have been out of place in any fine dining room in London. August had worked hard with Charleaux to ensure that the service was impeccable. Along with the French chef, it added to the popularity of the dining room. The man produced a bottle of wine and set to pouring the ruby liquid into the glasses on the table with a subtle flourish.

"Tell Charleaux we are ready to be served," August instructed.

"Of course." The man set the bottle in the center of the table and vanished as silently as he'd appeared.

"I understand you had trouble with some soldiers," the baron said without warning.

August froze. "I beg your pardon?" An image of Clara trapped against a stone wall before they'd been interrupted suddenly filled his mind. Out of the corner of his eye, he saw Clara take a long swallow of her wine, which told him that she was imagining the exact same thing. Jesus, if he was going to start this negotiation with Strathmore calling him out, it was going to be a very short discussion indeed.

"Ran into a patrol southwest of town the other day while rendering assistance to a young boy, as I understand."

The boy. Of course. "I didn't run into them, exactly," August said. "Avoided them, more like. Though my horse was not so lucky."

The baron's eyes narrowed slightly. "Your horse?"

Strathmore had obviously been speaking to someone other than the staff at Avondale. The nameless child, perhaps. Or perhaps someone in his family. The baron was a doctor, after all, one who seemed to spend a great deal of time in the community, and it wasn't far-fetched that he might have heard the tale in the course of his travels.

"A flesh wound from a reckless bullet. The horse will be fine," August said.

"You never said anything." Clara sounded horrified. "Are you all right?"

"It was nothing, really. No real harm done. I was simply in the wrong place at the wrong time."

"Or the right place at the right time." The baron was still watching him.

August nodded. "Or the right place at the right time, depending on one's perspective." He didn't elaborate. Because that would provoke questions about his actions that he had no interest in answering. Neither Clara nor her brother needed to know why he had done what he had for a boy he didn't even know.

The baron was watching August intently. "The last years have been difficult. Hunger is a powerful motivator."

"I understand." Strathmore and Clara had no idea how much.

"You must eat here often," the baron remarked, looking around at tables of well-dressed ladies and gentlemen and the occasional table occupied by naval and military officers. "Given that you are on such ... familiar terms with the hotelier."

"Occasionally," August replied. He picked up his glass and took an appreciative sip. "I confess I enjoy the selection of wines."

Clara made an inarticulate noise. "The duke owns this tavern and inn."

"I had no idea," Strathmore murmured. Brother and sister exchanged a look that August couldn't decipher.

"I don't generally advertise it. Monsieur Charleaux manages the day-to-day affairs."

The baron fingered the stem of his wineglass. "If you own this place, surely you can do something about the sign out front. The first time I was here, I thought the place to be called the Rotted Raven."

August glanced at Clara, who had suddenly become fascinated with the edge of her napkin.

"As it turns out, Strathmore, that is being addressed as we speak. I shall have a new one in place in the very near future." August sat back in his chair. He had no interest in speaking of his businesses. "I was asking your sister about your own profession. Whatever made you decide to become a physician?"

Strathmore was eyeing him shrewdly. "It's something I'd wanted to do for as long as I could remember. And I was fortunate enough to have a family who supported me." The baron glanced at his sister. "We all were."

"Why not practice full-time?" August asked casually.

The baron's brows shot nearly to his hairline. "If I could make a copy of myself, I most certainly would," he said, and there was a faint bitterness to his words.

August sighed in commiseration. "Ah. I can understand that. The business left to you by your late father must be incredibly time consuming."

"Something like that," Strathmore muttered, downing the rest of his wine.

August took a moment to choose his words. "Have you ever considered taking on a partner?"

"A partner?" Strathmore repeated, going quite still.

Beside him Clara visibly stiffened.

"Your comment about making a copy of yourself made me think of it." August felt the first faint stirrings of misgiving. Perhaps he had misjudged—

"No," the baron said.

"No, you have not considered it, or no, you wouldn't consider it?" he asked.

"Both. I have two partners already. One of them is sitting next to you."

August forced a chuckle. "And a formidable one she is. I learned that the hard way, if you recall."

"I recall." The baron was unsmiling.

August tried a different tack. "Forgive me if I spoke out of turn, but in my experience, sometimes to make something truly flourish and reach its full potential, one must occasionally look for assistance. Or break things into pieces that might prove more manageable. A change to the structure, if you will."

"A change to the structure?" Strathmore reached for the bottle of wine and refilled his glass. "Tell me, Your Grace, is that what you suggested to Walter Merrill?"

August kept his expression pleasant. Now that was an unexpected remark. "You are, of course, speaking of the former owner of the Silver Swan."

"Indeed." Strathmore's voice was devoid of any sort of challenge, as though it were merely idle curiosity that had spurred that question. August wasn't fooled for a second.

"I believe Mr. Merrill's refusal to adopt change led to the failure of his business, if that is what you're asking."

"I suppose I am." Strathmore glanced out the window, over the darkening harbor. "Did you know that this place had been in Mr. Merrill's family for six generations before you bought it?"

August laced his fingers together, wondering if there was an accusation in that statement. But it would seem that Strathmore had more in common with his sister than just the color of his eyes. He, like Clara, was utterly inscrutable. "I did. Though I fail to see the relevance."

"The relevance." The baron seemed to be mulling that over. "I would suggest such information might be relevant with respect to the pride or self-worth that ownership might bring to a man like Merrill. Did that not give you pause?"

August frowned slightly. "Good Lord. Are you suggesting that I should have left this place in the hands of Merrill for the sake of...sentimentality?"

The baron shrugged. "That might be one word for it."

August's frown deepened. He'd believed the man to be much wiser than that. "No. There is no room in business for sentimentality. Nor do I do things by half measures. If Mr. Merrill had any sort of pride of ownership, he had a strange way of showing it."

"Ah." The baron turned back from the window, his fingers playing with the stem of his wineglass. August couldn't tell if there was censure or acceptance in that single syllable, and he wasn't sure he liked it.

"Mr. Merrill had his chance. And he failed. But amidst that failure, I saw opportunity. I buy things with potential, Lord Strathmore. And then I make that potential happen to ensure the safety and well-being of my family."

"Yet you did not offer Walter Merrill a partnership."

"No." Strathmore would know that only if he knew Merrill himself. Even given Strathmore's ties to the community, that sort of knowledge was a little odd for a man who called London home and Dover a very temporary residence. "The level of deterioration to which this place had fallen, both physically and financially, was extreme. Mr. Merrill was not supportive of my proposed changes to correct that. Though he was certainly supportive of the bank draft with which I provided him." He eyed the baron. "If he tells you anything different, he is lying."

"Walter Merrill died last year. Shot by soldiers while sneaking through the dark with a tub of smuggled French brandy strapped to his back."

"I'm sorry to hear that."

Strathmore lifted his eyes to August's. "I'm sure."

August met his dark gaze, unhappy with the direction the conversation had taken. He'd hoped to plant the seeds of a solution to the Haywards' financial difficulties, but when it came to business, it would seem the baron had some convictions and ideals that were going to prove difficult. Lord Strathmore seemed to be a man who would have to be backed into a corner first, the very real threat of total bankruptcy of his family presented before he started to see things the way August wished him to.

"Strathmore Shipping is not for sale, Your Grace." It came from Clara, and it was so quiet, August almost didn't hear it.

"I beg your pardon?" August turned toward her.

Her face was pale, her hands clenched in her lap. "It's what you came to Dover for, isn't it?"

~

You will not meet a more ruthless, cunning adversary than Holloway when he goes after something he wants.

It was what Harland had told her. Clara had heard him, but she hadn't listened. Not carefully enough.

But she had listened as she sat at that damn table tonight as August Faulkner made it clear why he was really here. Made it clear why he had really sought her out that day at the museum and why he had followed her to Dover. No, Clara amended, it wasn't she he'd been seeking. It had been Harland all along. He'd asked after Harland all along. She just hadn't paid attention.

She was such a fool. Clara had allowed herself to believe that he had really come to Avondale for Anne, because she had wanted to believe in the caring brother and not the ruthless adversary. And worse, she had completely fallen for every charmed word that had slipped from his silvered tongue and convinced her that he truly found her—what had he said? *Extraordinary.* She had kissed him. Would have done far more than kiss him.

Mortification and fury crowded into her chest, and she welcomed them. They didn't allow room for the sadness and disappointment that weren't welcome at all.

He buys broken things and breaks them apart further before building them back up into profitable ventures.

Harland had said that too. Things like the Silver Swan. Like Strathmore Shipping.

The duke's expression was closed, his eyes shuttered and his lips thinned. "Cl—Miss Hayward, I—"

"Yes or no, Your Grace," Clara hissed.

Holloway's features tightened even more. "The possibility came up."

"While you were dabbling in the tobacco trade?" Clara sneered, wondering for a moment if she shouldn't leave now. Before she said something that she would really regret.

From across the table, Harland laced his fingers together. "Good heavens, Your Grace, is that what you call what you do in the tobacco trade? Dabbling?" He glanced at Clara. "Did you know that Holloway is the largest importer of tobacco in southern England?"

His empire is bigger than most people realize.

Clara swallowed with difficulty, the wine turning sour in her gut. That certainly explained how he had discovered their financial struggles. If Holloway was that deeply entrenched in import, then he would have access to all sorts of information when it came to the London docks. She was such an idiot.

Holloway stared stonily back at her brother. "You are unusually well informed, Lord Strathmore."

"And so, apparently, are you."

"You have damaged, idle ships that will rot before you can repair and crew them. Without the capital to correct that, it will be difficult to recover. I am prepared to offer you a very fair price—"

"No." Harland said. "We are the custodians of the legacy left to us. We will ensure that it survives and, with time, continues to flourish, by whatever means necessary. It is not something that can simply be disposed of on a whim so that we might indulge in personal fancies or because it becomes *difficult*." He paused. "I can assure you, Your Grace, we have matters well in hand."

"Your Grace, your Lordship, pardon my intrusion." A uniformed servant suddenly appeared at Harland's shoulder carrying a salver. "A message for Lord Strathmore just delivered," he said, holding out the small tray. "I am made to understand it is an emergency."

Harland's eyes finally slid from August as he took the note, cracking a plain red blob of sealing wax. He scanned the message, then stuffed the paper inside his coat.

"Do you wish to send a reply?" the server asked. "The messenger is waiting just outside the tavern."

"No need. I'm on my way."

"Very good, Lord Strathmore." The man departed with brisk efficiency.

"I have to go," Harland said unapologetically. He glanced at Clara.

"I'll see her safely home," August said without looking at her.

"That won't be necessary, Your Grace," Clara replied

through gritted teeth. "I'll make my own arrangements. I've done it many times."

"I insist." The duke wasn't budging.

Harland's eyes flickered between Holloway and Clara. She bit her tongue against a scathing retort. Her brother would expect her to be angry at the duke's duplicity, but not irrationally so. And she had no desire to explain the extent of it. She just wanted to be left alone. Long enough to lick her wounds and collect what was left of her dignity.

"Very well." Harland turned his attention toward the duke once more. "I trust we have made our position clear regarding Strathmore Shipping," he said coolly.

"You have." Holloway had yet to look at her.

"Good. Then I bid you a good night, Clara. Your Grace."

Clara watched as Harland took his leave. "It never would have worked, you know," she said.

"What are you talking about?" Holloway finally turned to her.

"Using me to get to my brother. Did you think that if you could get me into your bed, I would put a favorable word in my brother's ear?"

A muscle jumped in his jaw. "What happened between you and me had nothing to do with—"

Clara laughed, but it was without humor. "Save your breath, Your Grace. You came here because you discovered our family company was struggling and wanted it for yourself."

He held her eyes with his. "That was one of the reasons," he said finally.

She already knew that, but the confirmation was like a slap. "Everything has been contrived, hasn't it?" Clara asked, feeling almost ill. "Your sudden appearance at the museum. Your convenient service to Rivers. Your concern over your sister. Us—"

"No. I care a great deal about Anne." He reached for her hand. "I care about you. You and I were—"

"A mistake." Clara snatched her hand away. "Just a titillating diversion for you while you pursued what you really wanted."

The duke looked away, his face set in hard lines. "No."

"I don't understand you," Clara said, forcing herself to keep her voice down, aware that they were still in a very public setting. "You have everything. Money, power, position. Yet you come after us like a vulture circling a wounded animal." She fought for composure. "When is enough enough for you?"

He turned back to her. "Never." The answer was swift and harsh. "Only a fool rests on his laurels."

Well, at least he was finally being honest. But it was too late. Clara stood, the duke rising as well.

"Where are you going?" he asked.

"Back to Avondale." She started toward the door.

"I'll see you home." Holloway was on her heels.

"Please don't do me any more favors," Clara said, threading her way out into the long shadows of the evening. She sucked in a deep, steadying breath of cool night air.

"I will see you home," the duke repeated, already signaling Miss Baker, who was hurrying across the yard.

She shook her head. "I—"

"I'll pick you up over my shoulder and put you in that damn barouche if I have to."

"Fine." Clara suddenly didn't have the energy to argue.

"I'm not letting you go, Clara."

An empty chasm suddenly opened up in the center of her anger, dark with desolation. "I was never yours in the first place."

Chapter 11

Given the way August had thrown himself into the evaluation of the Avondale estate, one would surmise that he owned it. Or that he was planning to.

Never had he immersed himself more deeply in assessments of soil quality and appraisals of forage crops. Estimations of lambing schedules and projections of breeding seasons. And of course, the potential costs and revenues from all of it put together. But no matter how hard he tried, nothing could make him forget the mess he had created at the Silver Swan. Never in his life had he handled anything as badly as he had handled his inquiries into Strathmore Shipping. And that knowledge had put him in a dark, dangerous mood this morning.

This was why August never mixed business with pleasure. Not that he'd ever really had the opportunity to do so in the past, but he should have been more careful. Instead he'd let his libido trump his intelligence and had blundered into another conversation that, in hindsight, he had been ill prepared for. Again.

The Haywards were nothing like the other entitled lords and ladies August endured and courted in London, something he'd known but had failed to truly comprehend until it was too late. He'd underestimated both the baron and Clara like a rank amateur. And now he found himself in a tangled mess of desire and ambition with no idea how to extract himself.

Did you think that if you could get me into your bed, I would put a favorable word in my brother's ear?

August flinched as Clara's words ran through his head again.

Those words had sat uncomfortably on his mind all night and all morning, adding to the foulness of his mood. Those words made him want to seek her out and apologize. Explain yet again that his interest in Strathmore Shipping had nothing to do with his interest in her. The urge was as unnerving as it was insupportable, because August Faulkner did not need to explain anything to anyone. He did what he needed to do to keep his family safe and financially secure without apology. He would never apologize for that.

But for whatever reason, the usual rules did not seem to apply when it came to Clara Hayward. And all of it was made even more complicated by the fact that the deed to Haverhall sat on his desk. She was slipping through his fingers again. And he had no idea what to do without risking the complete destruction of a relationship that was already in tatters. Which made his mood even darker.

The sound of a carriage rattling up the drive distracted him from his thoughts. He straightened where he had been leaning, near the gate of the west sheep enclosure, and idly followed the equipage with his eyes as it stopped in front of

Avondale. His own ride home with Clara had been taut with silence, neither finding any words that—

August's hand slipped from the gate as the occupant of the carriage emerged, dressed like a bloody popinjay in an orange coat of a hue most definitely not found in nature. The bright-yellow embroidery splashed all over the front was visible from where August stood. He felt his jaw slacken even as the rest of his body went rigid.

"Goddammit," August cursed sharply under his breath. What the hell was Mathias Stilton doing here? At Avondale? Now?

August started stalking toward the manor. Dover was a long way from London, and there was no way in hell that this was a casual social call, no matter how Mathias Stilton might try to frame it. The man was here for a reason. August of all people knew that. He just wasn't sure what that reason might be.

Though he had a pretty good idea.

August ground his teeth. No matter what had happened between them last night, Clara Hayward was his.

⁓

"A gentleman to see you, Miss Hayward."

Clara's head snapped up from where it had been bent over the pages of her book. The butler was standing patiently just inside the door of the library, his face expressionless. Clara snapped her book shut irritably, hating the unwanted spurt of expectation that had shot through her at the announcement. Whoever was here to see her, it wasn't August. Which suited her just fine. He had shown his true colors last night, proving himself as manipulative and ruthless as Harland had said. In the cold light of day, she reasoned that it was just as well her eyes had been opened when they had, before she had managed to do something monumentally stupid. Like become completely smitten.

"Who is it?" Harland asked from where he stood, at one of the long tables. Clara had been pleasantly surprised when she had found her brother in the library, though Harland had thus far proven a poor conversationalist, his attention focused on a pile of what looked like old maps of the county coast.

"A Mr. Mathias Stilton," the butler replied.

Harland's brows shot up as he looked at Clara in question.

"Tabby mentioned he had stopped by earlier," Clara told him with a small frown. "I had forgotten."

"Long way from the British Museum," he murmured.

"He told Tabby he was visiting friends."

The butler cleared his throat. "Shall I tell the gentleman you are receiving, Miss Hayward?"

"Of course. Show him to the library." She wasn't expected to meet with her students in Dover for another two hours. Entertaining Mathias Stilton was the last thing she felt like doing, but whatever he had to say surely wouldn't take long.

The butler disappeared and Clara set her book aside, pushing herself to her feet.

"You have yet to mention the Silver Swan," Harland remarked casually.

Clara stared out the long library window, her fingers clenching in the folds of her skirts. She forced them to relax. "I think we made ourselves abundantly clear to His Grace that we had no interest in selling Strathmore Shipping. I can't see it being a problem any further." Because for the rest of Holloway's stay, Clara had every intention of avoiding him completely.

"Mmm. I agree. I was, however, referring to the fact that the man owns the bloody inn and tavern. The very place where his sister—your student—is even now toiling away under the watchful eye of Monsieur Charleaux."

Right. That.

"Lady Anne is aware that it is her brother who owns it?"

"I believe so."

"Then perhaps she should have mentioned it to you at the very beginning?"

Clara frowned. "Perhaps."

"It might be best to tell Charleaux who his student really is," Harland prodded. "Sooner rather than later."

"Yes." As per custom, Anne had been introduced only as Miss Anne in the tavern. Not Miss Faulkner, not Lady Anne, and most certainly not Lady Anne Faulkner, sister to the Duke of Holloway.

Clara sighed, knowing that she just might be forced to find another placement for Anne. Given the duke's stifling aspirations for his sister, Clara couldn't imagine that he would condone Anne's industrious efforts in any sort of tavern. And Charleaux, as progressive as he might be, would undoubtedly fear for his job should the duke discover that the man had left the haggling for the week's beef and ale in his sister's hands. Though finding another mentor willing to take on a female student would be difficult at best.

Which was probably why Anne had never mentioned it in the first place.

Her irritation, which had been simmering, boiled over, and she bit back the urge to curse like a damn sailor. Not that it would do any good, but it might make her feel better. The duke needed to leave. Before he caused any more headaches and heartaches with his callous manipulation of everyone around him.

"You'll need to come with me, I expect," Clara muttered in the direction of Harland. "And bring your medical bag. Charleaux will have an apoplexy when I tell him who she is. He knows just as well as I that no matter how much money Anne saved the duke and his tavern yesterday by taking the collier to task over the price of coal delivery, Holloway will likely be horrified, not happy—"

"Miss Hayward." She spun away from the window to find Mathias Stilton striding into the room, a broad smile on his face.

Clara pasted a smile on hers. "Mr. Stilton. Welcome to Avondale."

"I'm so glad I caught you at home. You are a difficult woman to track down with all your little hobbies," Stilton said, coming to a stop just in front of her. "But I must say that you look absolutely dazzling. The sea air becomes you."

Perhaps it was her current mood, but Stilton's slightly patronizing tone made her want to throw something. Or reach for the whiskey bottle. Or maybe both, just not in that order. "Thank you," she said, trying to regain a hold on her decorum. It was not Mathias Stilton's fault that she had been wildly out of sorts since last night.

"Good afternoon, Mr. Stilton," Harland said, making no effort to move out from behind the library table and his pile of maps.

"Lord Strathmore." Stilton pivoted in surprise. "What an unexpected pleasure."

"Mmm," Harland replied, his eyes sliding to the doorway. "Ah. And good afternoon, Your Grace."

Clara felt herself freeze, her eyes snapping to the library door. The duke was leaning against the frame, his dark hair windblown, his dark coat dusty, and his expression positively black.

August's gaze was fixed firmly on Clara. "Lord Strathmore. Miss Hayward." His lip curled unpleasantly. "Mr. Stilton."

Clara averted her eyes, despising the way her stomach flipped. She glanced at Stilton to find that his smile had vanished, displeasure now etched across his face. If Stilton had had hackles beneath the confection he called a coat, they would have been raised, and his teeth would have been bared. Even a half-wit would have felt the tension that had inundated the room.

Resentment rose, competing fiercely with her irritation. Bloody hell, but she'd had it with men. Without considering what she was doing, she headed toward the hearth and the small table that rested beside it. She snatched a glass from the polished surface and poured herself a healthy measure of whiskey from the decanter.

"And here I was going to offer tea," her brother murmured loudly enough for her to hear.

Clara shot Harland a withering look. He sounded as if he was enjoying this.

She put the bottle back without throwing it at anyone, which was something. "Mr. Stilton, I confess it is a bit of a surprise seeing you so far afield of London." She tried to keep her voice pleasant and conversational while ignoring August, who was still looming menacingly in the doorway like a great, brooding crow.

"Visiting friends and seeing the sights," Stilton replied, smiling at her again. "You've spoken so often of the county's beauty on our many, many outings, and I just had to see it for myself." His eyes slid in the direction of Holloway's and then back.

Clara raised her glass to her lips so she didn't have to reply to a comment that had clearly been uttered for the duke's benefit. Her patience was rapidly deteriorating.

"How are you faring with your classes, Miss Hayward?" Stilton inquired.

"Very well, thank you," she answered politely.

"Your students must be enjoying the beauty of Kent."

It was like a death by a thousand cuts, this small talk. Usually she was a master at polite conversation. Today she just wanted nothing to do with it. "They are," she replied.

Stilton smoothed his hands over the front of his coat. "Forgive my forwardness, but I was wondering if I might have the privilege of calling on you sometime later this week, Miss Hayward?" Stilton asked gallantly. "I would be honored if you would accompany me for a scenic drive." He turned back to Harland. "If that meets with your approval, of course, Lord Strathmore."

From the corner of her eye, Clara saw August step farther into the room.

Harland shifted. "My sister has a very capable mind of her own," he said. "She doesn't need my approval to make her own decisions about how she chooses to spend her time."

The duke went rigid, setting Clara in mind of a bull about to charge. She suddenly understood how Anne must feel regularly.

"Miss Hayward?" Stilton prompted silkily.

No, she didn't really want to go driving with Mathias Stilton. Or the Duke of Holloway. Or anyone else for that matter, no matter how gallantly he asked.

"That is a very kind offer, Mr. Stilton, but I fear that I will be very busy with classes—"

Stilton pressed his hands together. "But surely, Miss Hayward, you'll have a moment of free time? I would love you to show me—"

"She said she's busy." August's words fell like an anvil.

Clara glared at him, her irritation spiking into something that was closer to fury. How dare August presume to insert himself into this conversation? He had no claim on her, her time, or whom she went driving with.

"Of course," Stilton said flatly. "My apologies, Miss Hayward, I did not intend to—"

"On second thought, I'm sure I could find time, Mr. Stilton," Clara said impulsively. Bloody insufferable duke. "Perhaps at the end of the week if that would suit. Sunday is a day off for both the students and me."

August crossed his arms over his considerable chest and glowered at her. She ignored him.

"Oh, indeed. That would be superb. I'm looking forward to it." Stilton shot August a smug, triumphant look that almost made her change her mind again. "I shan't take up any more of your time." Stilton offered a small bow in Clara's general direction. "I'll send a message on to Avondale, then, Miss Hayward, to find a time convenient for you?"

"Of course."

"Good afternoon, then. It's been a pleasure."

"Good afternoon." Clara was the only one who answered, and Stilton sauntered from the library, though he gave August a wide berth.

"You should not feel obligated to entertain Stilton just because he is here, Clara," Harland said, bending to peer more closely at a map. "Or just because he asked."

"I know that," Clara answered in clipped tones.

"The man is a hopeless fop."

"Perhaps, Harland, but that doesn't make him unworthy of friendship," she said.

August made a rude noise.

"You disagree, Your Grace?" Harland's question was almost mocking, and Clara sent another quelling look his way that was wasted on the top of his head. Her brother did not need to encourage the duke's bloody barbaric behavior.

"It doesn't matter if you disagree. Your opinions are not required in this matter, Your Grace," Clara bit out. "Surely there is a sheep pasture that needs another inspection at this time?"

"The man is clearly infatuated with your sister, Strathmore," August said to Harland, completely ignoring Clara. "Does that not concern you?" He made his way past her and retrieved the whiskey, then poured himself his own drink.

"Jealousy does not become you, Your Grace." And bitterness did not become her, but Clara couldn't help herself.

August turned an intense blue gaze on her. "Don't be ridiculous. I'm simply concerned for your well-being."

"If you weren't aware, I've been looking after myself for quite some time now, and I don't need your assistance."

The duke set the decanter back on the table with an angry thump.

"He may be a fop, but he's treated both my sisters with nothing but respect, Your Grace." Harland straightened from his map.

August made a face. "But—"

"Are you infatuated with Mathias Stilton, Clara?" Her brother asked, interrupting August.

"Of course not."

"Planning to elope this weekend with the man?"

"Don't be asinine."

"Start a very lewd, very public affair with him in the next few days that I should know about?"

"You're not funny, Harland. Mr. Stilton is a friend. One whose *honesty* I value." Clara knew she sounded like a shrew, but she didn't care.

Harland shrugged. "Then there you have it, Your Grace.

My sister has proven quite capable of managing her opinions, herself, and, in this case, Mr. Stilton. It is not my place to dictate whose company she can and cannot enjoy."

August's hand was wrapped around his glass so hard that Clara could see his knuckles were white. "So you're content to let the man take your sister on a drive. Alone."

"*His sister* is standing right here," Clara snapped. "And *his sister* drove all over Kent with you alone yesterday, didn't she?"

"That's not the same," August gritted.

No, it certainly wasn't. Mathias Stilton had never had her up against a stone fence, his hands in her hair and on her skin. Stilton had never kissed her senseless or made her whimper with want. Though those things were never going to be repeated. Clara had misjudged Holloway completely. She'd almost made the biggest mistake of her life because she had allowed a decade of romantic daydreams to obscure harsh reality.

"But it is the same." Harland put his hands on the table and leaned forward. "Don't mistake me, Your Grace. If I thought a man was a danger to either of my sisters, I would cut off his balls and nail them to his front door. As a battlefield surgeon, I'm handy with a knife like that, you see."

Clara pinched the bridge of her nose with her fingers. For the love of—

"Good." August held Harland's gaze.

Clara closed her eyes and tossed back the last of her whiskey, letting the liquor burn a trail of fire down her throat. She opened them to find Holloway standing directly in front of her, his eyes like blue fire in the light from the window.

"You and I need to have a conversation very soon," he said in a voice low enough that only she could hear. "Alone."

Clara pressed her lips together. "No, we don't. I've said everything I need to say." It was a harsh whisper.

"And I haven't." His eyes dropped to her lips, and need arrowed through her. Dammit, how, after everything, did he still do this to her?

"I don't—"

"Soon, Clara." August glanced over his shoulder to where her brother had returned his attention to his maps. "But in the meantime, there are some sheep pastures that need another inspection."

Chapter 12

Y our Grace!" The shout, accompanied by the sound of
pounding hoofbeats, broke his thoughts. August looked up
in the late-afternoon light to find Miss Baker flying toward
him on a lathered horse, her short curls disheveled, her expression panicked.

August vaulted over the stone fence of the sheep enclosure, reaching for the reins of his own horse as Miss Baker
reined hers to a sliding stop.

"YourGraceyouneedtocome." Her words were breathless
and hard to understand as her horse danced sideways.

"Steady, Miss Baker." He caught hold of her horse's reins
in his free hand.

"There are soldiers at the Silver Swan," she said, making
a visible effort to speak more clearly. "They're tearing it t'
pieces."

"What?" August froze for a moment before he let go of
Miss Baker's animal and swung himself up into his own
saddle. "Why?"

"They're lookin' for smuggled goods hidden there. They're sayin' they got anon—amenen—"

"Anonymous?"

She nodded her head, her eyes wide. "Anonymous information stating so."

"What are they looking for?"

"They wouldn't say. But they're makin' a terrible mess."

August cursed under his breath as his horse surged forward, Miss Baker right behind him. Anonymous information his ass. He might not live on the coast of Kent, but he knew very well that almost every soul on its chalky edges was quite aware of the covert trading that went on all along the shores. And if they weren't involved, either directly or indirectly, at the very least they certainly had a family member or a friend who was.

And there were very few who were willing to sabotage a system that often offered their only means of survival.

He had no idea why the Silver Swan had been targeted, but it didn't matter. August urged his horse to greater speed. If he hadn't already been spoiling for a fight with an officer who let his troops use children for target practice, he certainly was now.

It didn't take them long to reach the town. He slowed his horse only enough to navigate the busy main road that ran parallel to the harbor. Within minutes he'd reached the Silver Swan, the commotion audible even before he pulled his winded horse to a stop in the chaotic stable yard. Soldiers milled about, boxes of supplies that had been dragged from the rear storehouses strewn across the yard. Near the stables two soldiers were bent over a large crate, tools being tossed carelessly from its confines. A third soldier stood in front of Miss Baker's brothers, keeping them immobile against the exterior stable wall with the threat of his gun. From somewhere in the stables, a loud crash could be heard.

August dismounted, leaving the animal with Miss Baker, his fury rising with every passing second. Nearer the rear of the tavern, where the kitchens were accessible by large doors that led through an attached storage building, a cacophony of angry voices rose. He stalked forward and yanked the heavy door wide. And stared.

The interior of the kitchens was in shambles, much like the stable yard. Pots and pans had been left in haphazard piles, and a handful of soldiers were still hauling items from the depths of the cupboards. Crates of produce had been opened and emptied, the contents of the pantry shelves scattered across the surface of the large wooden table that had been dragged to the side amid broken crockery. Where the table should have been, covertly hinged pieces of floorboards had been thrown wide, exposing a deep, gaping hole that August hadn't known existed.

Charleaux, usually unflappable, was standing on the far side, snatching items from soldiers and cursing loudly in French. His customarily dapper appearance was disheveled, his trim frame almost vibrating with anger. In the center of the disaster, a bulldog of an officer stood, his meaty fist wrapped around the nape of a familiar threadbare coat. The man was sweating profusely, but an unpleasant smile of satisfaction had crept across his broad face. The boy in his grip struggled, much as he had once done in August's grasp in a shadowed hedgerow before he had darted away. But all of that was not what had August gaping.

Between the officer and August, two women inexplicably stood, blocking the officer's exit. The one with the dark hair so like his had her hands on her hips, her posture stiff with ire in a way he had seen many times before. The

woman closest to him, with the mahogany hair, had her
hand extended as if she could stop him from leaving with
his prize.

He strode forward, coming to a stop beside her.

"What seems to be the problem here, Miss Hayward?"

Clara froze at the sound of August's voice, her nape prickling in sudden awareness. Anne's head whipped around,
and her eyes widened slightly. The officer restraining the
boy turned, an unpleasant sneer on his face. Across the
room Charleaux fell silent, his face flushed in ire. The soldiers who were still pillaging the kitchens paused in their
mission, their attention transferred to the commanding new-
comer who stood utterly still in their midst.

The tavern and Anne had been Clara's last stop for the
afternoon, as she'd checked in with her other students already. She hadn't been at the Silver Swan long enough for
Anne and Charleaux to pull out the accounting ledgers before all hell had broken loose. Soldiers had streamed in as
patrons had scrambled out. And Clara and Anne had been
left trying to slow the carnage.

"There seems to be some confusion," Clara replied with
a coolness she wasn't feeling. She and Anne could talk and
plead and beg all they wanted, but if this red-coated officer
and his troops wanted to destroy the Silver Swan and then
leave with a terrified child, there was little they could do to
stop them. If ever there was a time for August Faulkner to
be an unyielding, entitled, power-hungry duke, now would
be it.

"I've noticed." August's voice was hard enough to cut diamonds, and never had he sounded so perfectly ducal. "And

I must say that I take great umbrage at the manner in which this property is being treated."

He didn't acknowledge Anne or let on that their presence was anything but expected. A measure of relief flooded through Clara. Clearly there would be a time of reckoning for her and Anne, but it was not now. Not given the scene before them.

The captain's eyes narrowed. "You cheat the king, you don't deserve any other sort of treatment."

"And what, exactly, makes you believe that anyone here is cheating the king?"

"I have information that says so."

"From where?" August inquired pleasantly.

"What?"

"From where or from whom did you receive your information? Because I fear that your source is badly in error."

"The cavity concealed in the floor begs to disagree. Big enough to store at least five dozen tubs smuggled ashore."

"I don't see any tubs."

"Doesn't mean there weren't any before we arrived."

"I'm sure there were hundreds."

The captain's mouth dropped open slightly. "I beg your pardon?"

"This tavern has been here for generations, Captain. It's not unreasonable to think that it has, at some point in the past, been used to store ill-gotten gains. However, this establishment is now under new ownership." August paused. "You may want to take that into consideration when flinging about accusations."

The captain's sneer faltered slightly. "And who might you be, exactly?" he demanded, his close-set eyes traveling the length of August, taking in his somewhat dusty, unassuming appearance.

"Ah. Allow me to introduce myself. I am the Duke of Holloway. The current owner of this establishment and, curiously enough, a friend of the king." He paused. "May I have the courtesy of your name?"

Clara took a moment to enjoy the sight of the color leaching from the captain's face, as petty as it was.

The officer cleared his throat. "Captain Buhler."

"Then I would appreciate it, Captain Buhler, if you would remove your men from my property before they do any more damage." August paused and Clara saw him eye the collar of the boy's ragged coat, still twisted mercilessly in the officer's hand.

Clara didn't know who the painfully thin, disheveled child was, but she had her suspicions. And the duke was once again in the right place at the right time.

"Additionally, I insist that you release the child." August's pretense of civility had been lost.

Clara studied the duke from the corner of her eye, struck not by the coldness of that demand, but by the bleakness that accompanied it. His expression, like his tone, was both chilling and stark.

Did you know his father was in debtors' prison?

Clara's stomach plunged to her toes as she considered for the first time what that might have meant for the rest of the family.

"He's not a child," the captain barked, having regained the color he'd lost and then some. "He's a plague on the country." His hand twisted a little more, and the boy flinched. "And he'll hang for his crimes like the thief he is. He might have got away from me yesterday morning. But not today. They start them small, you know, stealing food and whatnot. Best to squash them before they get big."

Clara hid her revulsion.

"That child is not a thief, Captain Buhler. He is my employee. And I will not ask you again to release him."

Clara shivered at the undisguised rage in August's voice, wondering if the duke would simply snatch up a weapon and run the man through. Even the soldiers shifted uncomfortably.

"His Grace is right. You have the wrong boy," Clara said into the silence. "This one is here every day before dawn, including yesterday. Fires don't light themselves." She moved then, her hand coming to rest on the head of the terrified boy, angling her body as if she was about to lead the child away. The captain took an awkward step back, his grip faltering enough for the boy to yank himself free. He skittered away, ducking behind Clara.

Buhler lunged forward but was brought up short as August stepped into his space. "Please leave, Captain, while I'll still willing to attribute this…disorder to an unfortunate error in judgment. And take your men with you." Very deliberately August stepped away and reached for the door, then held it open silently.

The captain looked as if he might argue before he looked at August's face and seemingly reconsidered. He yanked on the front of his coat, smoothing the heavy wool, and turned on his heel to exit the kitchens. The soldiers who had been searching the room trailed after him, casting hard if somewhat uncertain looks in Clara and August's direction.

August waited only long enough to assure himself that the soldiers were collecting their horses and departing the Silver Swan's stable yard before he closed the door with a loud bang. He turned and leaned against the heavy wood, his eyes lighting on each other remaining occupant before they settled on the boy still half-hidden behind Clara.

Beside her Anne squirmed.

"Come out from there," he ordered the boy.

The boy shuffled out from behind Clara, regarding August warily with eyes that were too big for his face. "You never said you were a duke before," he mumbled, and Clara's suspicions were confirmed.

"Well, in fairness, you never told me your name either." August crossed his arms over his chest.

"Jonas." The boy scuffed a toe against the stone floor and ducked his head.

August peered at him. "And how, exactly, did you manage to run afoul of the captain and his posse? Again?"

"We—I was hungry. An' I came here. Like you said I could." He stopped, staring resolutely at the floor, his thin face drawn. "Didn't see the captain till too late."

"Then I'm glad you came. Consider yourself hired."

Clara hid a smile, feeling as if she might cry at the same time.

The child's head came up. "You're bein' serious?"

August nodded. "If you're going to eat my food, I think it's fair you work for it."

"Yessir."

August didn't correct him.

"Is he goin' to come back? The captain?" Jonas asked uneasily.

"If he does, I'll deal with him." August's jaw was tight, and his eyes swung toward Clara. "You didn't need to lie."

"Yes, I did." Clara held his gaze. "Occasionally one is in the right place at the right time."

August nodded his head in a jerky movement before he turned his attention back to Jonas. "Perhaps you'd like to be introduced to the rest of the staff here? Make sure you understand your duties in the kitchens? Or your duties once we manage to clean up this mess." The duke raised a brow at Charleaux, and the man nodded in unspoken agreement. "This is Monsieur Charleaux, Jonas. You will do whatever he asks, understood? When I am not here, he speaks for me. You may go with him now."

"Yessir." He bounded toward Charleaux like an eager puppy. The hotelier shot Clara and Anne a worried glance before ushering the boy from the room. Clara sighed. Charleaux had no idea how worried he ought to be.

She straightened her shoulders as August's eyes returned to her and then slid to his sister. Clara watched as he studied Anne's stained apron, her heated cheeks, and the expression of defiance that had crept across her features.

"Will someone tell me why my sister is standing in the kitchen of my tavern, dressed like a scullery maid? Or are you really going to make me ask?"

"I work here," Anne said flatly.

August gaped at his sister as though she had said something in a foreign language he didn't understand. "Miss Hayward, perhaps you can try to say something that makes a modicum more sense."

Clara sighed in resignation. "As part of Haverhall's summer term, we place our students in a field of study that they choose as part of their curriculum."

August stared at her before turning to Anne. "And the field of study that you chose was lye soap and kitchen grease?" he asked acidly.

"The fields of study that I chose were lodging and food service management. Labor and inventory administration. Accounting and planning services. Shall I go on?" Anne's words were clipped.

"Why?" August asked, raking a hand through his hair.

"Because I'm good at it."

"But you don't have to—"

"I know I don't have to. I *want* to. And for the record, lye soap is sold at a more attractive price when you buy it in bulk locally." Her last sentence had an edge to it.

Clara watched as August pushed himself away from the door. "All of the students do this?"

"Not this, exactly, but something similar," Clara said.

"For example?"

Clara shrugged. "My brother is currently mentoring three aspiring physicians. Small-scale amputations are not a suitable conversation topic at Almack's."

"I— That's—" He was clearly struggling for words. He blinked suddenly. "And Charleaux knows about this? About Anne? About what you're doing?"

"Of course he does. Anne is my student, and consequently his. She isn't his first. The staff believe she is simply his assistant, hired on for the busy summer months." She sighed. "No one is aware that she is your sister."

"And I want to keep it that way." Anne's face was set in the same hard lines her brother wore so often.

"Jesus." The duke paced toward a pile of pans that had been abandoned near the center of the room. "Who else knows? The truth about Haverhall's summer school? About what you do here?"

Clara rubbed her forehead. "Very few," she said wearily. "Most people do not and will not see the value in it."

"Miss Anne?" The harried question came from the doorway to the tavern. A young maid was standing in the frame, wringing her apron between her fingers. "The brewer is here, spittin' mad because the soldiers took his kegs from the delivery cart. I can't find Monsieur Charleaux and I don't know what to do but the brewer wants to know if—"

"I'll deal with him," Anne said briskly, already hurrying forward.

Clara saw August frowning after Anne fiercely, but he made no move to stop his sister as she disappeared after the maid.

"You think you should have told me why Anne was really here?" he asked without turning around.

"You think you should have told me why you were really here?" Clara countered, though the anger she had wielded earlier was missing.

The duke dropped his head. "Fair enough."

Clara hesitated. She had expected a fight. "Have you taken a good look at Anne's plans for the Trenton Hotel?"

His back stiffened. "How do you know about that?"

"She showed me her drawings. She's quite good at this, you know."

August shook his head, his eyes still fixed on the far side of the kitchens, and Clara had no idea what he was thinking.

"What will you do?" she asked.

"Do?"

"You own this tavern. You hold all the power. But if you think to punish Charleaux for his role in this, or evict him from his position, I take full responsibility for—"

"Stop." The duke looked up at the ceiling. "What kind of person do you think I am?"

Clara bent to retrieve a discarded wooden spoon from near her feet and considered her answer. She had no idea who he was, other than a study in contradictions. He was a man who offered no apology for his ruthless pursuit of wealth but then offered charity to a ragged boy he didn't know. A man who loved his sister but refused to set her free. "I honestly don't know."

"Then ask me something."

"I'm sorry?"

"Ask me whatever you want to know about me. I promise you the truth."

Clara considered his offer. Her fingers toyed with the handle of the spoon. "My brother told me that your father was incarcerated. Debtors' prison."

The duke stilled, though he still didn't turn around. "And just how did he come across that piece of... trivia?"

"He said that he had treated your father as a medical student at Marshalsea. For dropsy."

"Ah." August put a hand on the edge of the heavy table. "I suppose I owe your brother a debt of gratitude, then. Not only for his medical assistance but for his discretion. And yours. Most people do not know that about me."

"I suspect most people don't know you at all."

The duke turned and stared at her then. She felt his appraisal like a physical touch. "Perhaps they don't." His quiet words echoed in the space.

"Is that what made you start? Your father's imprisonment?"

"Start?"

Clara made a helpless gesture with her free hand. "Doing what it is you do."

She heard August release a breath. "I suppose you could say that. Starvation motivates a man like almost nothing else can. Do you know what it is like to go for months and months without a proper meal? Reduced to scavenging the leavings of others just so that you might survive another day?"

He said it casually enough, but underneath she could hear the rawness of that confession. She had heard the same in his defense of Jonas, and it made her heart hurt. "No. I don't."

"It sounds counterintuitive, but I could not afford to spend the little money I had managed to put together on things like food. Or shelter. Everything I had went into my efforts to make that money work for me."

"But you won't starve now. You've achieved . . . more than you could ever have expected. More than anyone expected."

"And I've told you that only a fool rests on his laurels. Life is not a horse race with a pretty ribbon for the winner at the end. There is no finish line, just packs of challengers hoping to see you fail."

And enough would never be enough, Clara thought with a wistful sadness. August Faulkner would never have enough. "That sounds like a life of dissatisfaction and unhappiness."

August scoffed. "Hardly. I find satisfaction and happiness in a great number of things."

"Name one that doesn't include money or calculating your net worth."

"You."

"Your Grace—"

"Sharing dinner with you. Dancing with you." He took a step toward her. Her fingers tightened on the spoon as if her paltry weapon might be enough to keep him at a safe distance.

She was suddenly hot all over. "You're changing the subject."

"I was answering your questions."

"Pardon my intrusion, Your Grace." The interruption came from the same doorway through which Anne had vanished. Only this time it was Charleaux who stood in the frame, looking significantly more composed that the last time she had seen him, though worry shadowed his features. "Our guests are starting to ask questions," he said with a grimace. "I will address them, of course, but your presence out in the public room and dining room would go a long way in quelling the rumors that have already started to fly. Rumors that might make our guests worry that they are sleeping in a den of murdering thieves."

Clara heard August mutter a muffled curse. "Very well." He turned to Clara. "We're not done with this conversation."

Clara swallowed, that addicting mixture of anticipation and desire that she had thought she'd vanquished threatening to drown her good sense. Her anger toward him might have faded, but that did not mean she was going to let her romantic daydreams lead her astray again.

"Tomorrow, then," she said, relieved her voice was steady. "Perhaps after classes have been concluded for the day at Avondale?"

He caught her free hand in his and pressed his lips to the backs of her knuckles, leaving no room for misinterpretation. "Count on it, Miss Hayward."

Chapter 13

August strode into the hall at Avondale, the door banging loudly as it slammed behind him. The sound reverberated off the polished marble of the floor and off the papered walls, shaking the crystals in the chandelier hanging just over his head.

Lady Tabitha was standing in the center of the hall, artfully arranging a vase of garden flowers and wildflowers that sat on the circular rosewood table in the middle of the entrance. She stopped, her hand frozen in the air, a crimson rose between her fingers.

"Good heavens, Your Grace," she said, peering at him over a pair of round spectacles. "We have a butler who is very adept at opening and closing doors if you need assistance with that in the future." There was a note of reproach in her voice.

August frowned, knowing he was behaving rather coarsely. He tried to gather his composure. "Where might I find Miss Hayward?"

He'd agreed yesterday to wait until her classes were over before seeking her out, but as the morning had crawled by, he'd run out of patience. Had he not been at the Silver Swan until the wee hours of the morning last night, he would have hunted her down then. It had taken his staff hours to right the mess left behind by Captain Buhler and his men. Worse, his discreet and not-so-discreet inquiries into what, or who, had brought them to the tavern in the first place had generated no answers. He supposed he should feel lucky that this was the first time the tavern had been the object of their scrutiny. August knew that private residences and barns were regularly searched.

"I believe she is in the studio with her class." Lady Tabitha returned her attention to the flowers in front of her and tucked the rose into the vase.

"And where do I find the studio?" August demanded, already moving toward the stairs.

Lady Tabitha slid neatly sideways to block him with more speed than should have been possible. "I will fetch Miss Hayward for you, Your Grace," she said.

"There is no need," he said, stepping around her. "I can certainly fetch her myself. I need but a moment of her time."

"Miss Hayward expressly asked not to be disturbed." Lady Tabitha once again slid in front of him, blocking his path to the stairs, and August wondered if perhaps this woman shouldn't be instructing a lesson in footwork at Gentleman Jackson's.

"She'll see me."

"Your Grace—"

"Enjoy your morning, Lady Tabitha." He stepped around her firmly again, moving at a clip that probably couldn't be called a dignified walk. Lady Tabitha might be quick, but he had almost four decades on her. And some pride.

"Your Grace, I must warn you that—"

"The flowers look lovely, my lady," he called back over his shoulder, taking the stairs two at a time.

He'd said things yesterday to Clara that he hadn't said to anyone before, and that had left strange feelings doing even stranger things to his insides. The revelation that his sister was meddling in his tavern hadn't been enough to make him forget how Clara had lied to an army captain with the imperiousness of a bloody queen not only because it was the right thing to do, but also because she understood why it mattered to him.

He needed to see her again. Needed to make sure she truly understood how much *she* mattered to him. Needed to make sure she understood how he really felt about her, especially after the way he had handled things so far. And he wasn't willing to wait any longer.

August reached the top of the stairs and headed left along a paneled hallway hung with portraits of people long dead, judging by their clothing and coiffures. Sconces were lit along the length, supplementing the light streaming in from the tall window directly ahead at the end of the hall. He stopped, listening hard.

There. Somewhere up ahead he could hear the muffled sound of voices punctuated occasionally by a muted laugh. He moved forward silently, his fingers trailing along the smooth wood. The voices got louder, a musical composition of young girls chatting. He smiled slightly, imagining Anne in that room, finally being able to share her artistic talents with other young ladies. Whatever ridiculous ideas Anne had taken into her head about the Silver Swan, at least here she seemed to be making connections, building and strengthening friendships.

Perhaps Haverhall was exactly what she needed.

He stopped again in front of the heavy door that led to whatever room occupied the very northeast corner of Avondale. A small paper sign had been stuck to the door, *Please Do Not Disturb* written in a feminine hand. Clearly, based on the voices coming from beyond, he had found the studio. He heard the unmistakable voice of Clara, followed by another. Her sister, perhaps. Rose. The artist. There was another, deeper voice in the mix, and he thought it was that of Lady Theodosia. He frowned, wondering what she was doing in an art class. Not that it mattered. He knocked loudly and turned the handle, pushing the door open, then took four commanding steps into the room.

"I'm sorry to interrupt, Miss Hayward, but I need a moment of your…" The words died on his lips as he was presented with a tableau that he couldn't quite comprehend.

At the front of the room, on a raised dais of some sort, was Lady Theodosia, reclining provocatively on a long settee. Wearing nothing other than what looked like a silk scarf, draped discreetly over one hip. A braided circlet of wildflowers was set about her head, her long, silver hair draped artfully over her shoulder, and a posy of crimson roses held loosely in her hand.

Holy Mary Mother. He averted his eyes from the elderly Venus on the dais to find nine students, including his sister, standing in a loose circle behind their easels and canvases, looking at him with gaping surprise. Clara's sister, Rose, was standing in the center of the room, a color-stained apron over her dress and a paintbrush in one hand that had frozen in midair. Her other hand was braced on her hip as she met his gaze with a look of utter disdain. From the far side of the room, Clara was stalking toward him.

August closed his eyes for a long second, wanting the last minute of his life back.

"Have you lost something again, dearie?" Lady Theodosia asked from the dais, and she sounded completely unconcerned that a duke had just walked in on her in a most horrifying dishabille. In fact, she sounded much the same as when she had caught him crouching behind a stone fence. Simply amused.

"His ability to read, perhaps," Rose suggested, and her disdain had not diminished. "The sign on the door read *Please Do Not Disturb*. Perhaps I should have drawn it in pictures."

August hastily backed up a step. "My apologies, my lady, I did not mean to interrupt," he managed with as much authority as he could muster.

"And yet here you are." It was said cheerfully by Lady Theodosia. "Are you interested in modeling?"

"Modeling?" August repeated dumbly.

"I suspect you'd be quite a glorious eyeful."

August felt his jaw slacken. Holy hell. Was she suggesting—

Clara had reached him, and she snaked her arm through his, not breaking stride even as she stepped around the spattered paint. "Excuse us," she said in the perfectly composed voice that he would have expected her to use when confronted with a duke who had just walked in on a mostly naked elderly woman and a collection of young ladies painting her. "This will take but a moment. Please, carry on." She steered August back and pulled the door firmly shut behind her.

August went on the offensive, not even sure where to start but needing to reestablish control. "What the hell was..."— he waved his hand in the direction of the firmly closed door—"that?"

"That's funny, Your Grace, because I was going to ask

you the very same thing." She pulled her arm from his and stepped back, putting her hands on her hips, her cheeks flushed. "For once I think my sister may have the right of it. I must assume that you can no longer read."

August ignored that. "There is a naked woman sprawled out in some sort of Botticellian recreation of *The Birth of Venus*—"

"*Venus of Urbino*."

"I beg your pardon?"

"Botticelli's painting depicts a woman rising from the sea. We were recreating Titian's *Venus of Urbino* composition. Less the individuals in the background. And with just a little more clothing."

"With a woman old enough to be my grandmother?" August demanded.

Clara's eyes suddenly went cool. "I didn't realize there was an age at which one can no longer be considered beautiful. Or desirable."

August felt his mouth snap shut. "That's not what I meant," he said after a moment.

"Then what did you mean?"

"I meant that…that it is not…seemly." God, he hated the way he sounded right now. Like an old, self-important ass. When he got his wits together, he would blame it on the shock.

"Not seemly." She crossed her arms over her chest and regarded him. "Which part?"

"Which what?"

"Which part isn't seemly? The part where Lady Theodosia is comfortable and confident in her own skin? Or the part where we ask ten young women who have been and will continue to be judged on their looks to consider that beauty comes in many different forms?"

August opened his mouth and closed it again.

Clara sighed and leaned back against the wall, and August saw her studying an ancient portrait of a woman sitting ramrod straight, a small child on her lap. "Pretty is as pretty does," she said quietly.

"I beg your pardon?"

"What Rose says all the time. It's why she does what she does."

"Which is what?" August was confused.

Clara's eyes slid to his and then away again. "Teach painting classes here in perhaps a somewhat unconventional manner."

"Unconventional? That might be the understatement of the century."

"Well, the century is still young."

"I don't appreciate your flippancy."

Clara shook her head, her lips curling slightly. "Tell me, Your Grace, do you find me attractive?"

August stared at her, uncertain he'd heard her right.

"It's not a trick question," she prompted.

Did he find her attractive? Bloody hell, he'd been in permanent state of arousal since he'd kissed her. All he could think of was how much he wanted to kiss her again. And then take her to his bed and have his way with her six ways to Sunday.

"Yes."

"What is it about me that appeals to you the most?"

"What the hell kind of question is that?"

She'd turned her head and was watching him, that half smile pulling at her lips. "Very well, I'll go first." She studied him. "Your loyalty to your sister. Your willingness to defend someone who can't defend themselves."

"What?" A peculiar feeling was rising up within him like curling smoke, spreading through his chest.

"The things I find most attractive about you." She returned her attention to the painting opposite her. "You are physically striking. And there is, of course, your title and all your wealth. Yet those are not who you are. Those three things are simply what you are."

August stared at her, the light streaming in from the tall window beyond putting her profile in stark relief and catching the deep ruby in the curls brushing her shoulders. Her chin was tipped up slightly, exposing the graceful lines of her neck and the gentle slope of her breasts. He felt adrift here, as if he had lost sight of the shore and was in over his head. Had any woman ever really looked past his title and his wealth and his looks? Had he ever wanted them to?

He took a step closer, suddenly needing to anchor himself. "Your confidence." He took another step and found her hand with his. This, this was what he needed. She was what he needed. "Your unwillingness to apologize for who you are. Your convictions."

Clara closed her eyes.

"Those are the things that leave me humbled."

Her eyes opened and flew to his.

"That night I asked you to dance, you gave me a chance and an honor I did not deserve." He caught her other hand in his and brought both to his lips, pressing a soft kiss on the backs of her knuckles. "I came here to ask you for the same chance again."

"Your Grace—"

"I don't want a temporary tryst."

She was watching with hooded eyes, and he could see the rapid rise and fall of her chest. "What do you want, then?"

"I want you. Whatever you're willing to give."

"What I want and what I can do are two very different things, Your Grace."

"August, dammit," he whispered harshly. "When I'm with you, I am just August."

She shook her head almost imperceptibly. "I can't risk—"

"I don't want excuses, Clara. I don't want regrets either." His fingers tightened on hers. "No regrets. No wondering what might have been. What happened between us had nothing to do with anything else. Not your ships, not my sister, nothing. Tell me you believe that."

He heard her breath hitch. "Yes."

"Good." He turned her hands over and kissed the insides of her wrists. "Tell me you wanted what happened between us."

She made a soft noise in her throat. "Yes," she whispered.

"I am not going to accept less of you, Clara Hayward. I will have you, and you will have me. You will show me everything that you have ever learned about pleasure, and then I will show you more. I will be the man who kisses you until you can't breathe and you can't think." He leaned closer to her, pressing her back against the wall, his mouth inches from hers.

She looked up at him, the raw desire in her eyes unmistakable, and it sent lust ripping through him. He didn't just want her. He needed her. Needed to have her mouth, so hot and wicked, on his. Needed to have her skin, bared and slick, pressed against his. Needed to stroke her, to sink himself deep within her. A vision of her as she had been last night, wrapped around him, her heels digging into his back, made his knees suddenly unsteady. He was so aroused it hurt.

"Say yes, Clara. And keep in mind that I'm not accepting no."

The sliver of space between them was suddenly full of pressure, like the air just before a storm. Just before the elements unleashed everything that was wild and terrifying and thrilling.

"Yes," she whispered again.

"Good girl." They were both breathing hard. "Part of me wants to take you right here, right now, against this wall." He brushed her lips with his, just the briefest of touches. "But the other part of me wants to have you somewhere where I can lock the door. Somewhere where I will take my time exploring you, where I will learn what makes you whimper and writhe with pleasure. Somewhere where no one will hear you when you scream my name. Because I like to understand what I possess."

He could see his own arousal mirrored in the liquid brown pools of her gaze. Her eyes dropped down to his mouth, and he leaned into her, letting her feel just how much he wanted her. Her lips parted. When she was looking at him like that, it was impossible to think beyond his scorching need to have her. But they were standing in a hallway, in plain view of anyone who opened the door.

"I know how much your position means to you, Clara. And I will do nothing to jeopardize that with my actions." Which wasn't exactly true, if one considered that Haverhall would soon be nothing but a memory, her position along with it. The guilt washed through him again, and he shoved it aside.

You should tell her that you own it, a small voice whispered.

But to what end? To become the man who had taken everything from her? To have her accuse him of using her again? Nothing would change what had already been done. Haverhall would still be demolished and developed. It would be better to focus her attention on the future. She could start over. The school was more than just a building—in reality it could be run anywhere. A new property could be purchased eventually. In fact, he could help her find one if it came to that. It wouldn't be Haverhall, of course, but Clara could continue to do what she loved.

She'd be happier if she still had Haverhall, a small voice whispered. *The legacy left to her by her parents.*

August ruthlessly smothered another wave of conscience that assaulted him. There was still no world that existed in which he would turn his back on profit for the sake of sentimentality, legacies be damned. August knew all about legacies. He had, after all, survived his.

So for the moment he would take Clara Hayward's words to heart and not live with regrets and excuses. He would not live with another decade of regret that he hadn't made her his when he'd had the chance. "I will see you tonight," he breathed.

"Tonight?"

"I'm taking you out to dinner again. When you're done here."

She pushed a piece of hair back from her face. "Yes."

August took an unhealthy amount of pleasure from the slight wobble to her voice. "And for the record, I am sorry I intruded. I promise it will not happen again."

Clara suddenly smiled, a low laugh escaping under her breath. "It will be difficult to forget the look on your face anytime soon."

"I don't think I was adequately prepared for the idea of my sister painting naked women."

"You would prefer her to paint naked men?"

August glared at her. "That's not funny. Nor is it appropriate."

The smile slid from her face. "What is appropriate for Anne? Flowers? Trees? So long as they have all their foliage on, of course?"

August could feel his teeth grind. "Do not mock me."

"I'm not mocking you, I'm asking you a reasonable question about a young woman who has shown herself immensely capable in class. And at the Silver Swan."

"I'm glad you brought that up. Because I'm not convinced that's appropriate either," August growled.

An elegant brow rose. "I'm sorry to hear that." It was brittle. "For the life of me, I can't fathom which part of her skill you find so...inappropriate."

"She deserves more."

"More than happiness?"

"You're twisting my words."

"And you're making me wonder why you think Lady Anne should apologize for who she is."

August bit back a curse. This wasn't how he wanted to end this conversation at all. "Seven," he said abruptly. "Be ready at seven for dinner."

She didn't respond, just gazed at him steadily with those dark eyes. He did not look away.

"You told me not to stop asking you hard questions," Clara finally said. "And I won't." She turned and took a half dozen steps down the hall before she stopped and looked back. "So whenever it is that you find answers to those questions, you may take me out to dinner and share them with me."

Chapter 14

It had been four days since Clara had left the Duke of Holloway in the north hallway, seething. She had seen him only twice, glimpses of him about the property as she had carried on with her classes and he had carried on with whatever business kept him in Dover. He hadn't even appeared today to check in with Anne when she and the students had a day free. Clara told herself that it was better this way. That the distance was a good thing.

I want more than a temporary tryst.

Desire spiked and sent her insides fluttering. They had sounded decadent, those words that he had whispered in that hallway. Every wicked thing he had murmured in her ear had instantly infused her with a hot, achy restlessness that teetered on the edge of recklessness. Because she wanted the same thing. But no matter his words and pretty promises, whatever this was between them could only ever be temporary.

And the longer he avoided her, the more temporary *temporary* became.

She would never marry and sacrifice her hard-won independence to become a wife, and becoming his mistress was still out of the question. No matter how careful they might be, he was a duke and, as such, attracted far too much attention. Eyebrows would be raised in his direction at his odd choice, but such a relationship would destroy any possibility that she might ever teach again.

"My brother is avoiding me."

Clara started, lost in her thoughts as she had been. She found Anne standing near the garden bench where she sat, peering out in the direction of the sea to where Clara could make out the shape of a horse and rider galloping along the ridge. August, she realized, recognizing the dark-haired man who rode effortlessly, as was obvious even from this distance.

"I'm sorry, Miss Hayward, I didn't mean to startle you."

"Not at all. Please join me." Clara slid over on the bench, her eyes once again going to the figure racing the wind against the backdrop of the sky. "I would have thought the distance your brother has kept would please you," she said, shoving a pang of longing back into the depths from which it had risen.

Anne sighed and came to sit next to Clara. "It does, I suppose." She was frowning, her fingers wrapped tightly around the edges of a sketchbook. "He's probably certain that I am still furious with him after he walked in on our art class. Though if anyone deserved to be furious, it was Lady Theodosia."

"If Lady Theodosia stopped snickering long enough to be angry, I might agree with you," Clara replied with a wry smile. "But to be fair, it might be more a matter of your brother avoiding me."

"Avoiding you? Why?"

"Because I don't think he liked what I had to say after his theatrical entrance into that studio. And his subsequent exit."

"Whatever you said, I'm quite sure you were justified."

"Yes. But that doesn't mean he agreed."

Anne looked down at her book. "He's so stubborn sometimes. So unbending. Unwilling to look beyond the gilded box he's built for himself. I find it maddening."

"I can see that. But he cares a great deal for you, you know."

Anne flushed slightly. "I know. I'm sorry. I do him a disservice by speaking of him like this. I just don't know what to do sometimes. He refuses to listen. He refuses to see me. The real me. Not the person he thinks I should become." She was twisting her skirts in her fingers, and with her hair pulled back in a simple braid, she looked painfully young.

Clara was silent for a moment as the horse and rider disappeared from view. She reached out and snapped off an errant rose that was pushing up against the side of the bench seat. "Why?" she finally asked.

Anne looked over at her, her forehead creased. "Why what?"

"Why does your brother not listen to you? Why does he think he knows what is best for you?"

Anne's pretty blue eyes skittered away.

"You don't have to answer me," Clara said gently.

Anne put the sketchbook in her lap and smoothed her palms over the cover. "My father was incarcerated in debtors' prison."

"I know."

Anne's head snapped up, and she met Clara's eyes with startled surprise. "You know?"

"Yes."

Anne looked down again, her fingers worrying a loose thread on the binding that ran along the top of the pages. "My father was a wastrel. After my mother died, he was thrown into Marshalsea because the only thing that had kept him out up till then was what my mother had managed to earn sewing." She hesitated. "I lived there too, when he was there. In Marshalsea."

Clara felt the breath leave her lungs, even as understanding dawned. She should have guessed that. "For how long?" she asked carefully.

"Five years." Anne's fingers stilled on the edges of the book. "It's not as if I weren't free to come and go as I pleased during the day," she said. "And August somehow managed to scrape up enough to pay the gaolers to ensure I didn't end up in a workhouse. He managed to make sure that my father and I were fed, at least most of the time. And the roof over our heads may have sheltered more rats and flies than people, but all together, we didn't freeze in the winter. Which was more than August had in those years."

"Is that why you stayed with your father? And didn't live with your brother?"

Anne shook her head. "August never talks about it. But I know he had nothing, and anything he could spare went to us. I know he endured at least one winter on the streets, though I suspect it was two. And had I been left on the streets with him…" She trailed off, not needing to finish that thought. "After August managed to get my father out of prison, we all lived in a single room just off Fleet. August was barely there, and Father wasn't well, so I looked after him. There was a woman in our building who took in laundry, and I would do deliveries for her for whatever coin she could spare. We still had nothing to our name in those years that wasn't begged or borrowed, but I had everything. Everything that mattered." She looked down. "I know that doesn't make any sense."

"It makes perfect sense," Clara told her.

"I owe my brother everything," she said after a moment. "And I know that. And I'm grateful, and I want to make him proud of me. But now that he has power and a title and more money than we could ever spend in five lifetimes, he wants..." Anne stopped.

"He wants you to have all the things you didn't have before. He wants to make sure that you will never want for anything ever again," Clara finished for her quietly.

"He wants to put me in a safe cage with golden bars where the unpleasantness of life might never have the chance to touch me ever again. This is what he believes will ensure my happiness."

Clara ran the tip of her finger along the soft pink petals of the rose in her hand. "Have you told him this? What you just told me?"

"I've tried. So many times. He insists he wants me to be happy. I've tried to tell him that my happiness cannot be bought with silk gowns and strings of pearls. That my happiness cannot be guaranteed simply because I marry a man with just as much money as August." She tipped her head back and looked bleakly up at the sky. "He just won't listen."

A silence fell between the two women, Clara considering very carefully what Anne had said. "Knowing what I know of your brother, I suspect he feels guilty for every day that you were in that prison."

"That's absurd. I don't blame him. None of it was his fault. He did everything he could and has absolutely nothing to feel guilty for."

"Did you tell him that?"

Anne straightened and blinked. "I'm not sure." She was frowning. "But August is one of the smartest people I know. He must know that."

Clara tipped her head. "What if he doesn't?"

"I'm not sure it would make a difference."

"There is a singularly easy way to find out."

"Perhaps." Anne sounded thoughtful. "Do you know the funniest part about this all? And by funny, I don't mean humorous, but ironic. The time I spent in Marshalsea is what taught me about accommodating large quantities of people. How to feed them, how to house them, how to provide the necessities. Granted, it was a cruel and desperate education, driven by corrupt and greedy gaolers, but an education nonetheless. And one I haven't forgotten. One I want to be able to use. I want to be able to manage a real inn or a hotel, because I love the logistics. And I'm good at it. And the profits can outweigh those of a prison, if one does it right." She caught Clara's look. "Prisons are a thriving business that revolves around profit." She made a face. "I'm surprised August hasn't bought one."

"A prison? Surely not."

"If he thought he could profit from it, he would." Anne pressed her sketchbook to her chest. "There is no amount of money that will ever make my brother feel worthy. Or safe," she said a little sadly.

Clara felt her heart ache. "He certainly seems...driven."

"He's had to be. And I'm well aware I've benefited from all his determination and brilliance and ambition." Anne glanced around her at the lavish gardens. "But I can't change who I am simply because our circumstances have altered."

"Be patient," Clara said. "Rome wasn't built in a day. Keep talking to him. Tell him what you've told me."

"Thank you, Miss Hayward."

"For what?"

"For listening. Not judging. Understanding."

"You're welcome." Clara smiled at her. "Your brother is a good man, and I think he'll come to understand too."

Anne opened her mouth to answer, but her eyes suddenly flickered over Clara's shoulder. "I think you have company," she murmured.

Clara turned to find Mathias Stilton at the far side of the garden, walking toward them down the manicured path, his step jaunty and his smile wide. He waved, and Clara lifted her hand in greeting.

"Ah. Mr. Stilton. Early as usual, come to collect me for a drive." Clara tried to drum up some more enthusiasm.

"Why are you going if you would rather not?" Anne asked.

Apparently Clara's manufactured enthusiasm had failed to convince. She sighed. "Because I promised I would. He's harmless, if a little long-winded. Though I confess I might have been provoked into accepting Mr. Stilton's offer by your brother."

"August has that effect on people," Anne stage-whispered. "Provoking them, that is."

"You have no idea," Clara murmured. "Do you wish an introduction?" she asked Anne.

"By all means," Anne replied. "I do not want to appear rude."

Clara pasted a wide, welcoming smile on her face. "Mr. Stilton, how lovely to see you," she said as he approached. Good God, but it almost hurt to look at the chartreuse-and-burgundy-striped coat he wore.

"What a glorious day, is it not?" he asked.

"It is," Clara agreed. "Lady Anne, may I present Mr.

Mathias Stilton. He's the gentleman who oft accompanies Rose and me to the British Museum while we're in London. Mr. Stilton, this is Lady Anne, the Duke of Holloway's sister."

Stilton stared at Anne almost a second too long before he bowed low. "A great pleasure to make your acquaintance, my lady."

"And you as well," Anne replied.

"I do hope I am not interrupting," Stilton went on. "Lady Theodosia was kind enough to tell me that you could be found out here enjoying the splendid gardens. I almost think that perhaps we should simply tour the grounds of Avondale together as opposed to driving."

Clara kept her smile firmly in place, all the while envisioning Stilton and herself running into August somewhere along the way. No, it would be much more prudent simply to leave. "I'd prefer to drive, if it's all the same to you," she said politely. "The wildflowers at this time of year are truly a sight to be seen. I thought we might head up towards the castle where the views of the sea are best."

"Of course, of course, Miss Hayward." He smiled broadly at her. "Your wish is my command."

"Shall we?" Clara rose and Anne with her.

"Good day, Mr. Stilton, Miss Hayward," Anne said. "Enjoy your afternoon."

"Thank you." Clara watched Anne wander back in the direction of the house.

"I didn't realize that the duke's sister was also in Dover," Stilton said.

"Yes. Lady Anne is one of my students."

"Of course. How delightful."

They made their way around the side of the house, Clara's eyes sweeping the rolling fields one last time for a dark-haired rider but finding the horizon empty. They reached the front drive of Avondale, where a hired carriage sat, the team waiting patiently. Clara allowed herself to be handed up and settled back, determined to enjoy the outing and put all thoughts of a sulking, brooding, and provoking duke out of her mind.

⁓

August drew the winded mare to a stop, nearly as out of breath as the horse.

It would seem that no amount of galloping or trekking did anything to improve his mind-set. He was well aware he was acting irrationally and discourteously, but dammit, nothing had gone as he had planned since the day he had arrived in Dover.

To start with, he hadn't had a decent sleep in four nights. He was tormented by dreams of Clara Hayward and his distracting, all-consuming need to have her. Teased by images of everything that he had planned to do—with her, and to her, and for her—until that damn conversation in that damn hallway had suddenly gotten away from him. He had not appreciated her words, nor her pointed questions.

You're making me wonder why you think Lady Anne should apologize for who she is.

He'd never asked his sister to apologize for who she was. He loved her too much for that. But it wasn't unreasonable to ask that she alter her behavior and her expectations, was it? Which wasn't the same thing at all, was it?

Whenever it is that you find answers to those questions, you may take me out to dinner and share them with me.

He did not appreciate her ultimatum either.

Clara hadn't apologized. In fact, he had seen neither

hide nor hair of her since that afternoon, though it might have something to do with the fact that he'd avoided Avondale completely. Which, after his ill-advised entrance into the painting studio, made him wonder whom he was trying to avoid more—a coolly critical Clara, a hopefully clothed Lady Theodosia, or his undoubtedly furious sister. Regardless, this...cowering avoidance was very, very un-duke-like behavior. Hell, it was very un-August-like behavior, and it made him want to cringe as much as it made him want to curse.

And to top it all off, there had been no word yet from Duncan about any of the matters he had brought to the man's attention in the missive he'd sent to London. August was frustrated, impatient, and completely out of ideas.

He cursed under his breath and dismounted, then led his horse toward the back of the house. A stable lad appeared with the seamless, brisk efficiency that he was beginning to associate with this place. August handed over his horse and stalked toward the dower house, yanking his coat off along the way. Clean clothes, a decent meal, and something fortifying to drink were in order. He banged into the hall, narrowly missing a footman who caught his coat without even blinking. A pile of objects in the center of the small, gleaming hall caught his eye and stopped him short.

A large, flat, square item wrapped in coarse burlap and rope was propped up against a portmanteau. A smaller case, one that might be used to hold documents, had been placed beside these. August spun to find Duncan Down coming across the hall, a biscuit in one hand and another stuffed in his mouth. The man's clothes and boots were covered in dust and grime, and his hair and face hadn't fared much better.

Hallelujah. Finally. He nearly gave in to the urge to hug the man.

"Where have you been?" August demanded, instantly regretting his tone. He hadn't actually been expecting Duncan to come to Dover in person, only to forward him what he'd requested. But now that he was here, August was inordinately pleased to see him.

Duncan raised his brows above his spectacles and continued chewing. "Avondale House first, where a rather stodgy butler directed me in no uncertain terms to this dower house," he said once he had swallowed. "But before that? Stuffed on a bloody mail coach."

"I'm sorry." August ran a hand through his hair. "It's been a trying few days."

Duncan glanced around him at the polished opulence. "I can see that. The mail coach, however, was nothing but sheer luxury."

August scowled. "Point taken." He gestured to the pile. "What did you bring me?"

"Everything you asked for. I wasn't sure where you wanted everything or where you wanted me, for that matter, so I had the footmen leave everything here."

"You can have your pick of rooms upstairs," August replied, distracted, as he heaved the large, square bundle upright. "Is this the tavern sign?" he asked.

"Yes."

"And was it crafted as per the drawing?"

"See for yourself." Duncan took a bite of his second biscuit.

August pulled at the knots and tossed the rope aside, unwinding the burlap. He let the fabric fall to the ground with an appreciative whistle. "It's stunning."

"It better be, given what it cost to have it completed in

such a short time," Duncan mumbled through a mouthful of crumbs.

The sign stood a little taller than August's waist and was about equally wide. It was painted a glossy ebony, a carved silhouette of a gliding swan dominating the center. *The Silver Swan* was carved in an elegant script just below the image, while whimsical curlicues stretched out from the center above. All the carving had been painted a brilliant white, flecks of silver embedded in the paint to give it a sparkling sheen.

"She's going to adore it," Duncan said, dusting crumbs from his hands.

"Who?"

"Lady Anne."

August ran his hand over the top and fingered the two heavy hooks that had been mounted into the wood, one at each side. "And why would you think Lady Anne has any interest in a tavern sign?"

"Because that sign was her sketch," Duncan said slowly.

"And how do you know that?"

"Because she showed it to me." He was watching August a little uncertainly.

"When?"

"I'm can't quite recall, Your Grace."

August scowled again, wondering what the hell was wrong with him. He couldn't truly be thinking what he thought he was. That Anne and Duncan— He cut that notion off. If his sister had been badgering Duncan about the hotel books and laundries and fishmongers, it was quite likely she had been badgering him about tavern signs and God only knew what else.

"Is something amiss, Your Grace?" Duncan was peering at him with concern.

Yes, there was a great deal that was amiss. Nothing that concerned his man of business, however. "What about the other two matters I asked you to look into?"

Duncan glanced around the hall, but it was deserted. He dropped his voice anyway. "As of two days ago, there was still no sign of Strathmore's ships. However, his Lordship forwarded a payment on to his banker just before I left London."

"What? How?"

Duncan shrugged.

"For how much?"

Duncan shook his head. "I wasn't able to ascertain the exact amount, but it was substantial enough to prompt his banker to extend his loan an additional week."

August stared at the swan frozen in graceful lines in front of him. Where the hell had Strathmore gotten capital like that? "And he has no other assets? Something we missed?"

"I looked again but found no record of anything," Duncan confirmed.

"The man could have the map to El Dorado squirreled away, and I wouldn't know it," August grumbled.

"So it's not going well? With the baron, I mean?" Duncan asked.

"I've managed to have a single conversation with him about business in the entire time I've been here. One in which he left halfway through, but not before he made it clear that he had no intention of selling Strathmore Shipping. Ever."

"Your calculated charm has failed?"

August shot him a black look. His charm hadn't failed. It had deserted him altogether to be replaced with acute need and want and longing and a muddled sense of direction.

"He might yet change his mind," Duncan suggested.

"He will when his ships don't return and he's facing ruination. But maybe not even then if he's got more tricks up his sleeve that we don't know about."

"Well, you can't win them all, Your Grace. At the very least, you still have Haverhall."

August shook his head. That didn't make him feel any better. And probably not for the reason Duncan would think. "What about the other bit of information I asked you for?" he said, changing the topic.

"Mr. Mathias Stilton."

"Yes." August kept his expression stony. He hadn't told Duncan why he had asked for information on the dandy, only that it was a business matter.

Jealousy does not become you, Your Grace.

He wasn't jealous. He was thorough. If this man was in Clara Hayward's life, he wanted to find out how. And why. There was no such thing as too much information.

"I would have thought you'd heard enough of Stilton when you bought that damn lace factory," Duncan mumbled as he strode over to the leather case resting near the portmanteau and rummaged through it, coming up with a piece of paper and what looked like an aged newspaper sheet. His face was mercifully blank as he straightened. "Mr. Mathias Stilton. Age forty-one. Originally from Southwark, only child of the late Jerome and Ellen Stilton. You know the part about his dismal business acumen, so I'll skip that bit. Moved to London after that and married a woman of means named Emily Livet."

"He's married?"

"Widowed. She died two years after they wed, leaving him the substantial parcel of land she'd brought to the marriage, which kept him in fine style before, and certainly after, her death. Though from what I hear, he's no longer popular with the merchants on Bond Street. He has a great number of outstanding debts, the least of which is to his tailor."

August felt his fingers tighten on the edges of the sign. An unpleasant sensation curled through his gut. "How did his wife die?" he asked.

Duncan unfolded an aged and somewhat brittle page of the *Times*. "According to the paper, she drowned in a boating accident."

"Witnesses?" August couldn't believe he was actually asking this, but his instincts were demanding his attention, and he always paid attention to his instincts.

"Just her distraught husband. Though it says a good Samaritan pulled him out of the Thames half-drowned himself after trying to save her. A picnic and punt on an idyllic afternoon turned tragic. Or at least that was what the account said." He passed the sheet to August. "You don't think it was an accident."

Duncan was reading his mind again. "I don't know. Either way, it left him a man of property and free to marry again, should he wish it."

"May I inquire why you are asking about him now?" Duncan asked, his brows drawn together. "Is he—"

The sound of the knocker on the heavy front door silenced the rest of his question, and the same footman who had disappeared with August's coat reappeared almost instantly to open the door.

August blinked as Anne strode in, handing her gloves to the servant. She stopped short in surprise. "Good heavens. Mr. Down?"

"Lady Anne." Duncan offered her a bow. "Good afternoon. You look radiant."

"Thank you." Anne smiled at Duncan, a genuine smile

that caused her eyes to light up and made her radiant indeed. "I didn't know you were coming to Dover."

"Nor did I until very recently. But I'm very glad I did."

August stared at the two of them. Bloody hell, was his sister *blushing*?

Anne's gaze turned abruptly to August, and some of that radiance faltered. "Good afternoon, August. I was hoping to catch you here so that we could talk—" Her words died suddenly as her gaze fell on the large sign August still gripped. "Oh." Her hand went to her mouth.

Duncan took a step back as Anne approached, her eyes fixed firmly on the tavern sign. "That's my sign," she whispered, her brows drawn together. "The one I drew."

"Yes," said August, feeling suddenly uncomfortable. His sister had the most peculiar expression on her face.

Anne reached out a hand and traced with her finger the carved curlicues that ran along the top. "I don't understand."

August cleared his throat. "What is there to understand? The current sign is in deplorable condition. I thought to have a new one made, and I rather liked your design. It was... expedient."

"Expedient." Anne looked up at him, her eyes brimming with what looked like unshed tears. Holy hell, was she going to cry? He wasn't sure he had ever seen Anne cry.

"Mr. Down brought it with him," August rushed on. "I thought perhaps you might like to see it hung."

"Yes," she whispered.

August suddenly found himself in an awkward hug, his sister embracing him over the top of the sign. He slid an arm around her back and squeezed.

"Thank you, August," she mumbled into the front of his coat.

"You're very welcome." He cleared his throat again because it seemed to have thickened inexplicably.

Anne drew away and turned to Duncan, wrapping him in an impulsive embrace as well. "Thank you, Mr. Down."

"It was my pleasure," Duncan said, his eyes darting to where August stood. "You're very talented."

Anne extricated herself and turned back to the sign, crouching down and running her hand over the polished surface. "No more bats," she said with a shaky laugh.

"Or flamingoes," August muttered.

She looked up at him, almost shyly. "I have some other ideas for the Swan," she said. "Maybe later I could show them to you?"

August would have agreed to almost anything at that point, if only to keep the smile on her face. "That would be nice."

"This is the best present you've ever given me," she said with a sniff.

"But it's not even something for you," August protested. "I didn't really give you anything."

Her eyes were shining. "That's not true. You made me your partner. And there is nothing in the world I value more."

August opened his mouth to say something, but words escaped him. There was so much joy emanating from Anne right now that he just wanted to take a moment to bask in her happiness.

"I'll just head upstairs," Duncan murmured tactfully from where he still waited.

"Very well," August replied, still distracted.

"Was there any other information regarding Stilton that you needed before I go?"

"Stilton?" Anne stood up from her crouch and put a hand on top of the sign. "Mathias Stilton?"

"Yes." August frowned at her. "How do you know him?"

"I just met him. Not a half hour ago. He came to collect Miss Hayward for a drive."

August's eyes met Duncan's over her shoulder, and those dark suspicions that had been brewing bubbled up again.

"Land titles are public records, Your Grace," Duncan said, telling August that his mind had fallen down those dark paths too. "And they wouldn't have been changed that fast."

"Where did they go?" he asked Anne.

His sister shrugged, her forehead creasing in confusion. "I'm not sure. But there was a hired carriage waiting out in front."

"I have to go." It was absurd, he knew. It was likely nothing. August would probably find Mathias Stilton nattering away in the sunshine, waxing poetic about the breathtaking views of the cliffs and the sea. Because even if Stilton believed that Clara still owned Haverhall, that knowledge did him no good. If the man was angling to gain control of the land, he would have to marry her and convince her not to convey the property to trustees before he did. Which seemed wildly far-fetched. Didn't it?

Mr. Stilton is a friend. One whose honesty I value, Clara had said.

Marriages had been built on far less than that. Forget the land, the purported wealth behind the Strathmore name was still legendary. And very desirable, especially when attached to a beautiful woman.

August ran an agitated hand through his hair. He was overthinking this, and he needed to temper his paranoia and jealousy. But he couldn't. Not where Clara Hayward was concerned.

"August?" Anne's beautiful blue eyes were full of concern. "Is something wrong?"

"No," he said. "Just something I need to check on. I'll come and find you when I return," he said. "I shouldn't be more than an hour."

"I'll probably be in the art studio, then," she told him.

He bent and gave his sister a brief kiss on her forehead before he stepped away, leaving the tavern sign in her grasp.

"Would you like me to accompany you, Your Grace?" Duncan asked.

"No," August said, already headed for the door. "I'll take care of it myself."

Chapter 15

What do think of the view?" Stilton asked her.

Clara stepped sideways, as the man was just a little close for her liking. They were standing on the edge of the cliffs, the castle looming behind them, the carriage left up on the narrow, snaking road above.

Stilton had insisted that they walk down the sloping land, following the thick outer wall that led away from the castle proper and down toward the sea, and Clara had agreed, if only to pass the time before she could ask to return without appearing rude. To her right the town sat far below them, nestled at the edge of the ocean in its nest of rolling green fields and jagged white cliff faces. Above them gulls wheeled and cried.

"It's very lovely," she said, trying to keep her smile from slipping. Anne had been right. She should never have agreed to come. While she enjoyed Stilton's company in small doses, an entire afternoon of his nonstop talking was starting to wear thin. He meant well, she knew, and she couldn't really blame him for her lack of enthusiasm or her distraction. That was solely on the shoulders of one Duke of Holloway.

"I'm so glad you accepted my invitation," Stilton said, sidling closer once again. "There is a matter I wished to discuss with you."

"Oh?" Clara asked, wondering what he would say if she insisted that he take her back to Avondale now.

"We've known each other for quite some time," he started. "And I have enjoyed your company immensely."

"And Rose and I have enjoyed yours, Mr. Stilton—"

"Mathias."

"I beg your pardon?"

"I think we've known each other long enough that we can dispense with the formality, don't you think? I'd like to call you Clara, if I may."

Clara frowned. "Mr. Stilton, I don't think that is entirely appropriate. While I value you as an acquaintance—"

"And that is something I'd like to change."

"I beg your pardon?" Clara felt alarm start to slither through her. Surely Stilton wasn't about to suggest what she thought he was going to—

"I'd like you to be my wife," he hurried on, reaching for her hands and clutching them in his.

Clara stared at him. This was not happening. "While you flatter me, Mr. Stilton, I am going to have to respectfully decline."

"But why?" He looked genuinely confused.

"Because I don't wish to marry you."

"It's not like you're going to get a better offer," he said, and there was an edge to his words now. "Especially at your age."

"Mr. Stilton, I can assure you that even as a younger woman, I—"

"No one wanted you when you were younger," Stilton told her. "Even your family's wealth wasn't enough to buy you a husband then. Do you honestly think anything's changed?" He drew their hands up to his chest. His palms were cold and sweaty, and Clara resisted the urge to yank her hands from him in revulsion.

"Again, Mr. Stilton, I do not wish to—"

"No one else wants you," Stilton continued. "But I am prepared to make you my wife."

Clara felt a familiar anger rise, tempered with disgust. "I am not prepared to have you as my husband."

"Is it because I'm not a duke?" he hissed. "You think you're too good for me?"

"That's not it at all." She tried to extricate her hands, but he tightened his grip.

"You won't do better than me," he told her coldly. "With your wealth added to mine, we could live in grand style."

Clara tried pulling away again, but Stilton held fast, his fingers digging into the flesh of her hands painfully. "Mr. Stilton," she said through clenched teeth, "you must understand that I have no desire to marry anyone. Yourself included."

"You know nothing of desire," he said, yanking her closer. "But you will soon."

His strength caught Clara off guard, and she stumbled into him. Stilton let go of her only to dig the fingers of one hand into her hair and use the other to grasp her underneath her chin, pressing it against her throat. He made a sound of satisfaction and dragged her mouth to his. His kiss was wet and slimy, and Clara struggled to wrench herself away, but he only twisted her hair more painfully in his fist.

"Stop," Clara snapped, letting her fury overwhelm the very real fear that was starting to thrum through her. If she screamed, there would be no one to hear her. There had been no one in sight when they had walked down to the cliffs' edge. She pushed on his chest with her hands, managing to shove herself back a few inches, even though his fingers still held fast in her hair and against her throat. "This isn't what I want. This isn't what you want," she grated.

She'd never seen this coming. Looking back, she wondered if she'd missed the signs. Perhaps she simply hadn't been paying enough attention. Today, or at any point in the last two years that she'd counted him an acquaintance. And now she was paying for that lack of vigilance.

"I know exactly what I want," Stilton breathed. His hand slid from her throat to her breasts, and he shoved his fingers into the top of her bodice. She heard and felt some of the stitching give way.

His breath was hot on her face. "I want more. And you can give me that."

Clara twisted her head vainly.

"You've teased me for long enough," Stilton said, and his voice had a coldness that Clara had never heard before. "Years I've catered to you and your oddities. I'm done waiting. You will marry me. I'll make sure of it."

"She can't marry a corpse." It came from behind Stilton.

Stilton's head jerked up, and his hands loosened in Clara's hair enough for her to jerk herself away. She staggered back a few steps, out of his reach, her breath coming in harsh gasps.

The Duke of Holloway was standing just behind Stilton, his hands loose at his sides, his body perfectly still. But it was his expression that sent chills shuddering through her. His eyes were feral, his expression black, and there was a dark, barely leashed promise of violence rolling off his body in palpable waves.

"What are you doing here, Holloway?" Stilton spit.

"Deciding if I should just toss you off the cliff, or if I should kill you before I do it."

"You wouldn't." Stilton was backing away from him now.

"You have no idea what I would and wouldn't do."

"Stealing my birthright wasn't enough for you, was it? You need to steal my woman from me too?" There was utter hatred in those words. "She's been mine all these years, not yours, Holloway. It's been me who has put the time and effort into this. I know you think you can take whatever you want whenever you want it, but I came here to make sure you didn't. To make sure I finally got what is mine."

August moved faster than Clara would have thought possible. In a single second he had his hands fisted in the front of Stilton's coat and was lifting and pinning the man against the thick curtain wall of the castle. Stilton's boots twitched above the grass.

"I didn't steal your birthright. I bought a business that had been ruined. And Miss Hayward has never been yours," August growled.

"She damn well is."

"The lady's struggles beg to differ," August said conversationally.

"She is to be my wife!"

"Your wife?" His eyes flickered to Clara, lingering on her neck and the redness that she knew would be visible where the man's hand had squeezed. His gaze slid back to Stilton. "I didn't hear her say yes."

"She will." Stilton struggled to no avail.

"Do you wish to marry this cockroach, Miss Hayward?" the duke asked.

"No." Her voice was rough.

"I didn't think so." He pressed his forearm against the man's throat. "Should I kill him?"

"That would be messy."

"But satisfying. And the tide's going out. It would be at least a day until they found the body, if they ever did."

"Don't kill him," Clara said unsteadily. "He was just leaving."

"He was? Well, then, I suppose that is a lucky coincidence for you, Stilton."

Stilton was sweating, though his eyes were mean and hard. "You don't want me for an enemy," he spit.

Clara saw something shift in August's eyes. "You should go now, Miss Hayward," August said in a voice so chilling it made her shudder.

"No." Clara took a step toward him.

"Go, Clara."

"Don't do it. He's not worth it. Please."

She saw August hesitate, every muscle in his body rigid. He suddenly stepped back, and Stilton collapsed in an undignified heap at his feet.

"Leave here. Leave London," August snarled. "Or I'll make sure you're on the next hulk destined for Australia, provided I don't just kill you first. If you dare show yourself to Miss Hayward, her family, or myself again, Miss Hayward's words will not be enough to save you."

Stilton struggled to gain his feet, stumbling like a drunken jester. He yanked on the front of his gaudy coat and fled past August, staggering up the incline and to his waiting carriage.

Clara watched him go, suddenly racked with shivers. There was a maelstrom of emotion swirling through her, and the individual feelings were difficult to sort out—fear, disappointment, anger, shame, regret, relief.

August closed the distance and wrapped his arms around her, and she leaned into his strength, hating how unnerved she felt. "I was so foolish," she mumbled into the front of his chest. "I never should have come out here alone with him."

"You are not foolish to trust someone you've known for years," August told her forcefully. "What happened just now is entirely on Stilton, not you. You did nothing to deserve that."

"I never encouraged him," she said miserably. "And I certainly never wanted to kiss him."

"I noticed." August's voice rumbled in her ear.

"God." She squeezed her eyes shut briefly before pulling back. "How did you find me?"

"Anne told me you had gone for a drive. It wasn't hard to follow the sightings of a peacock in a chartreuse coat."

Clara made a muffled noise. "Why?"

"Why what?"

"Why did you come looking for me?"

August was silent for a long moment. "A brilliant woman once told me that jealousy did not become me."

"That woman knew nothing."

August was silent.

"I would never have married him," Clara said fiercely. "No matter what he did."

"I don't think Stilton anticipated that."

Clara bit her lip. "Would you really have killed him?"

"Yes. If it had been necessary to protect you." His voice was flat.

"How very barbaric of you," she said, and the tremor she could still hear in her words was no longer just from her ordeal.

"Did you know that *barbarian* was a term that the

Romans gave to everything and everyone who wasn't them?" he asked, and Clara knew he was trying to distract her now.

"The Greeks used it first," she mumbled.

August made a funny noise. "That is not the point. My point here is that in truth the barbarians were courageous, cunning, and ruthless and, in the end, drove the Romans all the way back to where they had started."

"Are you fishing for compliments, Your Grace?" She felt the pull of a smile.

"Possibly. Probably."

"Then I rather like your barbarian tendencies," she said wryly. "All of them."

"Good. So you won't mind if I do this." Without warning, he bent and scooped her up into his arms.

"What are you doing?"

"Taking you back to Avondale."

"What? You can't— Where— I don't—"

"Once we are there, if you are so inclined, you will ask me to stay for dinner."

"I will?"

"Yes. Because I finally have an answer that is good enough for the question you once asked me."

"Oh." She laid her head against his shoulder. "I'm having dinner tonight with the students. Lady Tabitha and Lady Theodosia as well."

"Splendid. I'll join you."

He heard her laugh softly. "You might be the only male in attendance."

"Splendider."

"That's not a word."

"It can be for a man who took to slaying dragons on behalf of his fair lady," he said lightly.

"You insult the dragon family, for Stilton is not so noble."

"You're right. I always fancied dragons to be green or blue and not chartreuse."

Clara sobered suddenly. "Thank you," she said. "For everything."

August pressed a gentle kiss to the side of her forehead. "You're welcome."

Chapter 16

The ride back to Avondale was a slow one, August not willing to risk the legs of his already-tired horse that now carried two. Which was just as well, because it took him nearly the entire journey to rein in his emotions and compose himself in a manner that wouldn't terrify the next unsuspecting person he came across.

When August had seen Stilton forcing himself on Clara, a rage such as he had never experienced flooded through him. When the red had receded from the edges of his vision, colors had seemed brighter, noises louder, every movement a little more pronounced. Looking back, he wasn't sure how he hadn't killed the man. How he hadn't simply ripped Stilton apart limb from limb or beaten him to a bloody pulp.

Perhaps he had recognized the need to defuse the situation for Clara's sake instead of making it worse. Battering a man to death would not have helped, though the man certainly deserved it. He did not want to take a chance that Clara would feel guilty about that too.

August hoped Clara's watching the man scurry away with his tail between his legs had lessened the impact of what he'd tried to do. What had happened had not been her fault in any way. Stilton was a coward and a cretin and not worthy of any further thought, and he hoped that Clara believed that.

Clara seemed to recover on the way back. She regained her color at least, and he engaged her in a debate over the theories of Aristarchus that had her talking and occasionally laughing. The feel of her body as it rested in front of his was torture. Her warmth and her scent enveloped him, and he wanted to keep her there forever, wrapped in the safety of his arms.

He reined his gelding to a stop in the drive and helped Clara dismount. She looked up at him, her eyes troubled. "Please don't say anything about what happened this afternoon. Not yet." She put a hand to where her bodice had been torn. "I'm going to change, and then I will speak to Rose. And Harland, when he returns."

Given the baron's chronic absences, August rather thought it might be Christmastide before her brother returned. But he refrained from pointing that out.

"No one else needs to know. Not the servants. Not my students." She was looking at him imploringly.

"I understand. So long as you understand that it wasn't your fault."

"I do."

"Good. I'll see you in and up to your room."

"That's not necessary."

"Humor the barbarian."

She nodded. "Very well."

"Besides, I have my own conversation to finish with Anne. She said I could find her in the studio when I returned."

"I might remind you to wait after you knock this time," Clara teased, and it made August happy to see her smile.

August led the way up the stairs. The house was silent, everyone seemingly occupied somewhere else, including the servants. Clara hurried down the south hall toward her rooms while August wandered in the direction of the studio.

He was almost at the end of the hall when the studio door opened and a woman stepped out, her blond hair tumbling in ringlets around her face. She was wrapped in a heavily embroidered robe, more suitable for a boudoir after midnight than a grand house in the middle of the day. She turned, and with shock August recognized her. More than recognized her. In fact, five years ago he would have recognized her more easily had she been wearing nothing.

"Lady Shelley," August said dumbly.

The woman froze. "Aug—Your Grace?" she replied with the same incredulity, her green eyes widening. "I beg your pardon for my appearance. I was hoping to make it back to my room undetected. We thought the house was empty."

"We?" August blurted.

"Miss Hayward. Rose Hayward," Lady Shelley clarified. Her initial surprise faded, and her lush lips curved into what August could only describe as a smug smile. "I've commissioned a portrait."

"In a robe?"

"In costume," she said vaguely, that same smile still playing about her lips, seemingly unconcerned about her dishabille. "I was on my way back to my room to change."

"You're staying here?"

"Just for the day. I did not know you were staying here as well. Goodness, it's like a house party."

"No such luck," August replied. "I'm here on business for the Earl of Rivers."

"Too bad. You know what they say about all work and no play, Your Grace," Lady Shelley teased. "And you work entirely too hard."

Rose suddenly appeared behind her, wiping her hands on a paint-smeared rag. "Who are you—" Her eyes went to August and narrowed, and her lips thinned. "You again. My apologies, Lady Shelley. I should have insisted you change in the studio. I should have known His Grace might be lurking about the hallways. This is unacceptable and most embarrassing."

"Oh, it is of no consequence," Lady Shelley said easily with a throaty chuckle as she headed down the hallway toward her room. "His Grace has seen me in far less than a robe."

August cursed inwardly.

Rose's eyes narrowed even further. "Of course he has."

Lady Shelley laughed again. "There are benefits to widowhood, Miss Hayward," she called back, with a saucy flip of her hair. "Many, many benefits. And I will never apologize for them."

Rose sent August another withering look before tossing the rag onto a small table just inside the door. "What do you want?" she demanded.

"I had come looking for Anne," he said evenly.

"As you can see, she's not here."

"Indeed. However, since I am, I'll extend the courtesy of passing along your sister's wishes to have a word with you as soon as possible."

"My sister is out for the afternoon."

"She is back now." He tried to keep any inflection from his words.

She shut the studio door firmly behind her. "Is she all right? Is she hurt? Is something wrong?"

"She is fine. She just needs a word. I believe she is in her rooms."

Rose brushed by him, heading toward the south wing, skirting the stairs and disappearing from view. August slowly followed her as far as the stairs before he stopped abruptly. He glanced in the direction in which Rose had disappeared and, still finding the hallway deserted, turned back the way he had come. He strode purposefully down the hall until he was standing in front of the studio door, wondering if he had completely lost his mind.

He had done more skulking and spying and sneaking in the days since he had become reacquainted with Clara Hayward than ever before in his life. Without wasting another moment on second-guessing himself and his motives, he opened the door, slipping silently into the room. On the dais the settee he remembered so vividly was still there, though it was empty and had been draped in a swath of brilliant emerald silk. Directly in front of the platform a large easel stood, holding a long, rectangular canvas. A small table covered with brushes and palettes and neatly organized pots of pigment rested beside it. Surrounding the dais in a wide arc were the students' easels and art supplies resting on small tables, one beside each station, waiting for their return.

August wandered around the room studying the drawings and sketches. They showed an eclectic selection of subject matter and no common thread, other than that the compositions had all been made with graphite and charcoal. Someone had sketched a garden the likes of which might have once been found at Versailles, complete with reservoirs and fountains and what looked like…plumbing lines? Alongside were sketches of plants and flowers, a jar half-filled with water and a small bouquet of roses sitting next to the easel, no doubt having provided some inspiration.

Next to the gardens were a completely different set of sketches, and it took August a good minute to comprehend what he was seeing. Anatomy diagrams. What looked like a heart dissected, with the tissue drawn back to expose the insides. A set of lungs, vessels reaching out from each like the branches of a winter oak. An empty tray rested beside that easel, and August chose not to consider what it had once held to provide inspiration. He took a step back, his eyes going to the next easel.

This was Anne's. He recognized the bold strokes and the clean lines right away. She had drawn schematics of what looking like a coaching inn, given the amount of space and detail dedicated to the stables and yard surrounding it. He peered more closely, noting the large rooms at the front, designed for eating, and the kitchens and storehouses in proximity. It was an efficient design, with careful consideration given to the flow of people from one space to another. Something the Trenton Hotel was lacking. He frowned. Perhaps he did need to reconsider the layout of the hotel. And perhaps he could consult with Anne.

You made me your partner. And there is nothing in the world I value more.

He found himself smiling reluctantly.

He turned away and found himself in front of the long canvas directly across from the dais. This must be what Rose Hayward had been working on because the brushes here were still damp and the smell of turpentine strong. The canvas had been covered with a light, filmy cloth, and before he could reconsider, he pulled one corner of it, letting the cloth flutter to the floor.

The woman gazing out from the canvas at him was instantly recognizable. And breathtaking. Not because she was beautiful, but because Rose Hayward had somehow managed to capture the sultry confidence in Lady Shelley's expression that August found so seductive in any woman. It was evident in every line of the body stretched out on the green silk, clothed only in the subtle light that the artist had captured with superb skill. Costume, indeed.

This was a woman who knew who she was. Who wasn't trying to hide the long scar that stretched over her generous hip or the purple birthmark that graced the upper half of her thigh. It was all there on the canvas with no apology. When August had been Lady Shelley's lover, she'd been ashamed of what she thought were imperfections. She'd tried to cover them with clothes or sheets, or darkness when that wasn't possible. He hadn't let her, and now, looking at the image of the woman, he was glad he hadn't. Perhaps he had, in some small way, contributed to the confidence of the woman gazing out at him.

"She's beautiful, isn't she?"

August jumped like a schoolboy who had been caught sneaking into the pantries. He hadn't heard Clara come in.

"She is," he agreed.

"Did you love her?"

"No. But she made me laugh," he said.

"Among other things."

"Among other things," he agreed again. "Her husband, the marquess, was not very kind to her during their marriage. I was her first lover after he died. Our affair lasted as long as it took her to understand that she deserved better than what her marriage had offered. That she was free to seek her own happiness."

"That's what she said when she commissioned Rose to paint her. That she wished to be painted like this because it pleased her. Just her. No one else."

"I'm glad she's happy." August bent and picked up the

sheet, then settled it over the painting once more. "I must assume your sister found you."

"She did," she said quietly. "I think it would annoy her to know that the two of you are more alike than she would ever care to think. She also offered to kill Stilton, though in a way that would have met with the Inquisition's approval." Clara paused. "And she too said that what happened wasn't my fault."

"Smart woman." He watched her out of the corner of his eye. "How are you feeling?"

"Much better." She let out a breath that was half laugh, half sigh. "I suspect listening to the merits of thumbscrews will do that."

He wanted to draw her into his arms. Hold her and kiss her senseless. Lay her down on that green silk and make her forget everything that had happened to her that day. Instead he clasped his hands behind his back, unsure if she was ready for that. "How did you know I would be in here?"

"Your barbaric tendencies."

"Very funny."

"You're not shocked." She gestured at the covered painting. "By this."

August let out a bark of laughter. "When it comes to this studio, I'm all out of shock," he said. "Get back to me next week, and I'll see what I can do to find some." He paused. "Though I admit to having been taken aback by what appears to be a set of lungs over there." He gestured to the smaller easels.

Clara smiled wryly. "The students were asked to sketch what interested them. There were no limitations or requirements, other than that they would present their work to the rest of the class with an explanation. You'd be amazed at what I've learned about swine organs this week."

"Why are you doing this?" August asked suddenly.

"What do you mean?"

"What do you hope to achieve? At the risk of sounding like an utter ass, once these girls go back to their families, back to London, they won't ever have another chance to do this sort of thing. Interests are not encouraged, not these, anyway. You know it, and I know it, and they know it as well. What can possibly come of all of this?"

Clara gazed at him. "You tell me."

"What?"

"Earlier, you said you had an answer for me that was good enough. I'd like to hear it now instead of at dinner."

August looked away. "I made Anne a sign."

"A sign?"

"A tavern sign for the Silver Swan. She had designed one. I had it made from her sketch."

An expression he couldn't decipher crossed her face. "Has she seen it?"

"Yes."

"And?"

He dropped his gaze. "She was pleased."

"I'm sure she was," Clara said gently. "Were you?"

"Yes."

"Was this a onetime overture?" she asked. "Or are you willing to admit that your sister has so much more she can offer?"

"I've never doubted her intelligence or her abilities. But nor do I want her to worry about...things anymore. The price of fish. The efficiency of the hotel kitchens. Laundry services." He threw up his hands in exasperation.

"Which is very noble, but by doing so, you've taken away her sense of purpose."

He ran his hand through his hair. "Anne doesn't need to—"

"Did you know that my father gave Haverhall School to my mother as a wedding gift?" Clara asked suddenly, interrupting him.

August blinked, hating the now-familiar guilt that instantly stirred every time the name Haverhall was mentioned. He didn't want to hear anything about Haverhall that didn't involve surveyors' reports and revenue projections. He did not want to know how deeply entrenched the school was in Clara's family or to be reminded of the legacy it represented to her.

"My mother grew up in a home where the only things she was responsible for were choosing which dinner dress she wished to wear and ensuring she used the correct dessert spoon." Clara continued. "If she were still alive today, she'd tell you what she told us. That she felt trapped, miserable, and so bored she could scream. Imagine her surprise on her wedding day when her husband presented her not with pretty jewels or a flashy horse or a fine house as a wedding gift, but an entire school, and the purpose, challenge, and expectations that came with it. Things that make a person feel alive. Useful. Important."

August could feel a muscle working alongside his jaw. Resentment edged out the guilt, and he clung to it like a drowning man. "It has never been my intention to trivialize Anne's existence, if that is what you're implying."

"That is not at all what I'm implying." Clara softened her voice. "I know Anne lived in Marshalsea."

August flinched. "How did you know that?"

"She told me." She gestured around her. "Look, I'm not trying to change the world. Well, maybe I am, but not overnight. Not in my lifetime, even. But what would happen if enough women believed in themselves? Believed that they could do more than what they've been told they can do?"

She sighed. "I'm not so delusional as to forget that the world we live in is real and we must all adapt to it. The classes I teach in London during my regular terms are not ground-breaking by any stretch of the imagination. But occasionally a young woman attends those classes who, like me, believes that things could be different. And I invite her out here to explore just how much."

August stared at her.

Clara exhaled loudly, her cheeks pink. "I'll stop talking now. Although you've passed on my earlier invitation to collect your sister and run screaming back to London, I wouldn't blame you if you did so now." She sounded as if she was only half joking. "But if you're sending the Bedlam stewards after me, can you at least wait until the end of next week?"

"You think I find any of what you said crazy?" he asked.

"I hope not, but it would put you in the minority."

"Good. I prefer to be in the minority. The masses don't know what they're missing out on."

"Oh." She looked up at him. "Thank you. For believing in me."

"Always, Clara." He bent and brushed his lips over hers, the softest of gestures. "Let me show you how much."

"Yes," she whispered.

Very deliberately August turned and walked to the studio door. Just as deliberately he turned the lock, the click sounding overly loud in the empty room. He returned and stopped just in front of her. He bowed low and straightened. "Dance with me."

Her lips parted. "I beg your pardon?"

"May I have the privilege of this dance, Miss Hayward?"

"Here? Now? But—"

"No regrets, Miss Hayward. And no excuses."

"And no music either," she said with a slow smile.

"Inconsequential details," August scoffed. He held out his hand. He saw Clara swallow before she reached out and took it.

Her hand was warm in his, and he pulled her to him, his other hand coming to slide around her waist. Her fingers tightened in his, and he heard her slight inhalation. "Close your eyes," he said.

"August—"

"Close your eyes."

She gazed at him for a second longer before her eyes fluttered shut. Her free hand went to his shoulder, her fingertips just brushing the back of his neck. "Perfect," he whispered before he led her in the first step.

It wasn't the reckless waltz that they had danced a decade ago, surrounded by glittering lights and glittering people. There was no orchestra to keep the time, no constant hum of those trying to make their voices heard over the voices of others. This was a private affair, meant only for them, danced in a small space and danced in silence. But it was no less powerful for it.

August tightened his grip on her waist, pulling her flush against him as they moved in slow circles across the floor in front of the dais. Clara's hand slid farther around the back of his neck, her fingers tangling gently in the back of his hair. He could feel her body, hot and supple against his, her chest rising and falling. She matched him step for step, and August wondered idly if she could feel the way his heart was thundering in his chest.

He drew the hand that held hers into the space between their bodies, tucking it securely against his chest, and lifted his fingers to stroke her cheek. She kept her eyes closed but her lips curled, and she tipped her head into his touch. God, she was so beautiful like this. So beautiful always, but like this, she was his. She belonged to him in this moment.

He bent his head and caught her lips with his, their steps slowing until they stopped altogether. As before, their kiss started slowly, only for different reasons this time. This time August wasn't afraid of scaring her or hurting her. This time he was afraid only that he wouldn't make this last the way he wanted it to. That he wouldn't be able to make good on his promise to her that he would take his time, learning what made her whimper and writhe with pleasure.

Because holy hell, he wanted her. Wanted her so badly that he ached everywhere. His skin felt two sizes too small, and his cock throbbed. The need to take her then, right there, on the floor in the middle of the damn studio, was pounding through him, making him dizzy with want. His hands slid from her face and over her shoulders and down her back, where they gripped her as though he was afraid to let her go.

And then she moaned, and her mouth opened and her tongue stroked his, and he was completely lost. His hands dropped to her ass, and he hauled her up against him the way he had done once before. She wrapped her legs around him, but her skirts hampered her movements, and it wasn't enough.

"I want you naked. Now." His voice was rough.

"Yes." She slid down the length of him, the friction sending all sorts of uncontrollable shudders through him. He set to work at her bodice, realizing that his hands weren't entirely steady. He fumbled slightly at the ties until he felt her hands on his, pulling them away.

"You can watch," she said, looking at him though heavily lidded eyes, her lips parted and her color high.

He cock twitched, and he groaned with need.

Clara took over where he had left off, with a slow, subtle

tease as one by one the laces and ties that held her gown and her stays were undone, the garments falling to the floor soundlessly. She stood before him in her shift, the outline of her body a tantalizing breath away. So close and yet so far.

Her eyes dropped to the bulge at the fall of his trousers, and a sultry smile touched her lips even as her fingers played with the ribbon at the neck of her shift. "Steady, Your Grace," she whispered.

August remained still, his breath coming far too fast. Very deliberately she pulled the end of the ribbon, and the top of her chemise loosened, slipping over one shoulder and then the other before it too joined the pile on the rug at their feet. And Clara Hayward stood before him wearing nothing but a smile.

His heart might have stopped momentarily before it resumed, thundering in his ears with the same rhythm that was pulsing through the rest of him. The sound obliterated everything around him, his eyes riveted on her fingers, which were now trailing over the slope of her left breast, coming to circle her dark nipple, hard and pebbled under her touch. She was watching him watching her, and he had never been as aroused as he was then.

"Don't stop there," he rasped.

Clara's eyes darkened, and her hand slid lower. Her fingers caressed the gentle swell of her abdomen before slipping through the dark curls at the juncture of her legs. He watched as she stroked a finger through the folds of her sex, her eyes fluttering closed and her head tipping back. Her hand circled low and hard, and a soft whimper escaped. She withdrew her hand, her finger wet with her desire, and it snapped whatever control he'd managed to maintain.

August didn't remember moving, but he hauled her up and against him, and in two steps he had mounted the low dais and deposited her on the edge of the wide settee in the center. He came to kneel just in front of her, her legs falling open as she leaned back. He placed his hands on the backs of her calves, running them up and over her thighs, spreading his fingers to caress as much of that smooth, soft skin as he could. His thumbs skimmed the indentation of her hip bones while his fingers cupped the firm roundness of her ass.

"Don't stop there," she whispered, and he might have laughed if he hadn't been so hot and so hard.

August bent his head and covered her sex with his mouth and felt her body tense even as she sighed. He caressed her with his tongue the way she had just done with her own fingers, the muscles in her thighs trembling under his touch. He found the bud at the apex of her folds and stroked it, her hips arching off the settee. He did it twice more, then stopped only to gaze at her, her head thrown back and her hands tangled in the emerald silk.

Her eyes opened, dismay clear. "Don't stop," she said, and he could hear the frustration and desire in each syllable. Her breasts were rising and falling with each rapid breath she took, and he couldn't look away. He rose, coming to kneel over her, bending his head to take one of her nipples in his mouth. He sucked and nipped and let the noises she was making in the back of her throat guide him. He let one of his hands delve between them as he kissed her, finding her center and slipping a finger deep.

She arched off the settee again with a gasp as he withdrew before sliding deep again. She was so hot and so wet, and it was just as well that he had yet to remove his clothes because that was the only thing preventing him from thrusting mindlessly into that heat. He dipped his head, catching her lips this time, stroking the velvety softness of her mouth with the same tempo with which his fingers stroked her sex.

Her hips rose to meet each stroke, each time with more urgency, and he slipped a second finger into her.

"August," she breathed, a second before she cried out. He felt her body beneath him stiffen as her hips jerked, and she rode his hand as she convulsed and shuddered. It was a long moment before she collapsed back on the silk, breathing heavily, a look of utter rapture on her face.

Christ, but she was incredible. To the day he died, the image of Clara beneath him, offering herself, letting herself go, letting him take control, would be forever burned in his mind.

He pushed himself to his feet, yanking at his clothes. He needed to be deep inside her. He needed to possess her completely. So, so badly.

Clara raised herself up on her elbows, watching him, her skin flushed and her eyes heavy with desire. The pins had long ago fallen from her hair, and it streamed in a glorious mess behind her. She looked like a woman who had been loved and loved well. And was anticipating being so again.

She didn't speak, made no move to touch him, just watched in much the same manner that he had. He finally stood before her in nothing but his trousers, letting anticipation build. She pushed herself the rest of the way up, coming to kneel on the settee before him.

"Come here," she said, and he obeyed. For now.

She lifted her hands and ran them down his chest, tracing the edges of his pectoral muscles and the ridges of his abdomen as though she had all the time in the world. She slid her fingers through the hair at the center of his chest and circled his nipples with her fingers. August forced himself to remain still. Her hands slid over his upper arms, along the small of his back, traveling along the waistband of his trousers.

With no hesitation she went to work on the buttons at the fall and slipped her hands inside, pushing the last of his clothing down his legs and away. His erection surged free, thick and aching. She smiled up at him, her hands circling his waist to cup his ass, her head dipping to—

Jesus. A sound he didn't recognize escaped from his throat, and he closed his eyes briefly as she took him in her mouth. His hands went to her head, his fingers buried in the wildness of her hair. His buttocks clenched, and he thrust up into her soft heat, unable to stop himself.

Clara made a soft noise of approval. Her hands were working their way over the curve of his ass to the backs of his thighs, and her tongue swept down his shaft and then back up, circling the crown. He felt his cock pulse, and lust pooled low and heavy.

"I'm too close, Clara," he ground out.

She sucked hard in response, and he moaned. Her hair fell forward, and the urge to thrust into her mouth again was overwhelming. August pulled her head back, and his siren looked up at him, her eyes glazed with the same desire that was coursing through him, threatening to undo him where he stood. "Not this time," he said.

He lifted her and laid her back on the settee, his hands sliding over the tops of her thighs and around to the backs, spreading her legs wide and lifting her hips toward him. His hand slid back up over the swell of her abdomen and along her rib cage, his thumb just brushing the underside of her breast.

Her hips flexed, a tiny, involuntary movement.

He smiled.

"August," she whispered, though it sounded like more of a plea.

He ran his finger across her lips, over her chin, and down

the column of her throat. He paused in the small hollow at the base before he slid his hand down the slope of her breast, palming its weight and brushing the tip of her nipple. He felt her shudder, and her hips moved again, this time more demanding.

"What are you doing?" she demanded hoarsely.

He brought his hand back to her hip, holding her steady. "Understanding what I possess." He positioned himself at her entrance and thrust into her slick heat.

Clara made a muffled noise and wrapped her legs hard around his waist, drawing him even farther. He could feel her inner walls flex around him, and he ground against her, stars starting to dance along the edges of his vision. Need was pounding through him with more urgency than he would be able to control.

He withdrew and thrust, once, twice, and again, each time harder and faster, never taking his eyes off her face. White-hot pleasure was streaking through him with each stroke, moisture gathering at his brow. His breathing was labored, and he could feel her heels digging into the tops of his buttocks, urging him on. She reached up and ran a hand over her breasts, rubbing her nipples. With a low growl, August knocked her hand away with his and set his mouth where her fingers had been.

"Yes," he heard her hiss, writhing beneath him.

She was so responsive, so goddamn perfect. He was never going to survive this.

He swirled his tongue around each nipple, sucking hard as he pumped into her. He lifted his head only enough to find her mouth. "I want you to come for me," he said roughly against her lips. "I need you to come right now."

Clara whimpered, a raw sound that sent another wave of pleasure slamming through him. He tilted her hips and thrust hard, grinding himself deliberately against the very apex of her sex, and just like that, she flew apart. She cried his name, a ragged, wild declaration of ecstasy as her orgasm crashed through her. She arched up and into him, her legs clamped around his waist as her inner muscles spasmed and pulsed around his cock. He drove into her, riding her climax, prolonging every wave of euphoria. His fingers dug into her hips as he caged them, his vision dimming as his own release bore down on him.

"Clara," he groaned, pulling out just as his own orgasm ripped through him, but she was ready for him, her hand fisting him between their heat-slicked bodies. He gasped and shuddered, pumping himself into the friction of her palm. Pleasure of an intensity he hadn't known rolled through him in unending, merciless waves, one after another without respite. His thrusts finally slowed, though it took them a long time to stop altogether, his body seemingly caught in the eddies of their lovemaking. It took him even longer to catch his breath and his wits, and when he did he rolled to the side, feeling a little out of control.

"We should have done that ten years ago," Clara said into the silence.

He laughed, a sound that caught him by surprise. "Agreed."

"Thank you." He felt her shift, and he turned on his side so he was facing her.

"For what?"

She smiled crookedly. "For your...ministrations."

"Twice," he teased.

"Twice," she agreed. The smile slipped. "And for your control and your responsibility."

"Oh." He was a little taken aback. No woman had ever thanked him for that.

"We should have spoken of it earlier."

August gazed at her. "I suppose we're speaking of it now."

"True. And I appreciate your...unselfishness."

He grinned. "You can make it up to me. I have some ideas."

She grinned back. "Good. So do I."

Desire surged through him and stole the breath he had just caught. He leaned forward and kissed her deeply, not wanting this to end. Not ever wanting to leave this studio and return to the real world. Not wanting to remember what sort of reality waited for them outside these walls. And the nagging guilt and discontent that came with it. He pulled back. "Are you happy?"

"Deliriously." Her forehead creased in puzzlement. "What a strange question."

He shook his head, wondering what he was doing. This was usually the part where he got up, set his clothing to rights, and left. Instead he found himself lounging naked on a settee in an art studio with a woman who had just shaken his world to its very foundations, and he was asking her about...happiness. Perhaps he was fishing for compliments.

"August?" she asked, sounding concerned. As she should. This whole episode was concerning.

"If you couldn't teach at Haverhall, what would you do?"

Clara stared at him. "Teach somewhere else."

He reached for her hand and threaded his fingers through hers. "Where?"

"I'd like to say Oxford. Maybe Cambridge if they'd have me." She made a wry face.

"I'm being serious."

She propped her head up on her hand. "Teaching is what gives me my purpose." Her eyes had a troubled, faraway quality to them. "I don't think I could ever stop, no matter what happened. Whatever circumstance might change, I'd always try to find a way."

That should have made him feel better. She was prepared to move on, even if she wasn't prepared to tell him why. Except there was something that was crowding into his chest, making his heart hurt. "Oxford or Cambridge would be lucky to have you." He looked down, staring at their entwined fingers. "If you ever need a recommendation..." He trailed off before he looked back up. "If you ever needed anything, Clara, would you tell me?"

She averted her gaze. "I'm not sure what you mean."

"Just that. If you ever needed...help." He wanted her to trust him. Needed her to trust him.

She looked at him again, her dark eyes unreadable. "That's very kind."

August swallowed his frustration. "My father never asked for help," he said.

"When he went to prison, you mean?"

"Even before that. My father..." He had no idea why he was talking about this, but now that he had started, he couldn't seem to stop. "My father was an inveterate gambler, reckless and selfish. He defied his family to marry an actress and embrace the wildly popular notion of true love. Except after they were married, he gambled away everything that they possessed and then everything that they didn't. And when that happened, he stole from his family to cover the debt."

Clara's fingers tightened in his.

"My mother was a good woman. I think she believed that she could change him up until the day she died. That love would change him. But of course, it didn't. And by the time he was finally thrown into debtors' prison, there wasn't anyone left who cared."

"I'm sorry," Clara whispered.

August shrugged. "I spent two years living on the streets," he said. "I know what it feels like to starve. I know what it feels like to be so cold that the skin on your fingers and toes burns and peels. I know what it feels like to have to defend yourself against those who would kill you for the shoes on your feet. But would I be where I am today without living that? I don't know."

"And does it make you happy?" she asked him suddenly. "Where you are today?"

He should have expected that Clara would turn his question back on him, yet it caught him off guard. What was even more disturbing was that he didn't seem to have an honest answer that he liked.

He untangled their fingers and reached out to push her thick hair away from her face. "I can't think of anywhere else I'd want to be right now," he murmured, dipping his head to kiss the smooth skin of her shoulder. "And you have no idea just how happy that makes me."

He heard her sigh, and he knew that he had fooled no one. But she didn't say anything, simply rolled onto her back, looking up at him with those knowing dark eyes. She reached out to touch his face with her fingertips, a gentle, butterfly-light touch before her lips curled into that half smile he knew so well.

"Very well, then, Your Grace. Why don't you show me how much?"

Chapter 17

Clara used to despise dinner parties.

Her parents had insisted on having them regularly, spectacles of wealth and extravagance that caused everyone who was anyone to angle shamelessly to secure an invitation. Clara would usually find herself seated between two eligible bachelors, and her mother had always made an attempt to ensure that each of them possessed an open mind. Or at least as open as the mind of one raised in male, titled privilege could get. On almost all occasions, Clara was vastly underwhelmed.

Only once could Clara ever recall having been captivated by her dinner partner, and he, it seemed, by her. He had spent ten years working for the Hudson's Bay Company in uncharted territory far to the north of civilized places like Boston and New York. His stories fascinated her, and he seemed to delight in answering each and every one of her pointed questions in complete, if occasionally shocking, detail.

Clara knew this dinner would be no different. Not because she already knew the conversation would flow freely, no question too improper or impractical, no answer too informed or too radical. Not because each and every person seated at the table had something fascinating to share. But because there would be a man seated at her side who took part in it all. Who knew her body, mind, and soul.

She had dressed with care that evening, or as much care as her limited wardrobe would allow. Since she had left the studio and crept silently back to her rooms, she felt a little as if she were glowing from within. She caught herself smiling and blushing at odd intervals, her skin tingling at the memory of August's touch, aching for him to touch her again.

It was different with August. She'd had only a single lover before—a young Italian artist who had been as skilled with her body as he had been at his craft. As her teacher, he had set her body on fire under the Tuscan moon, and as his willing student, she had learned to do the same for him. Yet neither had had any expectations beyond physical pleasure. There had been respect and admiration for each other, but no deeper emotion had been involved. Nothing that had sucked the breath from her lungs in his presence and made her heart ache fiercely in his absence.

She was well aware that somewhere she had crossed a line she had never intended to cross with August Faulkner. Or maybe that line had been crossed in a ballroom ten years earlier, and this was simply the inevitable culmination. But what she felt—the unrelenting longing, the constant desire—this was something that she hadn't been truly prepared for. It was an all-consuming, overwhelming emotion, like a cyclone that had borne down on an unsuspecting sailor. And she was caught right in the heart of it.

Which of course, changed nothing. While she might take advantage of these last weeks in Dover, far from the merciless scrutiny of London, when they were over, so was whatever was between her and August. If Clara wished to continue teaching, no matter where, she needed to retain her image of perfect propriety.

She was beginning to hate it. But that was simply fact.

Clara left her rooms, determined to push reality to the side for another night and enjoy the time she had remaining. With the end of summer, she wouldn't have August. With the end of summer, she wouldn't have the job that had given her such purpose for so many years. But for tonight, she'd leave worry for tomorrow.

She met Tabby and Theo in the hall as she descended the stairs. Tabitha was once again arranging flowers in the vase that was the centerpiece of the round table in the center of the hall, an embroidered blue shawl draped elegantly over her shoulders and her silver hair touched almost gold by the slanted rays coming in through the long hall windows.

"Those roses are stunning," Clara said as she approached, eyeing the profusion of blooms in fuchsia and soft pink.

"Aren't they? Amelia cut them for me from the gardens out back. Says certain types of roses do better if they are pruned a little more aggressively." She worked another bloom into the vase and glanced at Clara. "You look fetching tonight, dear," she commented. "You must have been out in the fresh air. It's put a lovely color in your cheeks."

"Thank you." Clara willed herself not to blush further. It wasn't the fresh air that had put color in her cheeks, but she wasn't going to argue. "His Grace will be joining us for dinner tonight," she said, and she hoped that it sounded casual.

"Oh, lovely," Theo said with a sly smile. "I was a little afraid I'd embarrassed him beyond repair. You know, when I asked if he'd like to model for the class." She grinned, her eyes twinkling.

"I think His Grace has gotten over himself," Clara said with a chuckle.

"Who has gotten over what?" Harland strolled into the hall with Rose on his heels and set a gallant kiss on Tabby and Theo's cheeks before coming to do the same to Clara.

"Harland," she said, blinking, "I didn't expect you for dinner."

"Got back from town earlier than expected," he said.

Clara's eyes darted from her brother to Rose, but she couldn't read anything in their expressions. If Harland had been in town, he would have picked up the post. Perhaps there had been word from London. Perhaps there was word of the ships—

"Not yet," he whispered, apparently reading her mind. "No news yet from the docks. But soon. I'm sure of it. Don't lose faith."

Clara nodded, her brow creasing and a renewed wave of anxiety rising. She knew very well that there was nothing they could do except wait, but the uncertainty became more pronounced with each day that passed.

"You look lovely this evening, Clara," Harland continued in a voice everyone could hear, distracting her from her grim thoughts. He was looking her up and down, a faint expression of consternation on his face. "You look...different. Did you do something new with your hair?"

She forced a smile onto her face. It had, in fact, taken her an age to fix what the Duke of Holloway had done to her hair. "I don't believe so, no," she said. "But thank you for the compliment." She took a deep breath. "I had just mentioned to Theo and Tabby that His Grace will be joining us for dinner," she said.

"Why?" Harland asked.

Clara shot him what she hoped was a look of cool admonishment. "Because I invited him."

"Did you send his invitation in hieroglyphs?" Rose asked sweetly. "Or has he learned to read since last week?"

From the center of the hall, Tabitha snorted with laughter.

Clara scowled and ignored her sister. "May I assume, Harland, from the lack of bloodstains on your clothes and what appears to be a fresh shave, you will be joining us as well?" Clara asked.

"I will." He stared hard at Clara. "Is Holloway done, then, with his business here?"

Clara shrugged, keeping her expression neutral, looking between her siblings. "I'm sure I wouldn't know. You can ask him tonight. But please try and be pleasant. Both of you. He'll be here shortly."

"I'm always pleasant," Harland replied.

Clara made a face at him just as a decisive knock echoed from the front door. The butler instantly appeared and pulled it open, allowing late golden sunlight to spill into the hall. The Duke of Holloway stepped in, squinting slightly in the relative dimness as the door closed behind him.

"Good evening, Your Grace," Theo said, moving forward to greet him. "So wonderful that you could join us tonight."

"Lady Theodosia." August offered Theo a chivalrous bow and caught her hand, bringing her knuckles to his lips. "My lady, may I compliment you on your appearance. That color of silk is spectacular on you."

The portly woman cackled with delight. "And here I thought it might be the dress."

"That too." He grinned at her, and Theo giggled like a

girl. "For what they're worth, my lady, you have my apologies for my earlier intrusion."

Lady Theodosia waved her hand. "Your apologies aren't worth anything, dearie, because I wasn't offended. It was your sensibilities I was concerned for."

"My sensibilities survived." He met Clara's gaze over her shoulder. "They might even have learned something along the way."

Clara looked down, feeling the heat creep into her cheeks. She was also avoiding the gaze of both Harland and Rose, who were both staring at her in silent contemplation.

"Oh, good," Theo said. "Shall we see if dinner's almost ready?"

"Indeed," Tabitha agreed. "The girls are already waiting for us in the dining room." Tabitha joined her sister, linking her arm through Theo's.

August made his way farther into the hall with the appropriate greetings, returned happily by Tabby and, as promised, pleasantly by Harland and Rose. He hung back until the four others had preceded him and extended his arm to Clara. "I've been looking forward to this all evening," he murmured.

"Dinner?"

"More like the dessert."

Clara blushed again. Bloody hell, but she felt sixteen years old.

His hand caressed the skin on her forearm, sending shivers of anticipation dancing through her body. "Do you suppose we can skip dinner altogether?" he whispered. "Do you think anyone would notice?"

"They might." Clara swallowed with difficulty, a pulsing desire pooling low in her belly.

"I can't get enough of you. And I can't stand the wait—"

"What are you two whispering about back there?" Rose asked, turning to look behind her suspiciously.

"I was just telling Miss Hayward how much I was looking forward to this evening," he said smoothly. August stopped at the doorway, his eyes scanning the dining room, where the chatter of seven young women filled every nook and cranny. "Where is Anne?" he asked, turning to Clara.

Clara frowned. Anne and Phoebe were both missing. "Perhaps they are late for dinner."

"Who's late?" Tabby had stopped and turned as well.

"Anne and Phoebe."

"That's odd," said the woman. "Those two are usually so punctual."

"I'm sure they just lost track of time," Clara said, though a strange trepidation was starting to blossom in her gut. "I'll have one of the footmen go up to their rooms to see if they're there."

"I'll go," said Rose, sliding past Clara and giving August a long look. "It'll be faster." She disappeared back the way they had come.

"I haven't seen Anne since this afternoon," Tabby said. "Right after Mr. Stilton dropped you off from your drive."

Clara went completely still. "I beg your pardon?"

"When you came back from your drive with that horribly dressed Mr. Stilton. He may be a friend of yours, but I declare that man is completely color blind. I saw Anne and Phoebe talking to him out on the driveway."

"Mr. Stilton did not drive me back to Avondale," Clara said carefully, afraid that, if she let herself consider the full implications of what Tabby had said, she might give in to panic. "His Grace did."

"When was this?" August demanded in a voice that Clara had never heard him use. "When was he here?"

Tabby paled slightly at his tone. "I don't know. Perhaps three?"

"Did my sister get in the carriage with him?"

Tabby blinked. "I don't know. I don't think so, but I can't be sure. I just saw them briefly out the hall window. Miss Phoebe had that doctor's bag of hers. I just assumed Miss Hayward was there—"

"Miss Hayward was not there," August said so quietly that Clara barely heard him.

"Why did Holloway bring you home, Clara?" This time it was Harland who spoke in a voice that sent fingers of ice down her spine.

Again it was August who answered. "Mr. Stilton expressed his desire to…further his friendship with your sister. He did not take her refusal well."

"What did he do to you, Clara?" Harland's face was like granite, and his fists were curled at his sides.

She felt her face burn in mortification and anger. "He tried to…kiss me and—"

"That was all he tried. I made sure he didn't have a chance to try anything else," August snarled.

Harland's eyes pinned August in fury. "And you're telling me this now?"

"I told him not to," Clara snapped. "It was handled. And it's none of your business."

Her brother turned. "None of my business?" he growled. "I beg to differ."

"Your Lordship?" This came from the butler who was now standing at the door looking harassed. "There is a…boy here who says he needs to—"

He was cut off by the sudden appearance of Jonas, who

skidded into the hall. The butler made a grab for him, but August waved him off. The boy's eyes were a little wild until they lighted on August.

"There's a bloke who has yer sister, sir," he sputtered, a little out of breath.

"What?" August asked, frowning fiercely.

"Miss Anne. The one who works at the Swan." He blinked at the expression on August's face. "She said it was our secret, her bein' yer sister an' working there an' all." The words were tumbling out of his mouth at a torrential rate. "But this bloke, he had a gun. I figured she'd want you to know."

A muscle was working furiously at the side of August's jaw. He was almost humming with the same barely leashed violence Clara had seen on that cliff. Only this time she wasn't sure that he would endeavor to exercise any sort of restraint.

You don't want me for an enemy, Stilton had said.

Clara hadn't taken him seriously. She closed her eyes, feeling sick to her stomach. If Stilton touched a hair on the head of either one of those girls, she would kill him herself.

"Where?" August demanded.

"By my ma's house. I can show you."

Clara whirled around to find August already stalking toward the door, Jonas darting at his side.

"I'm coming with you," she said, running to catch up.

"So am I," Harland said from just behind her. "In case you don't kill him right the first time."

"I don't need your help. Either of you." August was already demanding a horse be brought around, and Harland was doing the same.

"This is my fault," she mumbled.

"This is not your fault," August said. "This lies solely on

the shoulders of a man who failed and blames and despises me for that failure. A man whose first wife made him very wealthy when she died. A man who I suspect decided that he could do even better."

Clara stared at him in horror, understanding dawning. "You think Stilton killed his wife?" she wheezed.

"And now he has my sister."

Clara pressed her fingers into her eyes, making spots dance under her lids. "And Phoebe. Oh God." She would not consider that he might kill one or both of them out of spite or hatred. Or that he would force— She stopped, dropping her hands. In truth, Clara had no idea what the man was capable of.

They'd reached the stables, and August nearly shoved the hapless groom aside to finish the task of saddling himself. Another groom was leading two other mounts out, and Harland seized the reins of one and swung himself into the saddle. Clara followed on her own mount.

"I'm not waiting for either of you two," August snapped as he mounted. He hauled Jonas up in front of him and kicked his horse into a gallop before he'd even fully gained his seat. Harland and Clara were on his heels, panic and worry pushing them hard. Stilton had three hours on them. Three hours in which he could have— Clara cut herself off. Thinking the worst would not be helpful.

They thundered down the drive and out onto the twisting road. The wind whipped against Clara's face, making her eyes water and tears stream down her face. Jonas must have been giving August instructions, because he was weaving his way across a series of fields and rutted cart tracks without slowing as the miles slipped by. Up ahead a half-rotten, sagging thatched roof was just visible beyond the ridge—

Clara nearly pitched over the head of her horse as the

animal dropped its hind end and came to a shuddering stop in a frantic effort to avoid August's horse, which was sliding to a stop as well. Beside her dust spewed from under the hooves of Harland's mount as he hauled on the reins. Clara fought for her seat, bracing herself against the neck of her horse, which was now dancing sideways.

The dust slowly cleared, and Clara managed to calm her horse enough to see the figures of two women trudging up the track toward them. The one on the right was dark haired, the one on the left had tresses the color of chestnuts. They were dressed in simple gowns, but the one on the left had ominous rusty stains down the front of her skirts. August was already off his horse and running toward them. Clara dismounted hurriedly and followed him.

"Jesus, Anne," she thought she heard him say before he engulfed his sister in an embrace. Just as quickly he drew back, his hands going to her shoulders. "Are you hurt?" he demanded.

Anne smiled at him, her expression strained but steady. "I'm not hurt."

Beside Clara, Harland was crouching in front of Phoebe. "Do you need to sit down? Are you bleeding?" he asked urgently, touching the edge of her stained skirts. "What happened? Are you—"

"I'm fine, Dr. Hayward," Phoebe said. "It's not my blood."

"Then what— Who—"

"Mr. Stilton. He might need a doctor." A vicious satisfaction came into Phoebe's eyes. "Or not. I don't think he's doing very well. His putrid coat is most assuredly ruined."

"Ruined indeed," Anne said, her voice steely. "But it was unavoidable given the circumstances." The two girls exchanged a look.

"What were you thinking?" August thundered. "Why would you ever have gone with—"

"I was thinking that you and Miss Hayward were lying in a ditch somewhere, dying," Anne snapped with a disgusted shake of her head. "Stilton arrived just as Phoebe and I were heading inside Avondale. He told us you had been in a terrible accident. You and Miss Hayward. And that you needed me, and there was no time to waste."

"I went with her. To offer what medical assistance I could," Phoebe added.

Anne's eyes hardened. "I'd already met him and had no reason not to trust him," she said, and Clara felt her stomach clench. "He played the part of the worried, anxious, helpful friend quite convincingly," Anne continued. "He had the driver take us to an empty cottage north of town with haste. I was so terrified at the prospect of losing you, I never stopped to consider that Stilton could possibly have any ulterior motives."

August swore.

"He sent the driver on once we were there and it wasn't until he was gone that he leveled a pistol at us and said he'd shoot one of us if the other tried to run. He said he'd never had reservations about killing to get what he wanted. And apparently you stole something that was dear to him, so he was returning the favor in kind."

Clara kept her eyes trained on Anne, not daring to look at August.

"But I don't think Stilton had actually thought the logistics of a good kidnapping all the way through," Phoebe said coldly. "So many variables. So much…unpredictability."

"Unpredictability?" August was looking between his sister and Phoebe with alarm.

"I begged Stilton to marry me," Anne said grimly. "To

take me away with him. Away from my controlling, suffocating, impossible brother who would force me to marry a man three times my age just so that he could further line his coffers."

"And he believed you?"

"She was very persuasive," Phoebe commented.

"And he seemed to already harbor a vast resentment toward you, dear brother," Anne added. "Who am I to ruin such a perfectly good grudge?"

"Jesus Christ," August swore.

"That's what he said when I retrieved the gun he had left lying on the table in his haste to prepare for our joyous union."

"You killed him?" August choked.

"I did not," Anne replied primly. "But when I told Phoebe to fetch help and he tried to stop, well, my finger might have slipped on the trigger."

"You shot him?"

"Of course I did." Now she was looking at her brother with incredulity.

August dropped his head, his expression bleak. "I'm so sorry, Anne. I should never have allowed you to be caught in a position where you had to—"

"For the love of God, stop." Anne commanded loudly. "I grew up in a prison, August. And then, for a while, in places where one was required to look after one's own well-being with a little more diligence than others. There were many lessons to be learned, and make no mistake, I learned them well. Stilton took me for a fool once. I did not allow him a second opportunity."

August was staring at her.

"It'll take more than a vengeful, disorganized, badly dressed fop to break me, August. I'm not so fragile as that."

"No," he said, his voice sounding distant. "You're not."

"And where is Stilton now?" Harland asked into the silence.

"Still in the cottage, I would guess," Phoebe told him, gesturing at the rotten roof still visible. "It's hard to go far with a bullet lodged in your knee. I patched him up as well as possible. Though my medical experience is still limited, I suspect he may be in danger of losing his lower leg if not treated promptly. He might lose it anyway."

Clara saw Harland exchange a look with Holloway. "Leave him to me," her brother told the duke.

"No. I'll take care of him." August's expression was black.

"You'll do your sister no good if you're hanged for murder."

"They'd have to find the body first," the duke growled.

"But I can't have you running all over Dover looking for a place to hide a corpse. I have a stake in this too, Your Grace. Let me handle this."

August's lips thinned. He glanced at Clara before looking back at Harland. "Fine." August's face was glacial. "See it done."

Harland nodded. "Good." He stood, collected his horse, and vanished over the ridge.

"Well," said Anne, "I suppose we're late for dinner."

August made a muffled noise. "How can you possibly be jesting about this?"

"Because, August, I'm fine. Phoebe's fine. The only one who is not fine is the ass who deserved everything he got." Her eyes were steady and cool. "If you want me to dissolve in hysterics and tears, then you're going to have to give me some lead time and possibly a script. Because you haven't had the market on survival cornered all these years, dear brother."

August ran his hands through his hair in clear agitation.

"Now, if you would be so kind as to offer us a ride back to Avondale, I would be obliged. I can't speak for Phoebe, but it's been a long day."

Clara stepped closer to August and placed a hand on his sleeve, a fleeting, gentle gesture before she moved to collect the reins of the horses. "Come," she said. "Let's go home."

Chapter 18

The actions of one Mathias Stilton had shaken August to his core.

Not because of what might have happened, though that still kept him up some nights, but because he had suddenly realized that the dark-haired, blue-eyed little girl who had been his sister wasn't at all who he had chosen to pretend she was. For these last years he had used yards of pretty silk and glossy pearls and watercolor lessons to try to bury the fact that Anne had grown up in conditions that only the strongest and the most cunning survive. She had become a beautiful, poised lady to be sure, but one who had a core of pure steel.

Stilton, it seemed, had vanished from Dover, though his belongings at the boardinghouse where he'd been staying had never been claimed. Harland had said nothing, other than that the man had been alive when he arrived at the cottage and still alive when he left. August hadn't asked for any further details, and the Baron Strathmore had offered none.

And then there was Clara.

He hadn't seen her since that night, which had been hard. Harder than he'd ever thought possible. She'd been fully occupied with her classes during the day, and he'd spent the evenings buried in his own work and the correspondence that Duncan had brought him. There were inventories to be accepted, blueprints to be reviewed, payrolls to be approved. Legal documents to be signed, bank drafts to be transferred. All activities that usually consumed him and brought him satisfaction and pleasure. Except he was struggling to find distraction and reassurance in what was familiar. Because everything that he'd thought he'd known, everything that had seemed so clear to him in London, had become blurry and indistinguishable in Dover.

The dinner that had been missed two nights prior had been rescheduled, and August had been reinvited. Anne had specifically asked him to come, though at that point he would have come anyway, if only for the excuse to see Clara.

He arrived early to find Lady Tabitha in her now-familiar spot, arranging a new profusion of flowers in the center of the hall. Her deep-pink gown matched the roses in the center of the bouquet.

"Good evening, Your Grace," she said with a smile as she tucked a brilliant purple flower into the side of the arrangement. "You're early. No one's down quite yet."

"I can leave and return," he replied, bending to pick up a sprig of greenery that had fallen. "Make a grander entrance later."

"You could." Tabitha laughed. "But I get the feeling that you're not one for grand spectacles." She glanced at him over a cut fern. "We haven't seen much of you in the last couple of days."

"I've been busy. My man of business has come up from London with a number of matters requiring my attention."

"Yes, Mr. Down."

August started. "You've met?"

"Of course." Tabitha adjusted another stem. "Your sister introduced us last evening."

"What?" August wasn't sure where to start. "My sister? What was she doing last evening? With Mr. Down?"

"Playing chess in the drawing room. Beat him too. Well, at least the first time. He beat her twice after that."

"That's impossible."

"No, I can assure you that she had his queen—"

"That's not what I meant." His fingers tightened on the sprig.

Tabitha was watching him, another purple bloom in her fingers. "Your sister is a remarkable woman."

"Yes." He didn't know what else to say.

Tabitha smiled slightly. "I've always maintained that a woman should never trust a man who spends more on his clothes than she."

A bark of laughter escaped, surprising him.

"It's hard, isn't it? To think of Anne as a capable woman and not a child?"

The stem snapped in his fingers.

"I had a daughter once," Tabitha said suddenly. "I would like to think that, had she had the chance to grow up, she would have become a woman like Anne. Fearless. Strong." She ran a gnarled finger over the delicate petals of the bloom. "Trust that your sister will live her life not perfectly, but well."

August looked down at the crushed greenery in his hand and uncurled his fingers. "You sound like Miss Hayward."

"Mmm. Another strong woman. Though perhaps not as fearless."

August tossed the crumpled sprig onto the table. "Miss Hayward is the most fearless woman I know," he scoffed.

"Mmmm." Lady Tabitha picked up the broken stem and straightened it. "Not in matters of the heart, I think."

August stared, not knowing what to say.

Lady Tabitha tucked the sprig into the vase and approached August, pressing the last purple bloom into his hand. "Clara deserves a great love, Your Grace. But that is the single thing she cannot accomplish alone."

⁓

Dinner was an informal, raucous affair.

Someone had taken the liberty of placing a small, petrified creature, caught for eternity in its prison of rock, at each place setting before everyone arrived. This was not a dinner at which polite conversation was limited to the weather, the inconveniences of traffic around Bridge Street, and the latest and most shocking French fashion. Instead debate raged over the identification of each creature and theories about how and when it had lived. How creatures that didn't exist now had existed then. And of course there were the inevitable tangents that sprouted when evidence did not match accepted knowledge.

Anne had caught August's eye as she put forth her own ideas about the small creature she held in her hand. She grinned at him and then proceeded to draw him into the fray by asking for his opinion. He looked across the table and caught Clara watching. She held his eyes with a soft smile before looking away, as though she understood exactly what he was thinking.

For an instant August wished he could live in that moment forever. He wished he could capture it like the creatures that lay on the table encased in stone. Preserve everything just as it was. Because this feeling that was coursing through him, that was twisting all his insides, pressing the very breath from his lungs and making his chest ache, was truly like nothing he'd experienced. And he realized that he was happy, and that it had nothing to do with acquisitions or profits. It just... was.

He spent the rest of the meal simply listening. Watching as Clara encouraged her students to present opinions on a variety of topics, prompting them to fill in gaps in their reasoning with logic and evidence. That kind of clever guidance was something that August might have expected at a medical school or a philosophy class taught at Cambridge.

And Clara should be teaching at Cambridge, he thought fiercely. The more he observed, the more he understood that her skills went far beyond mere intelligence and competence. She was a truly gifted teacher, something that very few could say. Any school would be lucky to have her.

Starting with Haverhall.

August looked away, that chronic leaden guilt bursting his fragile bubble of happiness. He was taking that away from her.

No, he forcibly reminded himself, he had simply bought a property. A very lucrative property that he'd wanted for years. Clara, with all her skill and ability, would easily find another position with another girls' school. She was simply too good at what she did not to. People faced changed circumstances all the time, and they adapted. Moved on. Thrived. He knew that better than anyone.

And perhaps, if she would allow him, August could even help her do just that. A title like his could open a great number of doors, he had discovered. This could be a great opportunity for her, even if she didn't know it yet. Yes, he decided, he would quietly do everything he could, even if she refused his help. Especially if she refused his help.

That decision should have assuaged his guilt, but it didn't. Not entirely. Instead August was left doubting himself and his motivations and his ambitions in a way he never had before. If he thought he'd felt adrift before, he was well and truly lost now.

He didn't return to the dower house after dinner. Instead he slipped into the library on the pretense of finding something to read should anyone ask, but he was met only with a silent room. He discarded his coat, chose a book from the shelves at random, not even looking at the title, and sat in one of the wide leather chairs that flanked the massive hearth. He should go, he knew, but he couldn't bring himself to leave. Couldn't bring himself to return to more empty rooms, devoid of the laughter and happiness that had surrounded him here.

He wasn't sure how long he had sat silently in the library, lost in his thoughts, but the house grew dark and quiet around him. The single candle that he'd brought with him into the library had burned down to almost nothing and now flickered and threatened to extinguish altogether.

"*The Mirror of the Graces, or The English Lady's Costume*," a voice beside him said. "Are you reading that for research or is it a new business venture you're planning?"

August jerked upright, the book that had been left forgotten on his lap crashing to the floor. "You could make a man's heart stop doing that," he accused, his pulse proving that his was still working just fine.

"Mmmm." Clara retrieved the book from the floor and perched herself on the edge of the chair. It was all August could do not to simply reach for her and draw her into his lap.

His heart was still pounding, but for a different reason entirely now.

"What are you doing in here?" he asked, looking up at her. The tiny pool of light his struggling candle afforded put her features into shadow and made her expression difficult to read.

"I saw you come in earlier. The better question is, What are you still doing here?" she responded.

"Waiting for you." It wasn't something he'd intended to say, but he recognized it for the truth that it was.

"Mmm." She paused. "Will you be returning to London with Mr. Down tomorrow?"

August hesitated. He should. There was no reason for him to stay. Anne didn't need him here. His report to Rivers was complete. There would be any number of things demanding his attention in London. And being in the city certainly had the added advantage of immediate and direct access to information from the docks. There was no logical justification for lingering here. But then, when it came to Clara Hayward, logic was in short supply.

"Maybe," he finally settled on.

Clara was silent for a long minute. Then she rose, setting the book aside, and he could hear her soft footfalls as she crossed the room. It was like a physical pain, her departure. He wanted to call her back, but he couldn't seem to make his voice work.

"Clara?" he finally asked.

There was a sound then. The soft snick of a lock sliding into place. He remained frozen, his hands wrapped around the arms of the chair.

The candle was suddenly snuffed out with a sigh and a spiral of smoke.

He felt her hand on his neck first, the softest of touches as she came around the back of his chair. Her fingers caressed his cheek. "You were quiet at dinner," she said.

"You were extraordinary at dinner," he replied.

"Thank you. Though your flattery will not distract me. That's my trick, remember?"

He reached up and caught her hand. "God, I've missed you."

He felt the brush of her hair at his cheek before he felt the soft press of her lips on his skin. "And I you."

"I wanted to come to you."

"Why didn't you?"

"I don't know." That at least was the truth. He didn't have an answer.

Just as he didn't have an answer for why he still hadn't been completely honest with her about Haverhall, other than that she hadn't been honest with him either. Which was no excuse at all. The truth of the matter was that he didn't recognize himself any longer. Every vow he'd made to himself, every driving ambition he'd pursued with a single-minded determination sat uncomfortably on his skin now. His old self didn't seem to fit quite right.

Clara pressed another kiss to the hollow behind his ear. "What's bothering you?"

August closed his eyes, letting his head tip back. "I think Anne is in love with my man of business." It was the coward's way out of that question.

"I agree," Clara murmured, pulling her hand from his and letting her fingers slide through his hair, smoothing it back from his temples in a hypnotic rhythm. "And he is very much in love with her. One doesn't need to sit through three chess games to see that." She paused. "Is he a good man?"

"The best," August groaned, and Clara laughed softly.

Her fingers were at his cravat and were deftly loosening the knot. "So what is bothering you, then?"

I think I'm in love with you.

It was there, a truth threatening to be freed. But he didn't want to be in love with Clara, because that made everything impossibly complicated and confusing and went against all the meticulous plans and preparations he'd so carefully put into place for his life.

"I don't know why I'm here anymore," he mumbled.

"Well, first, there was your pursuit of Strathmore Shipping. Unwanted, unsuccessful, but understandable, given what you do," Clara replied. "And then there was the requisite crawling around on your hands and knees spying on your sister. Probably best no one gave her a pistol earlier," she mused.

August chuckled, even as self-reproach stabbed at him. Because none of those reasons were the truth. Not really.

"Clara, there's something—"

"But then," Clara whispered, cutting him off, the knot of his cravat unraveling in her hands, "there was this." She pulled the linen away from his neck and pressed her mouth to his heated skin, her lips sending bolts of electricity straight through him.

He was hard instantly, his body straining for something he was starting to need the way he needed air. Straining for her. He reached back and caught her hand, pulling her around the side of the chair. He didn't care that he wasn't gentle. "I want you," he said thickly.

"Yes," she whispered.

⌒

Clara felt it the moment he changed.

There had been a strange air of unsettled...something

about him this night. Something unsure. Uncertain. Something that was not August Faulkner. But then he took her hand and all of that went away, his intention blindingly clear even in the darkness of the library. Which was good, because her intentions had also been clear from the moment she had left her rooms in search of him. Soon she would return to London. Soon whatever this was that existed between them would be over. But for now, she would not think on that.

August leaned forward, his hands finding her hips and tugging her toward him. He dragged her onto his lap, shoving her skirts up her legs so that she could straddle him on the wide chair. She lowered herself against him, feeling the hard ridge of his erection bulging through the fall of his trousers.

"Clara." His hips flexed, his hands tightening on her waist.

She angled her own hips just slightly. Just enough to send scalding pulses of pleasure tearing through her. She rocked against him, unable to help herself.

His hands slipped up and caught her face, forcing her head down. He found her mouth with his, stroking with his tongue, his teeth scraping her lips.

Clara wrapped her arms around his neck, her breasts crushed against his chest. August dropped his mouth from hers, and his tongue played over the column of her neck, into the hollow beneath her jaw. "Undo my trousers," he ordered, his breath hot against her skin, his teeth pulling at the soft flesh of her earlobe.

Clara shuddered. She unwound her arms and pushed herself a little higher on her knees, sliding her hands between them. She worked the buttons, taking her time, letting her fingers caress his cock.

"Witch," he hissed.

Clara leaned forward and set her lips to the side of his neck. The tendons beneath his skin were corded and straining, and Clara traced them with her tongue.

"You don't know what you do to me," he groaned.

"I have an idea." The last button slipped free, and she pushed the fabric aside, allowing his erection to surge free.

August hissed again as she took him in her palm, running her fingers over the head and down his shaft, cupping his balls. He groaned again, his breathing becoming ragged. Lust raced through her veins at the sound. God, this man aroused her like no other. He made her feel all-powerful and utterly vulnerable all at once. A devastating combination of emotion that left her feeling drunk and dizzy.

His hands left her face to slide over her shoulders, finding the edge of her bodice and yanking it down. Her breasts spilled into the cool night air, heavy and tight with need. He covered them almost instantly with his palms and fingers, and every one of his touches sent new spirals of pleasure swirling deep within her. Her inner muscles clenched, and dampness pooled hot and slick between her legs.

He took her nipple in his mouth, and Clara whimpered, her hand tightening on his shaft.

"Jesus, Clara." His thighs were like rock beneath her. "I need to be inside you."

"Soon."

"Now." His hands dropped to her waist, his fingers digging into the flesh at her hips as he urged her down.

She allowed herself to sink lower, her hand still stroking the length of him. Very slowly she guided the head of his cock to her entrance, letting it slide through her wetness. His hips bucked, and he made a rough, desperate sound. She closed her eyes and sank down on him, letting him fill and stretch her, spasms of pleasure already flickering through her at the friction.

"Oh God, Clara, yes," August managed through clenched teeth.

She rocked her hips, feeling him slide deep within. A hunger slammed through her, so intense it stole her breath. This was what she wanted. Him. Here, just like this, deep within her where he was hers.

He was hers.

His hips thrust up and back. Clara grasped his arms, feeling his biceps flex through the thin fabric of his shirt. Beneath her touch, his body trembled, shaking with restraint.

"Don't," she whispered hoarsely, finding his lips with hers in the darkness. "Don't hold back."

He caught her lower lip, his teeth tugging as he thrust again, and she rocked her hips in time. His strokes became faster and harder, and Clara bore down on that pressure, feeling the beginnings of her release building within her.

"Harder," she begged.

He tore his mouth from hers, his head buried in her neck, his body straining as he pumped into her. "Clara," he gasped, "we have to stop. I can't—"

"You can," she said hoarsely. "I want you to come inside me, August."

He faltered, though she could feel him still hard and throbbing deep within her. "Clara—"

"Trust me," she said against his ear, wrapping her arms around his neck again. "Take me."

He made a tortured noise and surged up and into her, thrusting with hard, deliberate strokes. She hung on to him, closing her eyes, letting the waves of unrelenting pleasure build. They came, more quickly now, until they crested with a sudden explosion, sending fiery sparks ripping through her as she bore down on the tidal wave of ecstasy. Brilliant spots of white light danced behind her lids, and she might have cried out.

August was panting, and she felt his cock pulse within her, and then he drove up into her with a shout, holding her tight against him as he jerked in the throes of his own pleasure. She collapsed against him, her head on his shoulder, her own breath coming in heaving gasps. She made no effort to move, wanting to keep him with her just a moment longer.

It was long minutes before she felt him stir under her, his hand coming to stroke her hair where it had tumbled over her back. "You were quite extraordinary after dinner too," he said, his voice low against her ear.

Her fingers played with the collar of his shirt. "We were extraordinary."

"I can't— You are— This is..." He stalled.

"Yes," she agreed. If she'd had to put the last moments into words, she wouldn't have done any better. If she'd had to put their entire time together into words, she wouldn't have done any better.

"I've never come inside a woman," he said after a moment of silence. "I don't—"

"There is more than one way to be responsible," she said, "if that's what you were worried about."

He stilled. "Yes," he said after a beat of hesitation.

"A pessary, soaked in an infusion and placed before—"

August pulled back to stare at her. "You came down here to seduce me."

"I did." Clara ran a finger over the shape of his lips. "I hope you are not—"

"Don't you dare ask me if I am shocked. Or if I disapprove. Or if I found any of this to be unexpected."

"Very well." Clara grinned. "How did I do?"

August's head fell back on the chair, and he chuckled, the sound rumbling through him. "You almost killed me. And no, I don't disapprove. I'm hoping you'll try it again."

Clara leaned forward and kissed him, a slow, languid kiss. "I hope so too." She rested her head on his shoulder, silent for a moment. "Will you stay?" she asked.

"I'd prefer to take this somewhere with a real bed, but if you insist, I won't move. Not sure if I can, anyway." His hand was stroking her hair again.

"No." She listened to the steady thump of his heart beneath her ear. "Will you stay in Dover? For the time left before we return to London?"

August's hand paused, and she felt his fingers slide against her scalp. His other arm wrapped around her back, and he pulled her even more tightly against him.

"Yes," he whispered.

Chapter 19

T he ships are missing."

As the weeks had passed, Clara had known she had to be prepared for the very real possibility, but that hadn't made it easier to hear. Her brother was sitting in one of the embroidered library chairs, his head in his hands and utter exhaustion etched into his face. The rays from the setting sun were slanting through the windows and spilling across the fine rugs, their golden color seemingly mocking in its splendor.

Rose got up from where she had been sitting and went to a tall window to run her hand down the edge of the velvet curtain, staring out onto the sun-washed grounds. "How do you know that?"

Harland reached into his coat and pulled out a crinkled, folded paper. He read it again, as though he hoped to discover something different within, before he tossed it on the small table beside him. It missed and fluttered to the floor, and he made no effort to pick it up. "There are reports from other vessels that have come in of unusually stormy weather. Our ships could be a thousand miles off course or at the bottom of the Atlantic for all we know. We need to make a decision."

"I think we're past that," Rose said quietly. "We all knew it might come to this. We need more money, and there's no more to be had. We're out of options."

"I might be able to—" Harland stopped.

"To do what?" Clara prompted.

Her brother shook his head. "Never mind. Yes, we're out of options. Save one, of course. Sell a share of Strathmore Shipping."

Clara took a deep breath. "That's not true."

Harland pinched the bridge of his nose with his fingers. "You have a buried treasure stashed somewhere nearby that you didn't tell us about?" His attempt at humor echoed hollowly.

"I could ask His Grace for a loan."

Rose turned from the window, and Harland's head snapped up. "I beg your pardon?" her brother said into the silence.

"I could ask Holloway for a loan." She held up her hand at Harland's expression. "Just a loan. Not a share in the company, but a short-term loan until our ships return."

"At what price?" Harland demanded.

"What do you mean?"

"The Duke of Holloway is not known for his charity," he said darkly. "You might as well sell him the entire company right now. If we offer a share of the company to someone looking for a simple investment, but who is not interested in swallowing the entire business whole, we will still retain control. We will still have the ability to make our own decisions, control our future. If Holloway covers our debt, he will take away that control. Maybe not at the beginning, but eventually. The second we lose a load of cargo to bad weather or bad luck, the second we default on a loan payment, we've lost. The duke will annex Strathmore Shipping into his own empire without even blinking. He's made his desire to do so very clear already."

Clara winced. "But maybe he would consider—"

"If you think he'd be more forgiving based on sentimental reasons, or because he has a soft spot for you because you were his sister's headmistress, think again. Better yet, ask Walter Merrill, who lost the Silver Swan to him."

"You make him sound so...mercenary," Clara said.

"Because he is. Because he's had to be," Harland replied wearily. "If he thought there was even a chance that he could take advantage of our circumstances, he would do so with no hesitation. Not because he is cruel, but because he is a shrewd businessman and the interests of his family will always take precedence over the interests of anyone else. No matter what."

Deep down Clara knew that Harland was right. It didn't mean that she didn't hate it.

"Promise me you will not talk of this with Holloway," Harland said. "Promise me that you will keep him out of this."

"I promise," Clara mumbled. She stared sightlessly at the rows of books towering silently around and above her. The sacrifice of Haverhall hadn't been enough in the end, and it made her want to scream with frustration and unhappiness. "I should never have sold it," she mumbled.

"What?" Harland asked.

"I should never have sold Haverhall. Because it was for nothing."

"Not nothing," Harland said fiercely. "Without that money

we wouldn't have a ship at sea, let alone two. We would have had no chance at all of fixing this." He suddenly reached into his coat and pulled out a second letter. "This was also waiting with the post."

"What is it?" Clara asked despondently.

"A notice from the solicitor that the new owner of Haverhall has expressed his willingness to allow the school to operate as per usual for a full year. You will not be required to vacate the premises unless, of course, you wish to."

Clara stared at him. "Why would he do that?"

Harland shrugged. "Probably because you are already a convenient tenant he can collect a rent from? Or because it suits his purposes to have the buildings occupied?"

Rose had come to stand closer to Harland. "But if that's the case, the fall term's tuition—"

"Still won't be enough," Harland told them heavily.

A dismal silence fell.

"We'll fix this," Harland said into the silence. "Together. Haywards always find a way."

Clara nodded. Harland was right. No one had died. Her family was still together, safe and healthy. They were not destitute, nor would they be forced onto the streets. They would be able to afford rooms, food to eat, coal to keep them warm.

"Whom will you ask?" It was Rose's question. "To invest?"

Harland looked away. "Leave that to me. The Duke of Holloway is not the only wealthy man in London who might be counted on for discretion. I had hoped never to have to do this, but we no longer have a choice."

It had been her hair that had first caught his attention.

It whipped behind her in the wind, and the sinking sun set fire to it, sending flames of dark red streaming behind her. August had been on his way home from Dover, along the worn road that skirted past the castle, when he'd seen Clara trudging up the incline toward the small church that sat in its shadow. He hesitated before he reined his mare toward her, urging the horse into a canter as it surged up the hill.

The church grounds were deserted at this time of evening, and August dismounted, leaving his horse grazing in the long light. She hadn't gone into the church but was standing against the ancient Roman lighthouse that flanked it, staring out in the direction of the sea. She had her arms wrapped around herself, her expression distant and drawn.

He knew why.

He'd been in Dover to collect his correspondence, including a letter from London that the Strathmore ships still hadn't come in. Harland Hayward had finally been backed into a corner, and August had already shown him the perfect way out. He would approach the baron again once they were back in London. August's purchase of Strathmore Shipping—or, at the very least, a significant share of it—would get him what he wanted and also ensure that Clara and her family would be taken care of.

He should have felt exceedingly pleased. Euphoric even, because this was what he lived for. The culmination of diligence, logic, timing, patience, and a little bit of luck. Yet this victory was strangely hollow.

August covered the rest of the distance with feet that felt heavy and sluggish. He came to stand beside her, gazing out in the same direction. Clara didn't look at him, didn't give him any indication that she was even aware of his company. Presently she pushed herself off the wall and circled the lighthouse, then slipped inside it through a darkened entry. August followed, letting his eyes adjust to the dim light.

"Why do you think they built this?" she asked.

"Who?"

"The Romans." She gestured to the walls around her. "Why did they spend centuries fighting? Why invest so much blood and effort to build something that, in the end, they simply abandoned?" Clara didn't move but stayed as she was, leaning back against the rough wall, her head tipped up to the clouds far above, visible through the round opening at the top.

August looked up at the swirl of scarlet-and-tangerine clouds reflecting the setting sun against a darkening sky. For a moment he could almost imagine the light was from the flame that would have burned centuries ago, guiding sailors home safely.

"I would suggest that the men who built this lighthouse had no intention of abandoning it." He scuffed his boot in the dirt scattered across the floor, scattering a small collection of stubborn, light-starved weeds. "I suspect that they knew they were building something greater than themselves. Something that would survive long after they were gone."

The wind was whistling through the openings set above their heads in the circular structure, and it tugged at the hem of Clara's skirts and the curl that was forever escaping. She shoved it back behind her ear. "Do you think greed was Rome's ultimate downfall?" she asked. "If they had stopped sooner in their quest to take over every corner of the world and had been happy with what they'd already conquered, would they still be here?"

"Perhaps *greed* is the wrong word. *Ambition*, maybe. Men will always want more," August said, his voice echoing against the circular wall. "More land, more wealth, more control, more security."

"I think my father would have said the same thing." She sounded bitter. "Both of you would have made good Romans."

"How so?"

"Enough is never enough. You told me that once. My father, I think, believed that too. I just…" She shook her head. "I just hope that…ambition ends better for you than it did for the Romans." *And my father*, he heard her add silently. Because August knew she was speaking of her father's failed ambitions and the mess he'd landed his children in.

"Clara…" He stopped, unsure what he wanted to say. The guilt was starting to overwhelm his resolve. He couldn't tell her. He couldn't tell her that he had bought the legacy that her mother had left to her and, after this year, would raze it to the ground. He couldn't tell her that that purchase had been what had led him to pry into her life and then take very deliberate steps to capitalize on her family's misfortune. He couldn't tell her any of that without losing her forever.

In his old life, such steps had made him clever and pragmatic. Yet standing here, in an ancient lighthouse with a woman who had illuminated his world, he didn't feel clever and pragmatic. He felt utterly wretched. His moment of triumph had somehow become a moment of failure.

"Tell me what's wrong," he said. He couldn't tell her what he had already done. But he could undo this, maybe, without losing her. Without risking her ever discovering what he had done. "I can help."

She shook her head. "No, you can't."

"I can. Is it money that you need?" The words tumbled from him in a desperate rush. "Because whatever you need is yours."

Clara had gone completely still, her eyes narrowed. "No," she said after a long minute. "I can't... We can't..."

August wanted to shake her. He couldn't reveal what he'd known all along without exposing his hand. He needed her to tell him the truth. He needed her to ask him for help.

He needed her to trust him.

"There's nothing you can do," she said.

Frustration skewered all the foreign emotions that were making it hard for him to think straight. "Horseshit," he said loudly, his voice bouncing around him. "You won't accept my help. Why?"

"Because this is a family matter and doesn't concern you," she said. "And you are not family."

That hurt more than it ever should have. "Then what am I?" he demanded. "A friend? A lover? A mere distraction?"

"You were never a mere distraction."

"Yet you keep me at a distance. You won't let me in. Just like everyone else."

"What's that supposed to mean?"

"Why are you still alone?" he demanded.

"Because being alone gives me my freedom. My independence."

He took two steps closer to her. "Independence and freedom don't mean you have to do everything by yourself. They don't mean you have to do everything alone. True freedom and independence allow you to recognize when you need help. And give you the ability to ask for it. Know when to ask for help, Clara."

She looked away. "You're speaking of your father."

"No. I'm speaking of you. You think I am the only man in the world who sees you and admires you for who you really are? You think I am the only man who would never take away that freedom and independence you speak of should he find himself lucky enough to have you? You, Clara Hayward, have become very good at using all the rules of society, the very rules you profess to despise, to keep yourself apart. And I can't figure out why."

She was staring at him, her chest rising and falling rapidly. "You can't figure out why?" she said in a strangled voice. "Why don't we start with your friends? The ones who dared you to dance with me. What did they call me that night?"

"They were never my friends, and you know it," August snapped. "They were the companions of a man who didn't know enough to call himself such. Who erroneously thought that he could regain what status his family had lost in society by gaining their approval."

"You never answered my question."

"Because their words don't bear repeating."

"How about if I do it for you? Unnatural. Bluestocking. Queer. Wallflower." She stopped. "How am I doing so far? Because even if those weren't the adjectives your friends used that night, I'd heard them all before. Many times."

"Clara—"

"How about Mathias Stilton, then?" she said, her voice ragged. "A man I had actually believed to be a friend, someone who had not weighed the value of my dowry against my intellect. But he too reminded me that no one wanted me then, and no one wants me now."

"I want you," he snarled.

"But not forever," she replied sadly.

August could feel his fingernails digging into the flesh of his palms. He'd never considered forever. But now that the word was out there, shimmering just beyond him, it was enough to make him reel.

"I'm tired of it all, August," she said, and her voice was

barely a whisper. "Maybe I grew tired of it long ago, if truth be told. It is far easier just to keep myself apart. Where there are no motivations to evaluate, no disappointments to endure. I have the freedom to seek my own happiness without depending on anyone else. Experience has taught me I am better served expecting the worst."

"That doesn't sound like the woman who once spoke of changing the world."

Clara smiled sadly. "I didn't say I would ever stop hoping for the best."

August reached out and smoothed her hair back from her face. "Don't ever stop. You deserve to be happy, Clara."

"I am happy," she said. "With you."

August made a muffled noise, and then he wrapped his arms around her and pulled her against him, crushing his mouth to hers. Clara melted into him instantly, wanting to lose herself in him. Wanting to lose herself in everything that was this man. She let him kiss her, let him set the pace, let him wipe her mind clean of everything that was not August Faulkner.

He swept his tongue across the seam of her lips, and she opened willingly, letting him plunder what had always been his. This kiss, more than any of their kisses, tasted bittersweet. Tasted of what-ifs and lost opportunities and desire realized too late. Standing in a ruined lighthouse, the sky blazing above their heads, it tasted of goodbye.

"Tell me what I am to you, Clara," August whispered against her mouth.

Everything, she wanted to cry. Everything that she had always dreamed of from the very first second he had taken her hand in a reckless waltz. And maybe that was why she had never entertained another man seriously. Maybe, somewhere deep down, she had given her heart away on a dance floor long ago.

But she didn't think, for one second, that she was his everything. She knew better than that. There had been no professions of love, no declarations of undying devotion. She had his respect and his admiration, to be sure, but not his heart.

She closed her eyes. "A friend. A lover." He had never pretended to be anything more.

"Yes. Always." August traced the outline of her lips with his thumb. "And that is not good enough to let me in?"

Clara opened her eyes. Not for this. Not if there was ever a hope of their remaining friends or, even more unlikely, lovers when they returned to London. Not if she was to keep her promise to Harland and keep the Duke of Holloway out of the Strathmore family's affairs.

"I want us to stay friends," she said. "So please don't ask me again."

August's hand fell to his side, and for the briefest of moments, he looked utterly bereft. "I need to tell you…" He stopped again, anguished frustration stamped all over his face. "I can't…" The words died on his lips.

Clara went up on her toes and pressed her lips to his. "Tomorrow I return to London with my students. And I understand that everything will change. But know this, August Faulkner. No matter what happens tomorrow, or a year from now, or another decade from now, I will always treasure the friendship that exists between us. I will always treasure what we were to each other here." Her throat had thickened, and it was all she could do to keep her voice steady. "And if you are ever dared to dance with me again, I promise I will always say yes."

Chapter 20

Outwardly, Clara's return to London had been peculiarly ordinary.

Haverhall continued to operate as it always had, which meant that the routine of Clara's life remained unchanged for the time being. The only difference being that all financial transactions and communications were handled through a solicitor. Harland had secured an investor, though he was tight-lipped about his identity, citing his desire to remain anonymous. It had been enough to clear them from debt and see the remaining ships refitted and crewed.

They had also received a letter from Boston, written by the captain of one of their missing ships, stating that both had taken damage on the way there, but that the damage had been minor, the cargo unharmed, and that they would be departing for England within a fortnight. They were expected back before the winter weather set in. The ships were too late to keep Strathmore Shipping intact, but Clara knew she should be thankful for small mercies.

The last days of summer had faded into fall, and Clara had started the term as she always had, Haverhall full of young London ladies anxious to partake in the usual curriculum. She was determined to enjoy whatever time she had left and make the most of it. She wasn't entirely sure what she would do when the year was over, but the success of this year's summer program was still fresh in her mind. Perhaps Haverhall would simply become a summer program, the classes small but the students still unique.

But despite her determination to stay positive and not wallow, she recognized that she had been different since she returned from Dover. The things that she used to find joy in seemed grayer, as if the color had been leached from them. She wasn't sure if that was because the future was more uncertain or because she was missing August with an intensity so great it hurt. Missing turning to him to share something. Missing his conversation, his laughter, his touch. Missing everything about him. She had thought she had been prepared to relegate their time together to memory. As she had the waltz they had once shared in their youth.

Except it hadn't been that easy.

She had visited the museum since her return and had stood in front of the relief of the Lapith and centaur, lost in her memories and her thoughts. Stood for so long, in fact, that one of the attendants had approached her and asked if she was unwell. She had startled, her cheeks flushing, wondering if perhaps she was. August hadn't called at Haverhall, nor had their paths crossed anywhere in London. Distance was easier, she supposed, in some respects. It would be infinitely harder to have him close and untouchable. And it would make the regrets that continued to linger even harder to ignore.

So when the message from the Holloway residence had arrived, Clara's reaction had been instantaneous and intense, turmoil reigning supreme. The butterflies stormed back, banging against the inside of her rib cage. Longing pooled hard and fast, deep within her, even as her mind intoned caution and curbed hope. She opened the neatly sealed missive and realized her hands were shaking. She closed her eyes and took a deep breath, feeling foolish.

The note was clear and concise, just as she imagined all correspondence from the Duke of Holloway to be. It asked her to attend him at her earliest convenience. There was no hint as to what he wished to see her about. No statements that he missed her, no declarations of affection. No suggestions that anyone could ever misconstrue as anything other than cool and impersonal. But it didn't matter.

Because the regrets that lingered had told her everything that she needed to know. Those festering regrets had made it clear that she had fallen utterly in love with the Duke of Holloway. She should have told him that in Dover. She shouldn't have said goodbye without telling him how she really felt. She should have told him everything.

And now, it would seem, she had the perfect opportunity to rid herself of those regrets. She didn't know what it would bring, but she was done hiding behind excuses.

⁓

The Holloway residence was a town house located in an older, established neighborhood, a location still distinguished and elegant, if not new. It would seem the duke had bypassed the more popular addresses, the wildly expensive squares where prices reflected nothing except the novelty of the residences. Clara almost caught herself smiling. August

Faulkner would pay for realized luxury but he would not pay for affected vanity. How very like him.

The interior of his home was exactly as she had expected as well. The finishings were fine but practical. The furniture was well made but not extravagant. The entire place exuded wealth but not excess. Clara was shown not into a drawing room but into a cavernous study by a quietly efficient butler. Tall bookshelves lined all the walls except the one that boasted a lit hearth, the fire lending light and a welcome warmth to the room. A heavy, masculine-looking desk sat just to the right of the hearth, its surface covered with papers. The entire room, in fact, had a very masculine feel to it, except, oddly enough, the second desk that sat just to the left. This desk looked new, and it was made of carved rosewood. It was something that, despite its practical, functional construction, looked as if it would be more at home in a lady's morning room.

Clara wandered over to it, taking in the neat piles of ledgers, an assortment of what looked like receipts, a small collection of writing tools, and lists in a familiar feminine handwriting. Anne's desk, then, by all appearances. Clara wondered if it had always been here. Or perhaps August had given Anne back her sense of purpose. Either way, Clara was intrigued.

There was no sign of the duke, or Anne for that matter, and Clara wandered over toward the hearth and August's desk. She knew she should return to the long sofa on which the butler had indicated she should wait. But the emotion and restless energy humming through her made it impossible to sit still. She didn't know what August had summoned her for. Didn't know what he wanted from her. But she was trying to remain composed. Trying not to hope.

She stood near the side of his desk, staring at the glowing

coals. A loud crash somewhere outside the study made her jump and whirl, her hip knocking a long, rolled sheaf of papers off the side of the desk. Clara put a hand to her chest, feeling foolish at the nervous tension that had her strung so tight. A maid hurried by the open door in the direction of the disturbance, a broom and pail in her hand, and Clara bent to retrieve the roll of paper from the floor. As she did, her eyes fell on the top corner, a word written in ink that had bled through to the back of the top sheet, easily distinguishable. *Haverhall.*

She stood, the heavy roll still in her hand, and gently placed it back on the desk as if it were a viper. The rolled sheets were huge, the sort that architects and shipbuilders used. Clara poked at them, even as something in her mind was screaming at her to turn around and leave. To turn around and walk away and not look at what was in front of her. Once she saw what was there, it would be impossible to unsee it. But it was already too late.

She took a deep breath and flicked the edge with her fingers, and the paper rolled out with a soft thump as it reached the end of his desk.

"Haverhall" was written in small letters along the bottom of the paper, followed by "Wilds and Busby, Brighton. July, 1819." She understood exactly what she was looking at even as she understood that it seemed August had solicited the services of architects and planners long before he had ever ridden for Dover. She swallowed with difficulty, her throat suddenly constricted and a feeling of sick certainty rising in her stomach. She smoothed the wide documents flat with her palm.

Across the paper she saw a drawing of the property that she knew like the back of her hand. The building that housed the school, the old carriage house and mews. The gardens

that spilled out from behind her office and the pond near the
northwest corner where the land dipped and the oaks grew
plentiful and tall. The drive that curved graciously in front of
the school and straightened toward the road, lined with ma-
jestic beeches.

Clara pushed the top sheet away, and underneath she
found another drawing of Haverhall. Only this one she
didn't recognize. Where the school now was, rows of town
houses swept gracefully over the space, forming perfectly
ordered squares. The carriage house and mews had also vanished, replaced with a central garden that was beautifully
symmetrical and soothing, walking paths surrounding what
looked like a fountain. The pond was gone too, more town
houses wrapping around another paved square, a wide avenue marching across the center. It was a stunning plan, a
work of art rich in detail and elegance. And it shattered her
heart into a million pieces.

Clara didn't need to be an architect or a banker to understand that the development staring at her in stark lines and
neat measurements would be worth a king's ransom. Perhaps not now, perhaps not even in five years, but soon. The
stench of money fairly bled from the very lines of the drawings, and even as gutted as she felt, she could recognize
the brilliance of the plan. Developing Haverhall would make
August richer than God.

*There is no amount of money that will ever make my
brother feel worthy. Or safe.*

She heard Anne's words echo in her mind, though Clara
had not truly heard her then. But with the proof staring her in
the face, she heard her clearly now. She had wanted so badly
to believe in him. He had been forced into honesty about his
intentions toward Strathmore Shipping, but given the choice,
he hadn't been honest about this. And he had known what

Haverhall meant to her. But in the end it hadn't mattered. She hadn't mattered. Not enough.

She would never be enough for a man like him.

"Clara?" It was his voice from the doorway. "What are you doing in here?"

Looking at the truth of us, she wanted to say.

"Just taking a look at the plans for Haverhall," she managed, and the steadiness of her voice surprised her. Because if there was ever a time that she might wish to act like a hysterical, weepy female, now would be it. "Imagine my surprise to discover that you are the owner of a school." She heard his boots on the floor as he crossed the room, though she didn't turn around. "I received your summons," she continued. "Was it this that you wanted me to see?"

"No."

"What does your sister think of these plans?"

He came to a stop behind her. "Anne doesn't know."

"Ah. You really are good at subterfuge, Your Grace. Have you considered a career as a spy? The navy, I'm sure, would be happy to have you."

"Clara—"

"Does anyone know?" Not that it mattered, really. Eventually everyone would. Legacies died, priorities shifted, and progress ruled. The rational part of her knew that if August hadn't bought this land, it would have been bought by another who would have eventually seen what August had. But another hadn't kissed her on a stone fence with a sunset at their backs. Another hadn't danced with her in a studio before he made love to her. Another hadn't made her believe that she might have what she had long ago thought lost to her.

She became aware that August had moved and was now standing in front of the desk beside her, staring down at the drawings.

"You weren't meant to see these," he said.

"Why not?" She would not cry. "They are remarkable."

"I had these ordered long before...us."

"Us." Clara made a rude noise, unable to help herself. "There was no us, Your Grace. There was, however, what you would probably call unexpected benefits from good business."

"No." He said it harshly. "The idea of Haverhall's potential came up long before I...before we..." He stopped. "What happened with us, what we are, what we have become, has nothing to do with any of this."

Clara blew out a shaky breath. "I think I've already heard that line before." She needed to leave. Get out of here, away from him, and recover her composure before she did or said something that she would regret. That she wouldn't be able to find an excuse for. Because they hadn't become anything. Not anything lasting, anyway, which was exactly what could be said for her school. All good things must come to an end at some point, and this was simply one of them.

"When will you start?" she asked, still feeling numb. "Developing the land?"

"I don't know," he said. "I don't know if I...Not until you..."

"Until I what? Find a position as a governess in a wealthy house?" She flinched, knowing she sounded bitter and petty. And she was better than that. "That's why you gave me a year's grace, isn't it?"

"A governess?" August made a rude noise. "You are a brilliant teacher, Clara. There are many schools that would be lucky to have you," he growled. "Your brother has somehow managed to set Strathmore Shipping to rights with no help from me. The fortune that your father lost will soon be recovered and then some. You will be able to do anything."

He was right, she knew. Even if it felt like a betrayal now, she needed to keep it in perspective. She needed to think like August. Needed to believe that it was an opportunity, not a loss. The only loss here was that of her heart.

"I wish you had told me about this," she whispered.

"I tried," he said. "I tried to tell you."

"For a man known for his ruthlessness and determination, you didn't try very hard, then."

"I couldn't."

"Why?"

"Why?" He raked a hand through his hair. "Because then you would have looked at me the way you're looking at me right now. I would have been only the man who had stolen your legacy from you."

"Perhaps," Clara said sadly. "But I would like to think I would have respected you for it. I would have liked to have believed that you trusted me—that you believed in me enough to know that I would have understood why you were doing what you did."

"Yet you wouldn't trust me with the truth," he said quietly. "You didn't trust me enough to ask for help."

"I suppose I didn't," Clara whispered sadly. "And now I can't say that I was wrong. I thought that I might have been worth at least something. That *we* were worth at least something, but you've made it very clear that you will never put anyone before your need to have more."

"That's not true. Clara, I don't want to lose you," he said.

"You can't lose something that you never had. I am not something else to be acquired."

"Clara, I want us to—"

"There isn't an us, August. *Us* implies that we would have faced the difficult things together the same as we would have faced the things that were easy. There was a *you*, doing what you thought was right for yourself and your family, and there was a *me*, who did what I thought was right for my family." Clara took a shuddering breath and rolled the drawings up neatly. She stared down at them for a minute before she turned. "I wish you well, August. I know that this will be beautiful when it's done."

He was looking at her, those intense blue eyes conflicted. "Don't go. Not like this."

"Goodbye, Your Grace," Clara said, hanging on to her composure by the tiniest of threads. And then she fled.

Chapter 21

Hours later, it was Rose who found Clara in her office, staring miserably out the window at Haverhall's gardens, watching the first leaves fall and litter the ground.

"There you are," Rose said, coming in and flopping herself down on one of the chairs in a most unladylike manner. Her hands were still stained with paint, and the apron she wore to cover her skirts was similarly streaked. "I was watching for you, but I must have missed you coming back. Did you go to see Holloway?"

"I did."

"And?" Rose asked, leaning forward. "What did you think of his idea?"

Clara felt her jaw slacken, another spear of betrayal stabbing at her. "Jesus, Rose. You knew?"

Confusion spread over Rose's delicate features. "Knew what?"

"About his plans for Haverhall." It was bad enough Holloway had kept it from her, but Rose had too?

"What the hell are you talking about?" her sister demanded. "You're not making any sense."

Clara scrubbed at her eyes with her hands. So Rose didn't know. It should have made her feel better, but all she felt was empty. "The Duke of Holloway bought Haverhall."

Rose sat back with a thump. She was silent for a moment, and Clara couldn't quite determine what she was thinking based on her expression. "I see," she finally said.

"'I see'? That's all you have to say?" Clara was aware her voice had risen, but she didn't care. "He had architects draw up development plans for Haverhall months ago."

"What do you want me to say?" Rose asked. "I'm still saddened that we—that you—had to sell it. I'm not surprised Holloway, or someone with his sort of vision, bought it. But it helped save our family."

Clara did not need Rose's practicality and logic now. "He lied," Clara spit.

"About what?"

"About why he was in Dover."

Rose considered her for an unnerving moment. "I don't think so."

Clara stared at her. "You're defending him? You hate him, Rose. The Duke of Doxies and all that? Remember?"

Rose winced slightly. "I might have been a little hasty in judgment."

Clara gaped at her. "What?"

"I don't hate him. Especially since my sister is in love with him."

"I'm not in love with him." She didn't want to be in love with him. She could not be in love with him. Not after what he'd done.

"You're a terrible liar. That is why you're so upset right now. Not that he bought Haverhall, but because he bought it without telling you."

"No." Clara was shaking her head, anger and hurt boiling through her. "You were right about him, Rose, from the beginning. I was such a fool. He told me what I wanted to hear. He pretended to listen, pretended to agree with me, made me think he might...respect me."

"Stop." Rose brought her hand down on the desk with a smack.

Clara jumped and, with horror, realized that there were tears running down her cheeks.

"Just stop," Rose said, a little more gently this time. "You're wrong. The duke may have bought Haverhall, and yes, maybe he should have told you. But the rest...You're wrong about him." She sighed. "I don't know how he feels about you, though I think I have a good idea. But I know he listened, Clara. Very carefully. And he...respects you very much."

Clara wiped angrily at her eyes. "What August Faulkner respects is money. For him there will never be enough, and there is no room in his life for...anything that is not cold-blooded ambition. I was simply a means to an end—"

"Clara—"

"No, let me finish. I have no one to blame except myself. So if I'm upset, it is because I had delusions that I could change his priorities. Yet I knew who August Faulkner was. I knew where he came from and what drove him. People don't change."

"No, I don't suppose they do." Rose was examining the streaks of blue and red staining her fingers.

"You're not making me feel better," Clara mumbled. "You're supposed to be on my side here."

"Oh, I am." Rose reached behind her neck and untied her apron, then passed it to Clara. "Dry your eyes. There's something you need to see."

⁓

The building sat on the very southern edge of London, where the tentacles of the city hadn't yet engulfed the countryside completely.

The structure was solid and wide, three stories tall, and had the straight, clean lines that could be found in London only in new construction. It wasn't fancy by any stretch of the imagination, the walls a nondescript stone, the roof a dark slate, the wide front door painted an equally dark gray. Plain, buff-colored curtains hung in the rows of windows that lined each story at regular intervals, fluttering gently where a pane had been opened to allow in the autumn air. A huge chimney ran up the east side, and a kitchen garden sprawled away from the side door, the backs of women and the occasional youth bent over garden tools and baskets visible in the still-lush greenery. On the southwest side, poles had been driven into the ground and clotheslines strung up between them, an array of sheets and petticoats flapping in the sunshine. A handful of women were pulling dry clothes down and replacing them with wet garments, and Clara could hear their faint chatter.

Behind the main building a second structure sat, even more plain than the first but with large, long windows. It put Clara in mind of a small warehouse, the likeness heightened by the wagon sitting in front of it, loaded with long wrapped bales of what looked like fabric.

"What is this place?" she asked as she and Rose stood on the short, wide drive.

Her sister remained silent.

Clara narrowed her eyes as a group of children, the oldest not more than six or seven, ran through the maze of drying sheets toward a knotted rope tied to a low branch of a massive oak just beyond. "An inn?" she ventured.

"Sort of."

"A boardinghouse?"

"Sort of."

"How many guesses do I get before you save me from myself?"

Rose studied the toe of her boot, not even cracking a smile.

Clara turned her attention back to the scene before her, noticing for the first time that there seemed to be only women and children present. "There are no men here."

"No."

She blew out an exasperated breath. "No hints? A convent, then. Holloway's concubines and their offspring?"

Rose looked over at her, a strange expression on her face. "No. You don't really think—"

"Well, of course not, Rose. But I'm out of ideas."

"This place is…" Rose looked as if she was searching for the right words.

"This place is what?"

"Is Anne's birthday present."

Clara blinked. "I beg your pardon?"

"This place—it's called Brookside, and the Duke of Holloway plans to give it to Anne for her nineteenth birthday in a fortnight. The buildings, the land, and the responsibility of managing it."

"And what is it, exactly?" Clara asked quietly, a strange sensation starting to rise through her chest.

"It's a home. For families whose fathers or husbands are

in debtors' prison. It's a safe place for women and children to live until their…circumstances change."

The world suddenly seemed to have become muffled, as if it had faded around her sister and her words. Clara's throat thickened, and the backs of her eyes burned.

"The duke built it five years ago," Rose said quietly and deliberately. "The children have chores, and they are expected to work in the garden and the chicken coops and the goat sheds, but they learn reading and arithmetic here too. The women who live here are responsible for the upkeep. Those who do not work in the house work out back."

"Out back?" Clara managed.

Rose gestured to the large building at the rear. "They weave. Holloway imports raw product from India, and it's processed and woven here into book muslins, checked, striped, and sprigged muslins. He can, of course, sell those faster than he can have them made, and at a very competitive price and for a very tidy profit. He's also invested in and purchased some new loom technology that he believes will change the way cloth is produced, and the women and girls here are quick learners. He told me that foresight will only benefit his bottom line in ten years' time." Rose said it wryly, and Clara could almost hear the words coming from August himself. They would be defensive, as though he had to justify his actions.

"Oh." Clara was searching for words that would express what she was feeling right now. *Admiration* was too weak. *Approval* too inadequate.

"It's not a charity," Rose continued. "No one lives here for free. They work, and they work hard, and if anyone refuses to do their fair share, they are asked to leave. Everyone has a purpose here. It's a mutually beneficial arrangement."

Love. Love was what she felt. What she'd always feel.

Love for a perfectly imperfect man who had never apologized for who he was, ruthless ambition and all. Love for a man who had done something truly special. Who had taken it upon himself to make a tiny corner of the world a better place. She had told him once that she wanted to change the world just a little bit at a time. August Faulkner had already done that.

"How do you know all of this?" Clara asked numbly.

"He brought me out here yesterday. Asked if I would consider teaching art lessons here once a week. For the children, and maybe for any of the women who wanted to try." Rose was watching her. "He asked if I thought you might agree to teach here as well. Perhaps a few evenings a week. Arithmetic, reading, writing. He said you already know a student here."

"What?"

"A boy named Jonas? And his mother? They moved here from Dover at his urging. He said the boy didn't make a very good hotelier."

Clara pressed a hand to her lips, realizing that it was shaking. "He never told me about this place."

Rose cocked her head. "Would it have made a difference in how you felt about him?"

Clara shook her head, the truth inescapable. "No. I loved him already for who he was."

Rose smiled slightly. "I know."

"This just makes me want to cry."

"I'm all out of aprons, so pace yourself."

Clara laughed and hiccupped at the same time.

"This will make Anne so happy," Rose said, as both women watched the children on the rope swing shriek with laughter.

"Yes."

"What about you?" Rose asked.

"What about me?"

"I want to see you happy, Clara. You deserve it."

Clara looked down at her hands. "I love him. I've probably loved him since the first day I ever saw him. Which sounds absurd, I know. But I don't know where to go from here."

Rose leaned against Clara, linking an arm through hers. "I doubt he does either. You're both in uncharted territory, and I'm afraid I'm the last person who can offer you any guidance."

"You seem to be doing well so far," Clara sniffed.

"Perhaps."

"He's never promised me anything."

Rose gave her a long look. "And what have you promised him?"

Clara looked sightlessly out at the sheets swaying on the line. "Nothing." And there it was. Neither one of them had dared to take a leap of faith. Neither one had dared risk everything. Instead they had both retreated to what they knew. Loyalty to their families. Determination to handle whatever needed to be done. Alone.

"Good God, but you two deserve each other," Rose scoffed quietly. She sobered. "Just don't...turn away from him. Don't retreat. Your duke is not like the others."

"No. He's not." But she'd already turned away. She'd already retreated.

She wondered if it was already too late.

Chapter 22

It was just as well that Clara Hayward had never truly been in love before. Now that she had admitted it freely, now that it had been flushed from the dark, secret corners of her mind, it seemed to gain power with every minute that ticked by. It made logic difficult, and it made her emotions swing wildly between giddiness and terror. It had stolen her appetite and her ability to concentrate on a task for any amount of time.

She hadn't gotten much sleep that night, her sister's words and everything she had learned that day rolling through her mind incessantly. When dawn had crept around the edges of her curtains, she hadn't been any closer to knowing what she would say to August Faulkner. But she did know that she would say something. She would not turn away from this. She would take this leap of faith, and whether or not he would be there to catch her remained to be seen.

But she would not harbor any regrets. There would

be no excuses. And if the worst happened, if he turned from her, then she would at least have her answer. She would not spend another decade wondering what might have happened.

"Step and turn!"

The shout and stomp jarred her out of her musings, and she hastily returned her attention to her surroundings. She was in the middle of one of the dance classes that she always offered in the fall term at Haverhall. She had twenty young ladies with a collection of titles that read like a chapter in Debrett's, a London dance master, and a string quartet awaiting its cue, all arranged in Haverhall's small ballroom. The dance master was demonstrating the movements of a French waltz in the center of the room, counting loudly in time with his steps.

Clara turned her attention from the man and surreptitiously studied the girls. Some were watching the dance instructor, their lips moving in time with his count, their bodies swaying involuntarily as they followed his steps. Others were examining their fellow students with varying degrees of superciliousness, distrust, and judgment. Those were the ones whispering behind their hands the same way they would whisper behind their fans. Clara almost rolled her eyes.

Her gaze fell on the young lady standing slightly apart from the group. She was perhaps sixteen, with jet-black hair and pale-blue eyes. She was watching the entire scene with a look of bemused interest, as though she had discovered that she had the finest seat in a theater. Every once in a while she would produce a small notebook and the stub of a pencil from somewhere in the fabric of her voluminous skirts and jot something down. She caught Clara watching her and blushed, jamming her notebook back into the folds of her skirts and feigning interest in whatever the dance master was droning on about.

Clara smiled. She would be having a conversation with this young lady after class. Any young lady who had seemingly sewn pockets into her gown to conceal writing paraphernalia might just prove to be an excellent candidate for her summer school—

"Miss Hayward?"

The dance master was looking at her expectantly.

"I beg your pardon?" Clara said. There were a few giggles.

"I was wondering if you might care to demonstrate what a proper French waltz looks like to your students before they practice."

"Of course." She gave herself a mental shake and stepped forward.

The dance master took her hand in his cool one, and she stifled a sigh. Every waltz, for the rest of her life, would be a disappointment. The dance master held up his hand for the quartet, and there was a general shuffling as it prepared to play. He glanced back in its direction and dropped his hand for it to start.

Except it never did.

Instead there was a more pronounced shuffling, some frantic whispering, and then a flurry of giggles.

"Pardon my intrusion, but I believe that this dance belongs to me." The voice came from just behind her, and Clara froze.

The dance master's eyes widened slightly before they narrowed. "Excuse me, sir, but in case it had escaped your notice, you are interrupting a class. My class."

"My class," Clara corrected him abruptly. She pulled her hand free from the instructor's and turned very slowly to find August standing behind her, his hands clasped behind his back, his intense blue eyes fixed firmly on hers. His hair was a little windblown, as if he had just come in from a hard ride, and his clothing was simple and unadorned.

"Miss Hayward, if I may have the honor?" He straightened and held out a hand. "And keep in mind that I'm not taking no for an answer."

Her eyes flickered over his shoulder to where twenty young women were staring openly. Except one who was scribbling something frantically. She smiled.

"You may, Your Grace."

The dance master blanched and backed up, nearly tripping over his own feet. They both ignored him. Clara placed her hand in August's, and the warmth of his touch instantly sent heat skating across her skin and down her spine. She placed another hand on his shoulder, and he slid his over her waist to rest at the small of her back.

"You're going to scandalize my students," she murmured. She could feel her pulse pounding through her veins.

"We scandalized everyone the first time we did this ten years ago. Why stop now?" he replied, pulling her closer than was proper.

The quartet, which had hesitated, now started playing, and the first strains of music drifted through the air. August led her in the first steps of a dance that was so familiar, yet so breathtakingly new. She followed where he led, never breaking stride, never breaking eye contact. Their surroundings blurred and then faded altogether.

"I'm sorry, Clara," he whispered as they floated across the floor. "It was never my intention to hurt you."

"I know. I am sorry too," she said.

"For what? You did nothing."

"Exactly. I did nothing. I didn't trust you; I didn't ask you for help when I could have. I shut you out and tried to do everything by myself. And then, worse, standing in your library yesterday, I essentially demanded that you apologize for who you were. Something that I once accused you of doing to Anne, and for me to do it to you was unforgivable."

"I forgive you." He tightened his hand on hers. "You were in an impossible position."

"Not impossible. Just hard."

He was shaking his head. "It wasn't fair—"

"Life isn't fair," she whispered, moving her hand from his shoulder to touch his cheek. "You know that better than anyone." She paused as they turned, the music thrumming through her. "It's made us who and what we are, and I don't want anyone other than the man who stands before me now. I've never wanted anyone but you."

"Good," he whispered. "Because I'm not going anywhere."

"Don't ever change."

His lips twitched. "There might be room for a little improvement. Here and there."

Clara smiled. "I saw your gift to Anne," she said softly.

She felt August nearly miss a step. He danced on in silence for long seconds before he spoke again. "I hated what she was exposed to in Marshalsea," August mumbled. "The filth, the disease, the hopelessness. That's a hard thing to come back from."

"Yes," she whispered.

"Brookside is not a hotel exactly, but I think Anne will do an incredible job. Especially..."

"Especially because she understands."

"Yes. Did I do the right thing?" he asked in a voice so low she barely heard him.

Clara tried to find words but failed utterly.

She saw his jaw tighten. "You don't think I—"

Clara pressed her fingers over his lips. "You've done a beautiful thing," she whispered.

He gazed down at her, his hand coming up to wipe from her cheek a tear she hadn't even been aware she'd shed. "Thank you," he murmured. "But don't cry."

"I'm not crying. I'm just warming you up for Anne's reaction," she sniffled, her hand dropping to his chest.

August laughed, and she felt the vibrations through his chest where her hand rested. "I'll consider myself warned." He paused. "Rose told you about Brookside?"

"Yes." Clara smiled. "Don't look so surprised."

"I didn't think your sister held me in very high regard."

"Then you think wrong. Besides, Rose insists she could never hate a man her sister is desperately in love with."

August abruptly stopped dancing, and Clara stumbled into him.

"That was not very well done, Your Grace—"

She never finished what she was going to say, because his lips were on hers in the softest, most gentle kiss. She melted into him, not caring who was watching. Not caring if she scandalized the daughters of half the peerage or all of London. He pulled back, a peculiar expression on his face. "August," she whispered. At some point the quartet had ceased playing, and there was only silence all around them.

He reached into his coat pocket and pulled out what looked like a delicate piece of ribbon tied in a small circle. He grasped her hand and looked down at her, his chest rising and falling rapidly. "I should have done this ten years ago too," he said.

"Done what?"

He touched her face. "Danced with you. Discovered what you think of Lapiths. Spied on you from behind stone fences. Learned a thing or two about purpose. Fallen in love with you."

Clara tried to speak, but her throat had closed up.

August dropped to one knee and looked up at her. "You asked me once when enough is enough. You are my enough. You are my everything." August drew her hand into his and slid the tiny ribbon over her ring finger. "I love you, Clara."

She looked down at the ribbon and touched it with her other hand in confusion.

"This ribbon was tied around a deed to a parcel of land. This land has a small cottage in the back that someone told me is being used as an art studio, a pond that doesn't seem to have any fish in it, some gardens that are rather pretty in summer, and a building that is currently being used as a school." He tipped her chin up and found her eyes, the love that was coursing through her reflected in his own gaze. "I thought that it, more than pretty jewels or a flashy horse or a fine house, might make a good wedding present."

Clara made an inarticulate noise and dropped to her knees in front of him. "Yes," she whispered. "It would."

"Is that an answer?" he asked.

"Was that a question?"

"Marry me. Or don't. But promise me you'll never dance with anyone besides me for the rest of your life."

"I like the first option," she whispered again. "And the third."

He leaned forward and kissed her again, and this time she became aware of a smattering of sniffles and applause. August got to his feet and pulled her up with him. "I think we've properly scandalized your students."

"I hope so." She laid her head on his shoulder. "I love you, August," she whispered.

"And I you."

"This was a terrible waltz, by the way. All that crying and talking and stopping."

"And kissing."

"And kissing," she agreed, joy and love making it hard to speak. She felt, more than saw, August signal the quartet, and within seconds music once again filled the air.

"I'll make it up to you," he said, pulling her tightly against him. "Because I plan on dancing many, many more waltzes with my wife."

Eli Dawes, fourteenth Earl of Rivers, assumes that his name has been permanently etched in the long lists of soldiers who died at Waterloo. But now here he is, back on English soil, heading for the one place where he knows his arrival will go unmarked and his presence unheeded by anyone save a handful of servants.

Avondale. And, unbeknownst to him, Rose Hayward.

Please turn the page for a preview from *Last Night with the Earl*.

It wasn't the first time Eli Dawes had broken into this house.

The rain seemed to slow slightly as he headed for the rear, toward the servants' entrance near the kitchens. The doors of the house would be bolted, but there was a window with a faulty latch, which he had taken advantage of a lifetime ago when he would stumble back from town in the dead of night after too much whiskey. Eli gazed at the empty windows that lined the upper floors, relieved to find that the vast house was dark and silent. Avondale would be operating with only a skeleton staff—aside from maintaining the structure and grounds, there would be little to do.

Eli slipped his fingers under the edge of the lower window and tapped on the top left corner while gently pushing upward. The window inched up slowly, though with a lot more resistance than he remembered.

Above his head another roll of thunder echoed, and he cursed softly as the rain once again came down in sheets.

Quickly he wrestled the window the rest of the way up and swung himself over the sill, then lowered the window behind him. The abrupt cessation of the buffeting wind and the lash of rain was almost disorienting. He stood for a long moment, trying to get his bearings and listening for the approach of anyone he might have disturbed.

But the only sounds were the whine of the wind and the rattle of the rain against the windows. He breathed in deeply, registering the yeasty scent of rising dough and a faint whiff of pepper. It would seem nothing had changed in the years he'd been gone.

The kitchens were saved from complete blackness by the embers banked in the hearth on the far side. Eli set his pack on the floor and wrenched off his muck-covered boots, aware that he was creating puddles where he stood. A rivulet of water slithered from his hair down his back, and he shivered, suddenly anxious to rid himself of his sodden clothes. He left his boots on the stone floor but retrieved his pack and made his way carefully forward, his memory and the dim light ensuring he didn't walk into anything. Every once in a while, he would stop and listen, but whatever noise he might have made on his arrival had undoubtedly been covered by the storm.

He crept soundlessly through the kitchens and into the great hall. Here the air was perfumed with a heady potion of floral elements. Roses, perhaps, and something a little sharper. He skirted the expanse of the polished marble floor to the foot of the wide staircase that led to the upper floors. Lightning illuminated everything for a split second—enough for Eli to register the large arrangement of flowers on a small table in the center of the hall, as well as the gilded frames of the portraits that he remembered lining the walls.

He shouldered his pack and slipped up the stairs,

turning left into the north wing of the house. The rooms in the far north corner had always been his when he visited, and he was hoping that he would find them as he had left them. At the very least he hoped there was a bed, and something that resembled clean sheets, though he wasn't terribly picky at this point. His stocking feet made no sound as he advanced down the hallway, running his fingers lightly along the wood panels to keep himself oriented. Another blaze of lightning lit up the hallway through the long window at the far end, and he blinked against the sudden brightness.

There. The last door on the left. It had been left partially ajar, and he gently pushed it open, the hinges protesting quietly, though the sound was swallowed by a crash of thunder that came hard on the heels of another blinding flash. He winced and stepped inside, feeling the smoothness of the polished floor beneath his feet, his toes coming to rest on the raised, tasseled edges of the massive rug he remembered. This room, like the rest of the house, was dark, though unlike in the kitchen, there were no embers in the hearth he knew was off to his right somewhere.

Against the far wall the wind rattled the windowpanes, but the sound was somewhat muffled by the heavy curtains that must be drawn. Eli drew in a breath and suddenly froze. Something wasn't right.

The air around him was redolent of scents he couldn't immediately identify. Chalk, perhaps? And something pungent, almost acrid. He frowned into the darkness, slowly moving toward the hearth. There had always been candles and a small tinderbox on the mantel, and he suddenly needed to see his surroundings. His knee unexpectedly banged into a hard object, and something glanced off his arm before it fell to the floor with a muffled thud. He stopped, bending down on a knee, his hands outstretched. What the hell had he hit? What the hell was in his rooms?

It hadn't shattered, whatever it had been. Perhaps it—

"Don't move."

Eli froze at the voice. He turned his head slightly, only to feel the tip of a knife prick the skin at his neck.

"I asked you not to move."

Eli clenched his teeth. It was a feminine voice, he thought. Or perhaps that of a very young boy, though the authority it carried suggested the former. A maid, then. Perhaps she had been up, or perhaps he had woken her. He supposed that this was what he deserved for sneaking into a house unannounced and unexpected. It was, in truth, his house now, but nevertheless, the last thing he needed was for her to start shrieking for help and summon the entire household. He wasn't ready to face that just yet.

"I'm not going to hurt you," he said clearly.

"Not on your knees with my knife at your neck, I agree." The knife tip twisted, though it didn't break the skin.

"There is a reasonable explanation." He fought back frustration. Dammit, but he just wanted to be left alone.

"I'm sure. But the silverware is downstairs," the voice almost sneered. "In case you missed it."

"I'm not a thief." He felt his brow crease slightly. Something about the voice from just above him was oddly familiar.

"Ah." The response was measured, though there was a slight waver to it. "I'll scream this bloody house down before I allow you to touch me or any of the girls."

"I'm not touching anyone," he snapped with far more force than was necessary, before he abruptly stopped. Any of the girls? What the hell did that mean?

The knife tip pressed down a little harder, and Eli winced.

He could hear rapid breathing, and a new scent reached him, one unmistakably feminine. Soap, he realized, the fragrance exotic and rich. Something that one wouldn't expect from a maid.

"Who are you?" she demanded.

"I might ask the same."

"Criminals don't have that privilege."

Eli bit back another curse. This was ridiculous. His knees were getting sore, and he was chilled to the bone, exhausted from travel, and in his own damn house. If he had to endure England, it would not be like this. In a fluid motion he dropped flat against the floor and rolled immediately to the side, sweeping his arm up to knock that of his attacker's. He heard her utter a strangled gasp as the knife fell to the floor and she stumbled forward, caught off balance.

Eli was on his knees instantly, his hands catching hers as they flailed at him. He pinned her wrists, twisting her body so she was now on her back on the floor, Eli hovering over her. He heard her suck in a deep breath, and he yanked a hand away to cover her mouth, stopping her scream before it ever escaped.

"Again," he said between clenched teeth, "I am not going to hurt you." Beneath his hand her head jerked from side to side. She had fine features, he realized. In fact, all of her felt tiny, from the bones in her wrists to the small frame struggling beneath him. It made him feel suddenly protective. As if he held something infinitely fragile that was his to care for.

Though a woman who brandished a knife in such a manner couldn't be that fragile. He tightened his hold and cleared his throat. "If you recall, it was you who had me at a disadvantage with a knife at my neck. I will not make any apologies for removing myself from that position. Nor will

I make any apologies for my presence at Avondale. I have every right to be here."

Her struggles stilled.

Eli tried to make out her features in the darkness, but it was impossible. "If I take my hand away, will you scream?"

He felt her shake her head.

"Promise?"

She made a furious noise in the back of her throat in response.

Very slowly Eli removed his hand. She blew out a breath but kept her word and didn't scream. He released her wrists and pushed himself back on his heels. He heard the rustle of fabric, and the air stirred as she pushed herself away. Her warm, exotic scent swirled around him before fading.

"You're not a maid," he said.

"What?" Her confusion was clear. "No."

"Then who are you?" he demanded. "And why are you in my rooms?"

"Your rooms?" Now there was disbelief. "I don't know who you think you are or where you think you are, but I can assure you that these are not your rooms."

Eli swallowed, a sudden thought making his stomach sink unpleasantly. Had Avondale been sold? Had he broken into a house that, in truth, he no longer owned? It wasn't impossible. It might even be probable. He had been away a long time.

"Is it my brother you are looking for? Is someone hurt?"

The question caught him off guard. "I beg your pardon?"

"Do you need a doctor?"

Eli found himself scowling fiercely, completely at a loss. Nothing since he had pushed open that door had made any sort of sense. "Who owns Avondale?"

"What?" Now it was her turn to sound stymied.

"This house—was it sold? Do you own it?"

"No. We've leased Avondale from the Earl of Rivers for years. From his estate now, I suppose, until they decide what to do with it." She paused, and he could hear suspicion seeping from every syllable. "Did you know him? The old earl?"

Eli opened his mouth before closing it. He finally settled on, "Yes."

"Then you're what? A friend of the family? Relative?"

"Something like that."

"Which one?"

Eli drew in a deep breath that wasn't wholly steady. He tried to work his tongue around the words that would forever commit him to this place. That would effectively sever any retreat.

He cleared his throat. "I am the Earl of Rivers."

Kelly Bowen grew up in Manitoba, Canada. She attended the University of Manitoba and earned a master of science degree in veterinary physiology and endocrinology. But it was Kelly's infatuation with history and a weakness for a good love story that led her down the path of historical romance. When she is not writing, she seizes every opportunity to explore ruins and battlefields.

Currently Kelly lives in Winnipeg with her husband and two boys, all of whom are wonderfully patient with the writing process. Except, that is, when they need a goalie for street hockey.

Learn more at:
  http://www.kellybowen.net
  @kellybowen09
  http://facebook.com

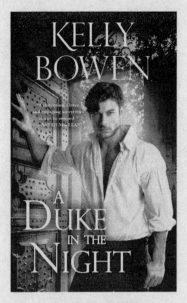

A DUKE IN THE NIGHT
By Kelly Bowen

Headmistress Clara Hayward is a master of deception. She's fooled the ton into thinking she's simply running a prestigious finishing school. In reality, she offers an education far superior to what society deems proper for young ladies. If only her skills could save her family's import business. She has a plan that might succeed, as long as a certain duke doesn't get in the way...

Fall in Love with Forever Romance

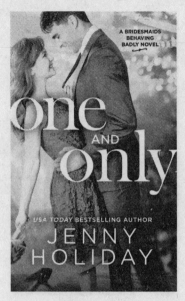

ONE AND ONLY
By Jenny Holiday

In this laugh-out-loud romantic comedy, *USA Today* bestselling author Jenny Holiday proves that when opposites attract, sparks fly. Bridesmaid Jane Denning will do anything to escape her bridezilla friend—even if it means babysitting the groom's troublemaker brother before the wedding. Cameron MacKinnon is ready to let loose, but first he'll have to sweet-talk responsible Jane into taking a walk on the wild side. Turns out, riling her up is the best time he's had in years. But will fun and games turn into something real?